PRAISE FOR #1 BESTSELLING

AUTHOR KEN FITE AND IN PLAIN SIGHT

★★★★★ "Grabs you from the first page."

★★★★★ "My heart is still racing!"

★★★★★ "I couldn't put it down!"

★★★★★ "A fantastic edge of your seat story."

★★★★★ "...twists that keep you turning pages."

★★★★★ "Blake Jordan is in a class with Jack Bauer."

★★★★★ "Reminds me of books by Vince Flynn."

★★★★★ "Keeps you wondering what will happen."

★★★★★ "...great read, sets up future adventures."

★★★★★ "If you liked the first two, you'll love this!"

—Amazon reviews

THE BLAKE JORDAN SERIES

IN ORDER

The Senator
Credible Threat
In Plain Sight
Rules of Engagement
The Homeland
The Shield
Thin Blue Line
Person of Interest
Abuse of Power

This is a work of fiction. The characters, incidents, and dialogues are products of the author's imagination and are not to be construed as real. Any resemblance to events or persons, living or dead, is coincidental.

For my wife, Missy.
I love you.

IN PLAIN SIGHT

A BLAKE JORDAN THRILLER

KEN FITE

1

Shawn Beckman lifted his empty beer bottle and nodded at the woman standing behind the bar. "We'll take two more," he said in response to her last-call warning.

AJ shook his head and looked at his friend. "I think I've had enough. I need to get up early tomorrow."

"Come on, man. It's your last night in Washington. Live a little," Shawn argued and smiled at the bartender standing impatiently with her arms crossed and head tilted. "Two more," he repeated.

The woman smiled and grabbed the empty bottles. After stepping away for a brief moment, she reappeared with two ice-cold beers and placed one in front of Shawn before turning to look at AJ. "This one's on me," she said as she set his down in front of him. "Sounds like congratulations are in order."

AJ nodded, realizing how loud his friend had been all night. "I'm starting a new job in Fort Meade on Monday," he explained as another man stepped up to the bar, waiting for the bartender to notice him.

"Fort Meade, huh?" she said. "I think I know what that means. You're one of *those* guys, aren't you?"

"Yeah," replied AJ, staring at his beer and nervously turning the bottle to look at the label while hoping the blonde wouldn't ask any more questions about his new job. He might have said too much already.

"I'll miss seeing you around. Your friend here, not so much," she said, looking over to Shawn, who laughed and told her she didn't have to worry about that, he'd be back tomorrow. She rolled her eyes. "Come back and see me sometime," the woman said, turning to AJ. "Maybe I'll give you another on the house."

"I'll do that," replied AJ as the bartender smiled again and shot him a playful wink before shifting her attention to the man standing a few steps away, wanting to order another beer before the bar closed.

Shawn reached over and slapped AJ's back. "I think she likes you, man. Did you see how she looked at you?" he joked and tried to contain a laugh while slapping AJ's back again. "You should have asked for her number. Wait, you don't have to anymore! Quick, take a picture of her! Run it through your database!"

AJ laughed and took another drink. The two men turned to the door as a large group of friends left The Bleeding Heart and stepped outside, causing a cold gust of wind to enter the room. AJ could see a fresh dusting of snow covering everything out on the street, casting a dark, gray filter over the outside world.

When the door closed, AJ stared at his beer again and continued to turn the bottle slowly. "The movers are coming tomorrow. Everything's boxed up and ready to go," he said. "Lisa said she might stop by, too."

Shawn turned to AJ. "Lisa? Why?"

AJ shrugged.

"You just need to forget about her, man."

"Trying to. It's why I took the Maryland job. Maybe she needs closure, you know? I sure could use some." AJ looked around the smoky room and watched as the bartender started wiping down the bar. "I hope I'm making the right decision leaving DC. Things were going great at the DoD. I have a lot of friends here."

"You'll make new friends, AJ. It's a good opportunity. The NSA's bringing all security work back in-house with Keller putting a stop to using contractors. That means more money for people like you and me."

AJ turned to his friend. "It's not about the money, Shawn. It's about trying to forget about Lisa," he said. "That's really why I'm doing this. I just can't work with someone who doesn't want to be with me anymore. Seeing her at work every day is torture," he added and stared at his beer again. "You think she'll ever come around?" When Shawn didn't respond immediately, AJ put a hand on his friend's back. "Hey, you okay?"

"Not feeling so good," replied Shawn as he put a hand on his stomach. "I'm ready to get out of here."

"Okay, give me a minute," said AJ. "I'll be right back." AJ stood from the barstool and walked down the long dimly lit hallway and entered the men's room. Once inside, AJ stared blankly at his reflection in the mirror, wondering what he was doing.

He had worked through one of the longest days of his life and was completely drained. His boss had made sure that everything he had worked on over the last year was documented and his coworkers fully trained to take over his work. It took three systems analysts to take on his entire workload. That made AJ smile. *They'll miss me when I'm gone*, he thought to himself.

The muffled music outside the washroom was lowered and replaced by laughter and loud, echoing voices. It wasn't until someone pushed the door open and stepped inside that AJ became fully present again.

He splashed water on his face and used his fingers as a comb, running them through his long dark hair. AJ took another glance at his reflection before he reached for the door and walked back toward his friend.

"Thought maybe you fell in," Shawn said with a smirk as AJ approached the bar and noticed that his friend was slurring his words. "Let me ask you something," Shawn continued. "Don't you think it's strange that your new boss was all over you today, checking on your access?" He swallowed the last of his beer. "We've worked together for a long time. I've never seen anyone provisioned access before their first day of work."

AJ thought for a second. "Not really, maybe he just wants to make sure I'm ready to go on Monday." Shawn stood from the barstool and started to fall over. AJ grabbed his friend and helped keep him steady. "Looks like I'll have to drive you home," he said as the lights flickered twice and the music turned off.

Shawn shook his head. "I walked here. Apartment's only a few blocks away," he said, putting on his coat.

"Good. I'll walk with you," said AJ as the two men followed another large group out the door.

Once outside, AJ looked down both sides of the street. He noticed a police car parked a block west of the bar. Shawn turned and started walking east on H Street. AJ followed. When Shawn turned the corner at Seventh and headed south, AJ looked over his shoulder and saw the police car make a U-turn and disappear.

"Think I'm gonna be sick, man," Shawn said as they approached G Street, and AJ watched as Shawn knelt and vomited into some nearby bushes. AJ blew hot air into his hands, trying to stay warm.

"I appreciate that. Hell of a way to send me off," said AJ as he looked north on Seventh toward H Street, where most of the traffic was. Without the headlights from the cars driving on the main road, AJ relied on the orange glow of a few streetlights to guide them toward Shawn's apartment.

Shawn stood and leaned against a fence in front of one of the homes on Seventh. As AJ waited for his friend, he felt the hair on his neck stand on end. He looked down both ends of the street, feeling like someone, somewhere, was watching him. *Nobody's out here*, AJ thought to himself as Shawn started walking again.

When they crossed G Street and passed an elementary school, AJ heard what sounded like a car door being shut somewhere close by. "Hold up," said AJ as he looked around. He didn't see anyone there.

When they reached the end of the block, AJ stopped and held his arm out in front of Shawn to keep him from crossing the street, and pointed in front of them. Crouched on the sidewalk half a block away was a man dressed in black, wearing a ski mask. AJ and Shawn stood still, overcome with fear, and watched the man closely. Then AJ noticed something metal shimmering in his hand. "He has a knife," he whispered.

2

AJ KEPT HIS EYES FIXED ON THE SHADOWY FIGURE STILL crouched in front of them and took a step backwards. He grabbed Shawn's coat. "We need to get out of here," he said and tried to get his friend to turn around.

Shawn broke free and held both hands to his mouth. "Hey, man, what the hell's your problem!" he yelled.

AJ grabbed Shawn and held him back while keeping his eyes on the man. "Shut up! I told you, he's got a knife," he said. "Let's head back to H Street. I saw a cop up there a few minutes ago. We need to go *now*."

"I have a better idea," replied Shawn, his speech becoming even more slurred now. "We're gonna have to split up. You run back to H Street and I'll go *this* way." Shawn nodded toward the road to their right. AJ looked up and saw that the street was Morris Place. His eyes returned to the man still crouched across the street. "Meet me back at the bar, okay?"

"No, *not* okay," whispered AJ as he watched the man in the ski mask stand and slowly tilt his head. His arms dropped to the side. AJ could clearly see the long blade catching the light from a nearby streetlight. AJ's blood ran cold as he slowly reached into his jacket, desperately searching for his cell phone. Adrenaline surged through his veins as he kept his eyes locked on the man in the mask.

"Go!" yelled Shawn as he started to run down Morris Place, catching AJ off guard. "Go, AJ! *Run!*"

But AJ was unable to move. He stood motionless, gripped by fear as he watched his best friend disappear down the dark street. AJ's eyes shifted back to the man with the mask. He slowly tilted his head to the opposite side and raised his hand, lifting the blade and pointing it at AJ.

AJ's gut was telling him to run back the way he came from, to H Street, where the heavier traffic was. Shawn's idea to lose the guy might work. But AJ knew his friend didn't stand a chance if he left him alone. AJ sprinted in the same direction as Shawn, leaving the man in the mask behind as he ran away.

His steps were loud as he ran down the one-way road. Cars were parked on both sides of the dark street, and AJ stayed in the center of the road as he headed west, trying to find his friend. "Shawn!" he yelled, hoping he was there somewhere hiding behind one of the cars, but there was no response.

AJ turned as he ran to look down the street, but the man in the mask wasn't following. "Shawn, where are you?" AJ yelled as he passed a basketball court and approached the entrance to the elementary school's baseball field.

The cold December air burned AJ's lungs as he breathed heavily and approached the end of the block. Reaching into his jacket again, he found his cell and started to call for help. But help found him instead.

The red and blue overhead lights turned on and bounced off the dark homes on the left side of the street. AJ watched as the officer slammed on the brakes, leaving the car blocking the street, and stepped outside.

"Show me your hands!" the officer yelled with what sounded like a Russian accent. He kept his hand resting on his holstered gun and walked around the front of the car.

AJ put his hands up, but took a step backwards.

"Stop moving," the officer said as AJ turned around again to look down the road behind him.

"That's not him," AJ heard a familiar voice yell from inside the vehicle, followed by frantic knocking on the window. AJ was relieved to see Shawn in the backseat. The cop glared at Shawn as he walked to AJ.

"Please, you have to help me," said AJ. "There's a man back there at the end of the street. He has a knife."

"That's what *this* guy just told me," the cop said, nodding to Shawn while keeping his eyes on AJ. "Thought maybe he had too much to drink, started seeing things, you know." The cop looked behind AJ, like he was anticipating, maybe even *expecting* the man with a knife to appear. "Turn around for me?"

AJ turned and kept his hands in the air. The cop kicked at his shoes, causing AJ to widen his stance, and began frisking him. When he was sure AJ wasn't armed, he turned him around. "Got some ID?" he asked.

Reaching into his back pocket while looking over his shoulder one more time to make sure the man in the mask wasn't approaching, AJ grabbed his wallet, unfolded it, and pulled out his driver's license for the officer. While the cop inspected the ID, AJ noticed a fading gold nameplate on the cop's uniform with ANDERSON embossed on it. The cop found a small flashlight, illuminated the ID, and looked back at AJ.

"Anthony," the officer began after putting the flashlight

back in his pocket while still holding onto the ID, "I need you to step into the vehicle for me."

AJ hesitated.

"For your *safety*," the officer added.

Anderson walked to his car, opened the back door, and motioned for Shawn to exit the vehicle. "Step out," the officer said. Shawn obeyed and cautiously inched his way out of the car. "Walk to the fence for me?"

After Shawn started walking, the cop gestured for AJ to step inside and take Shawn's spot.

Doesn't seem like an Anderson to me, AJ thought and took a seat. The officer pushed the door closed and followed Shawn to the fence on the other side of the street. AJ watched him say something into his radio, but he was too far away to hear what he had said. So AJ sat silently in the backseat, wondering what Anderson was doing, and why he wanted Shawn against the fence and needed AJ inside the vehicle.

AJ thought back to when he and Shawn had stepped out of The Bleeding Heart. He had turned the corner and watched as a police car made a U-turn and disappeared. *Was Anderson following them?*

He began to panic. Unable to open the door, AJ banged two open palms against the window. "He didn't do anything wrong! Please! Get us out of here!" he yelled, but Anderson ignored him. AJ watched the cop bring the radio to his ear to listen to a transmission, then attached it to his belt and looked behind the car.

Anderson pointed back at Shawn. "Don't move," he said, the words muffled to AJ, and started to walk.

The cop saw something. AJ's blood ran cold. He turned around and saw what looked like movement behind the car as a shadow passed across the back window. It was fogged up, keeping AJ from being able to see outside the vehicle. AJ reached over and used the sleeve of his jacket to wipe the window clean.

"That's him!" he yelled and turned to pound his fist on the car window. "That's the man!" he screamed.

Anderson rested his hand against the gun holstered on his belt and ordered Shawn to face the fence again.

AJ watched as the man dressed in black approached. He was still wearing the mask. As he passed behind the car, getting closer to the cop, the orange glow from the streetlight at the corner of Morris and Sixth clouded AJ's view. The window in the back of the car fogged up again as AJ started to breathe more heavily, forcing him to have to wipe it clean again. "Do something!" AJ yelled to the officer.

Anderson walked past his police car and met with the man dressed in black across the street, next to the townhouse on the corner. The cop kept his hand resting on the gun as they spoke. AJ listened, but the voices were too low to make out what was being said. "Do something," he said to himself. "Arrest him."

AJ watched as the officer handed the man in the mask the driver's license he'd given the cop only seconds earlier. Anderson pointed to the car. AJ was filled with terror as the man wearing black headed straight toward him. "What's he doing?" AJ whispered and slid across the back to the seat to his left.

The man stopped at the door. AJ watched Anderson walk closer to Shawn and draw his gun. He fired two shots. Shawn fell to the ground. Anderson jumped into the front seat as AJ's door opened. The man in the mask climbed inside. As the car sped away, he turned to AJ and removed the mask.

"Hello, Mr. Lennox."

3

JAMI RESTED HER HAND ON MY BACK TO KEEP HERSELF STEADY as she leaned over to set the dessert in front of Kate and me. "This might bring back some memories," she said, smiling at her sister and taking a seat at the head of the table just to the right of me. Kate's face lit up as she set down her glass of chardonnay.

"Jami?" said Kate as her eyes grew wide. "Is this Mom's pumpkin pie?"

Jami grinned and reached over to cut an extra-large slice, carefully set it on Kate's plate, and spooned a dollop of whipped cream on top. "It's not as good as Mom's, but it's close," said Jami as she watched Kate take a bite. "I try to follow the recipe just like she wrote it, but it never seems to turn out the same." Jami cut another slice and set it on my plate, followed by one for herself. "I still can't believe she's gone. Christmas wasn't the same this year."

"I know how hard it is to lose a parent," I said to Kate, who was sitting across from me. "I'm sorry."

Jami stared at her plate, lost in thought. "Is Matthew going to want some?" she finally asked her sister.

Kate had taken another bite, shook her head, and held up a hand. "He won't eat it," she finally got out.

Jami shrugged. "More for us, I guess," she said and shot me a wink to lighten the mood.

Kate set her fork down and looked at me. Her smile faded. "So how long will you be in Chicago, Blake?"

"Just for the week," I replied and took a sip of Jami's eggnog, trying my best not to overanalyze Kate's question. It always seemed like she had a wall up, like there was something more that she wasn't saying. I tried to ignore it. "Flew in Christmas Eve. I'll head back to DC after the first of the year," I added.

"Just a few more days to spend with Jami, then," said Kate. "Doing anything special for New Year's Eve?"

I smiled and looked at Jami. "I think we're going to head over to Navy Pier and watch the fireworks over Lake Michigan." Underneath the table, I moved my right hand to my pocket and felt the box I had been carrying since I arrived almost a week ago. I figured it was safer to keep it on me so Jami wouldn't find it.

Kate picked up her fork, turned her gaze back to her plate, and started playing with her dessert. "Sounds fun." She took a sip of wine, turned to Jami, and smiled. "It'll just be Matthew and me this year."

Jami reached her hand out and placed it on Kate's. "I know it's been a rough couple of months for you. First the separation, then Mom." She slowly shook her head. "Things will get better, Kate. You'll—"

Before Jami could finish, we heard the piercing sound of glass shattering a few feet away from us.

I jumped from my chair, turned around, and headed for the kitchen. Eight-year-old Matthew was startled and backed away from me. He stood next to the counter, looking at the shards of broken glass on the floor.

"Don't move," Jami said in a calm voice and walked past me to grab a broom so she could sweep up the glass scattered on the floor. "Don't want you to get cut, okay, sweetie?" she added.

Matthew looked like he was on the verge of tears, but held them back as I reached into another jar and handed him a cookie.

I knelt next to the boy and rested my hand on his back. "You okay, buddy?"

He looked at me and nodded.

"I'll take care of it," Jami said and motioned for me to go finish dessert as Kate watched from the doorway.

Kate and I sat back down. She pushed her plate away and stared across the table at me. "You okay, Blake?" she asked. "Thought for a second you were going to tackle my son back there." Kate reached for her glass and held it up as she continued. "You're not still in that line of work, are you?" she added and took a sip.

I leaned back in my chair. "A little on edge, that's all. It's not exactly the best neighborhood in Chicago. And I've told you before that I work as a domestic counterterrorism advisor to President Keller."

Kate took another drink and set the glass down. "Don't lie to me, Blake." There was an edge to her voice. Kate and I never got along too well. I didn't know why. But we somehow managed to hide it from Jami.

I rested my arms on the table and leaned in. "Look, did I do something wrong? Because you haven't been here long enough for me to offend you, yet," I said. "What's the problem, Kate?"

Kate looked over my shoulder and stared at the kitchen door. We sat in silence, listening to the sound of Jami sweeping the broken glass. "I'm worried about my sister. We already lost Dad; now Mom's gone." Her eyes returned to mine. "Jami told me what you *really* do for the president. She said your advisor job is a cover. Since January, you've been working in the field on counterterrorism assignments for Keller."

"Well, she shouldn't have told you that."

"She shouldn't tell her sister about what's going on in her life? Should she have *lied* to me instead?"

"Kate, Jami is a federal agent at the Department of Domestic Counterterrorism. A damn good one, too. Not exactly the *safest* job. She chose that life for herself well before she met me. And in case you forgot, she's responsible for the capture of Claudia Nazir, a wanted terrorist. I think she can take care of herself."

"I know she can take care of herself. That's not what worries me. I want her with someone who can keep her safe. She tells me things, Blake. She called just last week. Did she tell you yet that she's changed her mind about DC? That she's going to request a transfer to the new DDC field office that's opening so she can be with you?" Kate asked, trying to keep her voice down so Jami wouldn't hear her from the kitchen.

"I'm sorry about John walking out on you and Matthew. But what Jami chooses to do is her decision," I said. "I know how it feels to lose everyone you've ever cared about, Kate. But Jami's all I have left now."

Kate reached for the bottle of chardonnay and topped off her glass. "That's the problem."

I shook my head slowly. "What are you saying, Kate?"

"Your wife, Maria, was murdered because of you. Before he became president, James Keller was kidnapped and almost executed because of you. Your father died because of the decisions you made while trying to rescue Keller. And your best friend in DC was shot and nearly killed because of you, Blake. Now my little sister says she's going to leave Chicago and move to Washington *to be with you*."

"Say it, Kate."

"You're cursed. Anyone close to you either ends up dead or in the hospital. You can't have the girl and the job, Blake. At some point, you're going to have to choose."

I leaned back, keeping my eyes on her. My hand moved back to the box in my pocket. I pulled my hand back quickly when Jami pushed open the kitchen door and joined us at the table, followed by Matthew.

"Grab your toys, Matthew. We're leaving," Kate said to her son while standing up. Matthew protested to his mom. Jami tried to stop her sister, urging her to stay just a little longer. But Kate wanted none of it. "Thanks for dinner. The pie was lovely," she said at the door and hugged Jami. Then she and Matthew left.

4

Twenty-four hours later, Lisa Evans sat alone in an empty coffee shop two blocks away from her Pentagon City apartment. She had met with two of her friends, talking about AJ and listening to their encouragement, while wishing things had turned out differently between the two of them. After an hour, Lisa gave both of her friends a hug and, after they left, returned to the counter to get another cup of coffee.

She had spent the day shopping to keep her mind occupied. But she couldn't stop thinking about her ex.

Lisa and AJ had dated for just over a year. They'd met when she joined the forensics department at the DoD as an analyst straight out of college. AJ was her coach at work, tasked with getting her up to speed. They didn't teach what she needed to know in school, but with AJ's help, she caught on quickly.

AJ's confidence was what had attracted her to him. But as Lisa started to get better at the job, tension grew between the couple and things started to unravel. Working together had seemed exciting at the beginning, but excitement turned to dread each morning as Lisa left for work.

When Lisa returned to her table, she heard her cell phone ringing. She set her coffee down, pulled her phone out of her purse, and stared at the screen. *Why's Jason calling me on a Saturday night?* Lisa thought to herself and slid her thumb across the screen as she pulled the chair out and sat down.

"This better be good," she told her boss sarcastically. "I'm trying to disconnect on the weekends."

"You sitting down?" asked Jason with what sounded like a concerned tone of voice.

Lisa was just about to take a sip of her coffee. Instead, she set it down and moved the phone to her other ear. "Yes, what's going on? Did the server go down again? I'm not that far from work if you need me to—"

"Lisa, it's about Shawn Beckman."

"Shawn? What'd he do this time?" There was a pause at the other end of the line. "Jason? You still there?"

"He's dead, Lisa. They found his body a few blocks away from his apartment at four o'clock this morning."

Lisa's eyes widened. She turned to look around the coffee shop. Besides the two employees working behind the counter, cleaning up and getting ready to close for the night, she was still alone. "Are you sure?"

"I'm sure. He was shot twice in the back. His body was found behind an elementary school near H Street."

Lisa reached into her purse, grabbed a tissue, and dabbed it underneath her eyes. "Why would anyone want to hurt Shawn?" she asked, but there was just silence on the other end of the line. "Why, Jason?"

"I don't know. But I need to call the rest of the team so they hear it from me instead of on the news."

A thought crossed Lisa's mind. "What about AJ?" she asked. "Does he know what happened?"

"That's a good question. I'm not sure. You know his last day at the office was yesterday. I don't have access to his contact information from the employee records system now that he no longer works for me." There was a pause on the line. "Don't you live close to AJ? Could you relay the news to him?"

Lisa took a deep breath and slowly nodded to herself. "We live in the same apartment building. *Lived*, I mean. He's moving this weekend. I'll go see if he's still there so I can tell him in person."

"Let me know when you talk with him, okay? I'll see you on Monday," said Jason. "Hang in there."

The line disconnected. Lisa stared at her phone's screen and watched it dim and then turn off. She tried to remember the last time she had spoken to Shawn. It was late last night, back at the office. Shawn and AJ were sitting at their cubicles, working.

Shawn stepped away from his desk right when Lisa was leaving to head home. She stopped at AJ's cubicle, wished him luck, and said she might stop by before he left, which she regretted immediately. *Why are you dragging this out?* she asked herself on her way to the elevators.

That was where she ran into Shawn, who said he was going to be taking AJ out for some drinks and invited Lisa to join them, an offer she had to refuse. Now, sitting in the coffee shop, Lisa thought through what might have happened. Shawn could have left the bar at three in the morning, closing time on Friday nights. There were plenty of bars along H Street, which was close to where Jason said Shawn's body was found.

Lisa gathered up her belongings, pushed her chair in, and hurried to the exit.

She walked outside and quickly headed north on Fern Street and cut across when she got to Twelfth. Lisa wondered if AJ was still in Washington or if he had already left for Maryland earlier in the day.

After taking the elevator to the eighth floor, she stopped at apartment eight fourteen and knocked on the door. There was no response. Lisa knocked again, harder this time. "AJ, it's me. Please open the door."

Lisa pushed her hair back behind her ears, something she did whenever she was nervous, and knocked again. "I missed him," she whispered to herself before remembering that she still had a key to his apartment. Lisa grabbed her purse from her shoulder, set it on the ground, and knelt as she rummaged through it. After unzipping a small compartment and squeezing two fingers inside, she found the keycard.

Lisa stood, inserted the keycard, and pulled it out quickly, praying the reader would light up green. To her surprise, it did, and the door unlocked. She pushed it open, expecting to find an empty apartment. Instead, Lisa found a dozen brown boxes stacked on the left-hand side of the wall inside the entranceway.

She made her way through the apartment, looking inside every room. "AJ? Are you here?" she asked as her voice echoed across the empty rooms. After Lisa had checked everywhere, she walked into the kitchen and found the only thing not boxed up yet—a landline with a built-in answering machine. She didn't even know AJ had a landline. As she approached, Lisa noticed a red number three blinking on the display.

Lisa pressed play. The first message was from AJ's movers, confirming the appointment for earlier that day. The second was from the movers again, letting AJ know they were standing at his door, but nobody was answering, so he'd have to call back to schedule another time for a pickup. The third was from a man named Morgan asking why AJ wasn't answering his cell phone and to call back immediately.

Does AJ know about Shawn? Where did he go, and why isn't he answering his cell? she wondered.

Lisa's eyes moved back to the landline. She touched the display and saw the phone number from the last caller. She recognized the Chicago area code and thought about the last phone call AJ had received. Lisa lifted the receiver and held it to her ear, then pressed a button on the display. The line rang twice.

"This is Lennox," the man said on the other end of the line with the same accent Lisa had heard on the answering machine. "Hello? Is anybody there?" he asked as Lisa hesitated and almost hung up the phone.

"My name is Lisa Evans," she finally said. "I'm calling about my friend AJ. I think he might be in trouble."

5

Our waiter set the large plate on a rack in front of Jami and me. Giordano's was our go-to place for dinner whenever I flew back to Chicago to visit. Jami complained about the forty-five-minute wait for the deep-dish pizza to bake. But I looked forward to the wait. It made us press pause on life. It gave us time to talk and catch up. And it reminded me of the life we had together before I took the job in Washington.

The last year of my life had been a whirlwind. Working for President Keller, my longtime friend and mentor since I was a kid in high school, wasn't what I thought it'd be.

What Jami had told Kate was true. My job as the president's special advisor on counterterrorism was a cover. I attended all of the National Security Council meetings and, to the rest of Keller's team, I was just one of his advisors. But there was more to my job than that. Keller had asked me to create a special task force to partner with all intelligence agencies to investigate and prevent domestic terrorism across the country. I had accepted the assignment.

The idea was to cut out the red tape and remove the silos

between federal agencies. I had already recruited Chris Reed from the FBI, who had worked for me back when I ran the DDC field office here in Chicago.

It wasn't enough. I needed more people I could trust to join us. But building a team from scratch was harder than I thought it would be. At DDC, I had the full resources of the CIA, DDC's parent organization. But creating a covert black ops team to stop terrorism wasn't so easy. I took my time. I had to be careful.

"You're not going to make me eat this whole thing, are you?" Jami asked, and I realized I'd been lost in thought about work again. I guess sometimes it's hard to separate your work life from your personal life.

"Sorry," I said, grabbing the metal spatula and using my fork to guide a hot slice of pizza to my plate.

"You know what I love about Giordano's?" Jami asked as she stretched her hand out to grab mine and I set my fork down and squeezed her hand back. "They list the calories for the entire menu right here," she said and held up a menu with her other hand. "Over a thousand just for this slice alone." Jami dropped the menu, let go of my hand, grabbed her fork and knife, and cut a small square. "Keep bringing me here and you're gonna make me fail the next random physical that Shapiro puts me through."

"Between Christmas and New Year's, they're not calories. They're deliciousness points," I replied.

Jami laughed and looked out the window. "We're close to Navy Pier. Think it'll be crowded tomorrow?"

"Is it ever *not* crowded at Navy Pier on New Year's Eve?" I asked and noticed that Jami had a sad look about her as I took a sip of my pop. "It's been a tough year for us. We deserve to have a little fun, Jami."

She nodded and took a sip of her pop, too. "I just feel bad for Kate," she said. "Did you hear the comment she made last night about it just being her and Matthew this year? She's really missing Mom. Maybe we should just stay home. We can have her and Matthew spend the night. What do you think?"

I thought Kate was ruining my plans. And I thought about how the last person I wanted to see tomorrow night was Jami's sister. "I already made reservations and got the tickets. Kate and Matthew will be fine."

Jami cut into her pizza and took another bite. She was thinking. I listened to the sound of dishes clinking together, waiters yelling to the cooks in the kitchen, and the regulars chatting while waiting for their food to be ready. "Tell me, Blake," Jami finally said, "what were you and Kate talking about last night?"

I grabbed my drink and took another sip, trying to come up with something. "Kate was telling me about work. Said she was putting in long hours at the office," I replied, hoping she'd move on to something else.

"It sounded like arguing to me."

I shook my head and set my drink down. "It was nothing, Jami," I said, not sure if she would buy it.

Jami thought for a second. "Do you remember how things were last year when your dad passed away?"

"Of course I remember," I said. "Those were some of the darkest days of my life."

Jami set her fork down. "Then you know what Kate and I are going through with losing Mom, right?"

As I sat across from Jami, I started to think about Maria. It had been a year and a half since she was murdered, shortly after I took over as special agent in charge of DDC. Something about the way the light hit Jami's face from the side. For a moment, she looked just like her. It scared the hell out of me.

"*Right, Blake?*" she asked, leaning in and raising her eyebrows to get my attention again.

"Right," I said, trying to focus on our conversation and suddenly realizing why I didn't want Kate near us. I pushed my plate aside and leaned in. "I need to ask you something, Jami."

She crossed her arms and rested them on the table and stared at me.

I hesitated before I spoke again. "Do you believe in curses?"

Jami furrowed her brow and squinted her eyes. "Blake, I'm trying to have a serious conversation here."

"I am, too," I insisted.

"You of all people should know that curses aren't real. Our Cubbies won the World Series, didn't they?"

"Not for a hundred and eight years they didn't," I replied sarcastically and leaned back in my seat.

Jami laughed at that, but her smile faded when she saw that I was serious. "Do *you* think you're cursed?"

I thought before responding. "I don't know," I replied. "Maria, President Keller, my father, Chris Reed."

Jami slowly shook her head, gathering her thoughts. "Blake, what happened to Maria wasn't your fault. And Keller got kidnapped on *my* watch, remember? Chris is alive and well. And your father? Ben loved you so much and was so very proud of you. You are *not* cursed. *Okay?*" Jami said and reached across the table again to grab my hands. "And if curses *are* real," she added, "then they're meant to be broken."

I stared across the table. I loved Jami and I couldn't wait to show her that tomorrow under the fireworks.

"Everything good?" our waitress asked as she approached, shouting over the voices inside the restaurant.

I held onto Jami's hands and smiled. "Everything's great," I replied, keeping my eyes on Jami.

Our waitress dropped the check. I tried to grab it, but Jami held on tight. She squeezed my hands once before letting go. I grabbed the check and looked it over, then reached for my wallet and dropped cash on the table. When I looked up, Jami had her phone to her ear and looked worried. "Missed a call."

As she listened to the voicemail, my phone rang. I grabbed it from my pocket and looked at the screen. "It's Morgan," I said. "I'm gonna take this outside."

Jami nodded. It was getting louder inside Giordano's, so she held a hand up to cover her ear as I stood to leave.

"This is Jordan," I said as I walked outside.

"Blake, it's me," Morgan said. "I need your help, mate."

6

AJ TUGGED AT THE SLEEVE OF HIS JACKET AND CHECKED THE time. It was nine thirty Saturday evening. He had arrived seventeen hours earlier and stayed awake throughout the night, sleep not being a possibility, as his mind raced and he tried to come to terms with the reality that his best friend was gone. AJ sat on a black couch, the only item in an otherwise empty room, and thought through everything that had happened.

While Anderson sped away from the corner of Morris and Sixth, AJ had stayed on the left side of the backseat, paralyzed, and looking at the man seated to his right. He knew him as Mr. Wolf, a man in his early fifties with graying hair and dressed in a suit both times AJ had met him.

AJ looked at Wolf, his hair matted down with sweat, as the police car twisted and turned through the backstreets of Washington. AJ found it hard to believe it was the same man he had met just a few days earlier.

It only took twenty minutes for Anderson to get to his destination. As AJ sat on the couch, he remembered seeing a sign for Martin Industrial Park as the vehicle slowed and finally arrived at an abandoned factory.

The cop stopped in front of a large driveway and threw the car into reverse. AJ turned and saw two large bay doors behind them with an entrance on each side. Anderson parked and entered one of the doors. A moment later, the left bay door lifted open. Anderson returned to the car and backed it into the factory.

Once inside, the cop turned off the ignition and opened the back door. Wolf exited. "Out," he ordered and AJ quickly obeyed. Wolf patted AJ down and took his cell phone, but let him keep his wallet and watch. Wolf handed the phone to the cop, who took it into an office. Then Wolf walked AJ across the factory floor, past a large table, and locked him inside a room turned into a makeshift cell where he now sat.

That was it, the sequence of events that AJ kept going through. Now he only had one question: *Why?*

The walls were made of brick and there were no windows. If it weren't for his watch, he wouldn't have any idea what time of day it was. A single fluorescent light on the ceiling flickered, threatening to go out at any moment. AJ stood and walked to the door and tested it. It was locked, so he rested his ear against it.

AJ could hear two men talking. As he listened, AJ looked down and noticed light hitting his shoes.

He knelt and noticed a one-inch gap at the bottom of the door. AJ slowly dropped onto the cold concrete floor and looked out onto the open area of the factory that Wolf had walked him through earlier that morning. Not only could he see outside his room, the gap helped him hear the voices better, too.

There weren't many noises coming from the other room. No generators and no televisions or radios, just two men talking. But AJ's next problem to solve wasn't in hearing the men, but in understanding them.

AJ recognized the Russian being spoken immediately. It had been a few years since he had completed his undergraduate Russian studies coursework at Columbia University in New York. He was a bit rusty, but listened carefully, piecing words together to make sense of what the men outside his cell were discussing.

Wolf's voice echoed throughout the factory. He spoke perfect Russian and that bothered AJ. It wasn't the kind of Russian AJ's professors had taught, the kind they themselves learned at university. Wolf spoke the way one would by living in the country, fully immersed in the language and its people.

He continued to listen to the voices and closed his eyes to concentrate and decipher what the men were saying. The best he could tell, they were going over some kind of plan. As the men continued to talk, AJ started to realize *he* was part of the plan. AJ never heard his own name spoken, but he did hear the men repeat a word he was familiar with. They referred to him as *Avstraliyets*. The Australian.

His thoughts went back to Shawn. Why had the cop killed him? Why was *he* still alive and Shawn dead?

Twenty minutes later, AJ heard the sound of footsteps approaching. With his chest resting on the floor, he watched as a pair of black boots appeared in his field of vision as one of the men headed to the door.

AJ pushed himself off the floor, looked around the room, and sat down on the couch against the wall, opposite the door. He looked down and saw white dust on his chest. He brushed it off quickly.

The sound of two bolts being turned was loud. The door opened. "Mr. Lennox, follow me," Wolf said.

AJ hesitated and stayed seated on the couch, once again paralyzed with fear and unable to move.

"I said follow me," Wolf repeated in a harsher tone, this time with much more authority in his voice.

Unsure what the man wanted from him, AJ slowly stood, left the room, and walked into the open space. Wolf gestured to the conference table in the center of the factory's floor. The cop was standing at the head of the table. "Take a seat," he ordered, no longer in uniform and wearing a different set of clothes.

AJ pulled one of the chairs out from the long table he thought belonged in a boardroom somewhere and sat down. Wolf chose a seat across from the officer. Both men faced each other with AJ in the middle.

"My name is Nikolai Ivanov," the middle-aged man seated to AJ's left said. His accent was thick, like someone who learned English late in life and learned it out of necessity. "Did you have a good rest?"

AJ stared at Ivanov without a reply.

The man nodded in response. "Fair enough," he continued. "I believe you've met my business partner, Mr. Wolf?" he asked, gesturing to the man to the right of AJ.

"Why'd you kill my friend?"

Ivanov sat back, glanced at Wolf, and lifted his hands slightly, palms up. "Beckman was an unfortunate casualty," he said, interlacing his fingers on the desk and leaning in before shifting his eyes back to AJ. "We were hoping you would go home after work. We watched you pack your things days ago. We figured you'd go home, turn in early, and leave for Fort Meade first thing today. You made things difficult for us."

AJ shook his head. "But why'd you have to kill him? And what were you watching *me* for?"

Ivanov stared blankly at AJ before responding, "Because you were chosen, Anthony. That's why. You're the only one who can help me get what I came here for."

AJ turned to his right and looked at Wolf. "Chosen for *what?*" he asked. "What do you want from me?"

Wolf smiled. He reached down next to him, grabbed something, and stood. He walked behind AJ's chair and set a laptop bag down in front of him. From a pocket, he pulled out a wireless AirCard and set it down next to AJ as well. He walked into the office and returned, unrolling a long orange extension cord.

Wolf unzipped the bag and reached inside, gently set a laptop in front of AJ, and lifted the lid.

"I don't understand," said AJ as the laptop quickly booted up and an NSA log-in screen appeared.

AJ turned to his left and stared at Ivanov, who leaned back in his chair. "I need you to log in, Anthony. Unless you want to meet the same fate as Officer Anderson and Mr. Beckman. *Go on, log in.*"

AJ slowly typed the log-in credentials that his new boss, Wolf, had provisioned, and sighed. "I'm in."

7

A CAR PASSED QUICKLY IN FRONT OF GIORDANO'S, ITS headlights illuminating the dirty snow at the edge of the street. With the temperature rapidly dropping, it looked like it was about to start snowing again. A gust of cold wind hit me as the door to the restaurant closed behind me. I turned from it so I could hear Morgan.

It had only been a few days since I last spoke with Morgan Lennox, the Australian-born analyst who worked for me when I ran the DDC field office here in Chicago. Chris Reed, my FBI contact and partner, also leveraged Morgan's expertise whenever we worked our many domestic counterterrorism cases.

With a background in tactical surveillance and data analytics, Morgan had helped me more times than I could count. Anything I needed, from accessing security footage to manipulating a building's power supply to flush out a terrorist, chances were Morgan could do it. I owed him a lot. And I owed him my life.

"Okay, Morgan, go ahead," I said as a couple passed me on the sidewalk and stepped inside Giordano's.

"There's been a murder, Blake," Morgan said as another car drove by me on Rush Street and accelerated.

"Where?" I shouted over the noise of the vehicle speeding away.

"DC, two blocks south of H Street. A man named Shawn Beckman was gunned down early this morning."

I thought for a second. The H Street corridor was a long east-west commercial strip spanning much of downtown Washington. "What's it close to?" I asked, trying to better understand the location of the crime.

"By the elementary school on Morris Place," replied Morgan. "This is important. Can you check it out?"

I nodded to myself and pressed the phone closer to my ear as another car turned onto Rush and passed me, pushing more dirty snow against the side of the street. "Okay, I think I know where that is," I said. Being in DC for close to a year, I was starting to get more familiar with the backstreets of Washington. "I'll be glad to check it out. Give me a few days. I'll be back in DC early Monday morning."

There was a pause on the other end of the line. "Back on Monday? Where are you now, Blake?"

"I'm here in Chicago, visiting Jami for a few days. Chris Reed's still in DC if it can't wait until then."

Another pause. "I need someone to look into this right away," Morgan replied with panic in his voice.

"What's going on, Morgan?" I asked, but he didn't respond. "Who was Shawn Beckman?"

"Hang on," he replied as I heard the sound of him holding the receiver up to his chest and muffled voices in the background. Then he came back on. "Sorry, Shapiro won't leave me the bloody hell alone."

Roger Shapiro worked for the CIA, what we refer to as Base. When DDC was formed, Shapiro was appointed regional director for the new agency and its first field office in Chicago. When he fired me as special agent in charge because of the actions I took while saving then-Senator Keller from his kidnapper, he didn't hire a replacement. Instead, he kept the job for himself. It gave him the control that he craved.

Shapiro also fired my assistant SAIC at the time, Chris Reed, but Morgan and Jami got to keep their jobs. I made sure of that by taking full responsibility for every action I took in my after-action report on the Keller kidnapping. The only reason Reed lost his job was because Shapiro wanted full control of the office.

That was why a regional director was running a field office. And that was why he was still there, over a year later.

"Who's Beckman?" I asked again, trying to understand why Morgan cared about the DC murder.

"Shawn Beckman. Gunned down sometime before four o'clock this morning. Two shots to the back, mate," said Morgan and paused again. "Beckman was a Department of Defense senior systems analyst."

"Do we know what he was doing?" I asked. "Not the best part of town to be in after dark."

"I'm trying to figure it out, Blake. But what concerns me isn't what he was doing. Hang on."

Once again, I heard the sound of muffled voices in the background. Something was happening at DDC. "I'll be right there," Morgan told Shapiro and came back on the line sounding rushed and frustrated.

I looked inside the restaurant and saw Jami through one of the windows. She was still on the phone. We made eye contact and she looked worried. I watched her grab her things as Morgan started to speak again.

"Blake, I've been reading through the police report. The Metro Police tagged it as a robbery," he said.

"Okay?" I said. "Gunned down in the early morning in a bad part of DC. A robbery sounds about right to me."

Morgan sighed. "But the report said Beckman was found with a cell phone still in his jacket. He was wearing a Bulova watch on his wrist and also had a wallet in the back pocket of his jeans. Beckman had seventy-five dollars in cash stuffed inside the billfold. Is that what you'd expect to find after a robbery?"

I thought for a second. "I don't know, maybe it was botched. Maybe they got scared off or something."

Just then the door was pushed open fast and Jami jogged over to me. "We need to go *now*," she said.

"Go *where?*" I asked, still pressing the phone to my ear. I caught up to Jami and we jogged toward her car.

"Shapiro called, said I needed to get back to DDC right away," she replied with an annoyed tone of voice.

"Can I talk to Jami?" asked Morgan as we approached the black SUV parked on Chicago Avenue.

"Yeah, hang on," I replied and handed the phone to her as she unlocked the SUV and we climbed inside.

"This is Davis," she said as she started the engine and pulled the vehicle onto Michigan Avenue as we made our way to the office just west of downtown. She turned on the police lights, drove through an intersection, and picked up speed while listening carefully to what Lennox had to say to her.

As she drove, I thought about all of the people who worked for me at DDC who were probably still there. Working for the president, I'd have authority to join her and Morgan if this was a terrorism-related threat. Shapiro wouldn't like that very much, which made me want to find out what was happening all the more. But I hadn't been inside DDC in over a year, and my heart started racing as we approached the building.

Jami and Morgan spoke for a few more minutes before he put her on hold. She turned to me and said Shapiro was at his desk. He came back on the line and said he had to go, so Jami disconnected the call.

"What's this all about?" I asked as Jami slowed to exit from Interstate 290 and pulled out onto Damen.

"Shapiro got a call from Bill Landry over at the FBI. The East Coast's been hit by a massive cyberattack."

8

Morgan Lennox set the phone down and leaned back in his chair, looking up at Roger Shapiro. "She's on her way," he said, referring to Agent Jami Davis. "Blake's with her," he added with hesitation.

Shapiro's eyes grew wide. "Blake *Jordan?*"

Morgan nodded. The director was clearly not happy. "Jordan works for Keller. You can't stop him, mate."

Shapiro nodded back. "Send them to my office. I want to talk to both of them as soon as they get here; then I'll need you and Jami to get together and figure out just what the hell is going on," he said and stormed off.

As Shapiro walked away, Morgan stood in his cubicle and watched his boss return to his office. His thoughts returned to the conversation he had earlier with Lisa about AJ. Morgan picked up his cell and tried calling his nephew once again, but the call went straight to voicemail. "It's me," he said. "I'm really worried about you, AJ. Please call me as soon as you get this, okay?" he said and disconnected the line.

DDC personnel was light for a Saturday night, even

more so with it being between Christmas and New Year's. The intelligence analyst that sat in the cubicle behind Morgan was off work, allowing him to look into Beckman's murder and AJ's disappearance without anyone close by looking over his shoulder.

But soon, Jami would arrive, and Morgan knew he'd be pulled into a joint workroom with Shapiro to help with sorting out whatever was happening on the East Coast. Then it would get harder to continue looking for AJ, so Morgan knew if he wanted to find his nephew, he had to act now.

He sat down, leaned back in his chair, and rested his hands on the back of his head to think.

AJ's cell was going straight to voicemail. That told him the phone was turned off. It was possible AJ had found out about Beckman's death and needed time alone to process what had happened to his friend.

Morgan's brow furrowed as he considered another possibility—that maybe AJ was hurt and needed help.

It had been almost five years since Morgan's brother, Thomas, had called from his hometown of Sydney in New South Wales. Thomas was excited to tell Morgan that AJ had been accepted to Columbia University and asked if Morgan could keep an eye on his kid when he started school. Morgan agreed and even let AJ stay with him in his New York apartment. But soon after AJ arrived in America, Thomas and AJ's mother were killed in a traffic accident. Morgan became a surrogate father to AJ, and the two grew closer.

The next semester, AJ changed his major to computer science and was accepted to the security track. AJ said it was because there were more jobs in security. But Morgan thought that maybe his nephew wanted to be like him. So he took AJ under his wing and taught him everything he knew.

Morgan shook his head and tried to focus on what he had to do. He'd need to try to turn the phone on to locate AJ. He accessed DDC's location-tracking software, logged into the system, and grabbed his cell to find AJ's number. He entered it into the system and initiated the search to triangulate AJ's location.

"Come on," Morgan whispered and stood, looking over his cubicle and out onto the agency's floor.

More analysts and agents were arriving. Morgan looked across the room and saw Shapiro on the phone in his office, probably calling in support teams who'd thought they wouldn't be back until after the New Year. DDC analysts and agents spoke on phones and visited each other's desks while they all placed their current tasks and responsibilities on hold to look into the attack Shapiro had made them aware of earlier.

Morgan heard a chime from his laptop and leaned in to review the results.

The screen displayed DEVICE INACTIVE, showing that the phone was in fact turned off. Morgan began typing at his keyboard to attempt to turn the cell back on again. He knew that when a mobile phone was off, it wasn't really *off*, it was more like putting a laptop in sleep mode. Morgan was hopeful, knowing that AJ's phone would still technically be on, in a low-power mode, with the ability to be woken up if needed.

Plus, knowing the kind of phone AJ had and how difficult it was to remove the battery, Morgan knew it would be an easy task. But no matter what he did, Morgan couldn't get his nephew's cell phone to turn on.

"What's going on here?" Morgan muttered to himself as

he tried again, knowing that even if the battery was drained, there should be enough of a charge to at least turn it on once and ping the closest cell tower.

Morgan stared blankly at the screen, thinking. His heart started to beat faster as the reality that something might have actually happened to his nephew sank in. Morgan picked up the landline on his desk, found the phone number he had written on a notepad just a few minutes earlier, and called it again.

"Hello?" the woman said as she answered the call.

"Lisa, this is Morgan Lennox."

"Did you find AJ?" she asked. By the sound of her voice, Morgan could tell that Lisa had been crying.

"Listen, love—where are you right now?"

There was a pause at the other end of the line. "I'm still in AJ's apartment. I thought he might come back."

Morgan stood and switched the receiver to his other ear as he looked around the room. "Lisa, I want you to listen to me very carefully. I've tried turning AJ's cell phone on remotely, but it's not responding at all."

"What does that mean?" asked Lisa. "Is he in trouble? How will we find him if his phone's off?"

"Lisa, do you have a safe place to go?" Morgan asked. There was another pause on the line. "Lisa?"

"I think so," she finally replied.

Morgan watched as his coworkers stopped what they were doing and turned toward the entrance to DDC. He heard whispers from some of the agents and looked over to see Shapiro still on the phone in his office.

"You need to go there now. Do you understand?"

"Okay. I'm leaving," said Lisa as she walked to the window inside AJ's apartment and looked out onto the dark street. "I worked with AJ and Shawn at the DoD. That's about as safe as it can get. I'll go there."

"Be careful, love. I'll call you back at this number when I know more," he said and set the receiver down.

Morgan leaned over his laptop and minimized the screens he was using to try to locate AJ's cell phone. He looked up and saw Jami Davis walking past security and entering the agency. She wasn't alone.

As he locked his laptop, Morgan pushed his way past the other agents and overheard one of the newer analysts ask who the man approaching with Agent Davis was. "Blake Jordan," Morgan answered and passed Shapiro's office, knocking on the glass wall as he did to let his boss know that Jami had arrived.

9

Sweat began to bead on AJ's forehead as he stared at the laptop's screen and typed frantically.

"You need to hurry, before someone notices you," said Wolf as he raised an arm to look at his watch.

"Just another minute," AJ replied and continued typing, keeping his eyes fixed on the screen as he spoke.

Nikolai Ivanov stood behind AJ as Wolf sat to his right, both men watching the laptop screen as AJ navigated multiple mainframe sessions. "Okay," he finally said. "I'm done."

Wolf turned to Ivanov and nodded his approval. Ivanov stepped away, entered the office, and accessed his cell from the refrigerator he used as a faraday cage to prevent the government from locating him.

AJ leaned back in his chair and turned to his right. He stared at the man who had offered the NSA job to him, the man he was supposed to work for come Monday. "Why'd you have me do that?" he asked. "You of all people should know that within minutes of a server timeout, government field offices on the West Coast will execute their failover plan to bring all systems back online. The outage will only be temporary."

Wolf stood from his chair and started pacing around the table, waiting for Ivanov to return. "You're right. They'll execute their failover, but it'll take some time to do that. And time is all we need."

The men heard the sound of footsteps, and Wolf turned to see Ivanov approaching. "I've received confirmation," he said as he reached the table where AJ was still sitting. "The East Coast has been brought down as expected. The media is reporting that the public cannot make purchases online. No mention yet of any impact to government systems on the East Coast. Looks like it worked, Mr. Lennox."

AJ looked at the men, turned his gaze back to the laptop, and thought about what he had done.

Ivanov turned to Wolf. "What are the specific impacts within the FBI and NSA?"

Wolf started pacing again, thinking through the implications. "Any agencies on the East Coast will be brought offline during the failover. By now, they've executed their business resumption plans and are moving traffic to offices on the West Coast while they figure out what the hell happened to them."

"Then?" asked Ivanov.

"Then they'll start looking for us."

AJ turned to his right and looked at Wolf, then back to Ivanov. "I've done what you asked me to do. Please let me go. I won't tell anyone about this," he said and wiped his brow with the sleeve of his jacket.

"But, Mr. Lennox," Ivanov began, "we're just getting started. You've proven that you're more than capable. We need your assistance on one more assignment. Then we can talk about where we go from here."

Ivanov turned to Wolf and began speaking in Russian. Once again, the man in charge used the term *Avstraliyets*. It sent a cold chill down AJ's spine. The men spoke quickly. It was hard for AJ to keep up.

He heard a few familiar phrases. The men said something about the time of day. They used the word *poyezd* and AJ vaguely remembered its meaning. *Train*, he thought, and realized they might be preparing to leave for the train station. AJ wondered how an NSA manager ever got caught up with a Russian terrorist. He became so lost in his thoughts that he didn't notice Wolf standing directly behind him.

He jumped when Wolf reached past him and tapped on the screen. "Forgetting something?" he asked.

AJ looked over his shoulder and stared. "What do you mean?" he replied. "I told you, I'm done."

"Cover your tracks and close the connection," Wolf demanded. "Do it now!"

After a brief pause, AJ got back to work on the laptop, realizing the man he was supposed to work for knew more about what AJ was doing than he was letting on. And that was going to be a problem. What AJ had done to help bring down the many interagency systems had left significant bread crumbs. He had left them there on purpose, with the hope that someone might use them to track him down.

Wolf looked at his watch. "Mr. Lennox, we have less than an hour before normal business functions are resumed and traffic is back to normal. Before that happens, you need to cover your tracks, close your connection, and open a new one for us to start the next phase of the plan. I suggest you hurry."

AJ again wiped his brow with his sleeve. Closing the connection and establishing a new one would be easy. But it was the bread crumbs that worried him. He sat paralyzed, trying to figure out how he could do it.

Ivanov approached AJ from behind. He felt the cold barrel of a gun resting against the back of his neck. It made him shudder. "Mr. Lennox, I suggest you do what my friend here is asking you to do *immediately*."

Wolf watched as Ivanov nodded to the room where they had been keeping AJ, wanting to talk in private. When they arrived, Wolf leaned against the wall next to the door. Ivanov kept his back to AJ. "How much do you know about Anthony Lennox?" Ivanov asked, crossing his arms and leaning in close to Wolf.

"I know enough," he replied. "Why are you concerned, Nikolai?"

"Because the kid understands Russian," Ivanov whispered.

Wolf broke eye contact with Ivanov and looked over to AJ. "What makes you think that?"

"Because I used a word he recognized. He looked at me when I said it. I pretended like I didn't notice," he said and leaned in even closer. "But I noticed."

"I need to get back," said Wolf as he tried to sidestep Ivanov, but was pushed back against the wall.

"Tell me again about how this will work. When the government figures out what's going on, they're going to look into who did this, will they not? They'll see that the systems were breached by an NSA employee."

Wolf thought about it. "The bread crumbs are an issue, but his access shouldn't be a problem for us. It takes seventy-two hours for a new employee's access to fully propagate throughout the system. And most systems are orphaned until the analyst's profile is built by day three, and we don't need that much time."

"And if you're wrong?" Ivanov pressed. "If they figure out who he is, that he's responsible for all of this?"

"They'll look for him. They'll go to his apartment and won't find him. They'll locate his new place in Fort Meade. They'll go there, too. It'll be empty."

Ivanov thought for a moment. "Will his apartment in DC be empty as well, should they show up looking for him?"

Wolf shook his head.

"Then that's a big problem we'll need to take care of right away," whispered Ivanov. "They'll assume he's still somewhere close to Washington." Nikolai Ivanov turned and walked past AJ and retrieved his phone from the secure area in the office and dialed a number. "Sergei, it's me," he said after placing a call to one of his men. "I need you to do something for me *immediately*."

10

As Jami and I entered the field office, I looked all around, never believing I'd ever step back inside this building again. Everything was still exactly like I remembered it the day I left, from the security personnel out in the lobby that I had hired to my old office, which I could see on the other side of the room. It was like stepping back in time to another life I had lived a long time ago. It was a surreal experience.

I followed Jami into the main room, and familiar faces appeared and stared back at me, surprised to see me. I noticed someone pushing their way through the agents and analysts standing along the hallway.

"Good to see you again, mate," said Morgan as he approached and shook my hand.

I pulled him in to give him a quick embrace. Although Chris Reed and I had worked with Lennox many times over the past year, I hadn't actually seen the man in person since the day I was fired. It was good to see my friend again.

"Jordan," Shapiro barked as he pushed his way past DDC employees, "I want you out of here, *now.*"

Jami and Morgan turned to see how I'd respond. I crossed my arms and watched the man get closer. "Roger, I work for the president," I said. "A cyberattack is an act of terrorism, so I'm not going anywhere."

Shapiro didn't say a word. Instead, he just stood there, powerless, and looked me over while trying to figure out just what he was going to do about me standing in the field office that he took away from me. For a man who loved to throw his weight around and remind everyone that he was in charge, he had a decision to make, with Jami, Morgan, and the rest of the crew watching to see how this would play out.

"I need to assess the situation and understand what we're dealing with here. Then I'll get out of your way," I said, trying to give Shapiro a way out of the corner he had managed to paint himself into.

Turning to face the onlookers, Shapiro ordered, "Get back to work," and the staff slowly returned to their workstations. A few who had gathered around slapped my back as they walked by. I shook their hands. A few of us embraced. It was clear that they were glad to see me again. I felt the same about them.

Who you work for matters, and there's a big difference between a boss and a leader. Jami had told me many stories about the director and how differently he was running the field office. I couldn't help but think about the legacy I had left at DDC. Based on my old team's reaction, they had thought about it, too.

Shapiro took a step closer. "Follow me," he said in my face, his voice gruff, with an edge to it.

He left us standing together, and we watched him enter the JW7 joint workroom on the other side of the center floor. Morgan hung back, and we watched Jami follow Shapiro inside. Memories rushed back of the three of us working from the same room last August when we investigated Keller's kidnapping together.

"I need my laptop. Be right there," said Morgan as he headed back to his cubicle behind me. I walked into JW7, left the door open for Morgan, and sat down. Shapiro remained standing.

Jami was silent and kept her eyes fixed on the large conference room table in front of us. I kept my eyes on Roger Shapiro. He was clearly not happy about me being here, but knew he couldn't do anything about it. Shapiro walked to the window and, with two fingers, separated the blinds. "Here he comes," he said.

Morgan walked into the room and sat down to my left, across from Jami. I was sitting at the head of the table, and Shapiro took a seat opposite me. Morgan turned to his left, then looked back to me. We could all feel the tension in the room. "I hate to break up this lovefest," said Morgan as he typed his password to unlock his screen, "but we have a bit of a problem to work through now, don't we?" He turned to Shapiro.

Roger Shapiro nodded and cleared his throat. "Moments ago, I received a call from my friend Bill Landry over at the FBI. I believe you're familiar with him, Jordan?" he asked sarcastically. Landry had been with the FBI's Chicago field office before transferring to Washington last Christmas and recruiting Chris Reed.

Landry liked me about as much as Shapiro. That made working with Chris difficult. Reed was essentially a shared resource. His day job was with the Bureau. But Chris was also my first and, so far, only recruit for the black ops team I was tasked with putting together under the authority of the president. One of the reasons Keller authorized it was to cut through the red tape from people like Landry and Shapiro.

"Why don't you tell us what's going on?" I asked and leaned in.

Morgan, who had been typing frantically, stopped and turned his laptop around so Jami and I could see his screen. It was an interagency bulletin.

Jami and I read the communication while Shapiro continued to speak. "Landry called to let me know the FBI's system is down in DC and to see if we're having similar problems. While we were talking, Bill put me on hold to take another call. When he came back on, he said the NSA in Fort Meade is down, too," Shapiro said while pointing at Morgan's laptop. "That bulletin says the entire East Coast has been brought down. Federal agencies from New York to Tampa are all offline."

Morgan turned his laptop back around and started typing again. "Well, not *completely* offline," he said, correcting the director. "We can still send email and do our jobs, the programs are just extremely slow. Some of them are timing out. That's what happens when we execute a failover to the West Coast servers."

I turned to Shapiro. "What's the media saying?" I asked to understand what the public was being told.

"They don't know what's going on. I was monitoring the news in my office before the two of you arrived. They're reporting that major retail websites based out of the East Coast are down, which is true."

I turned to my right and looked at Jami. "So who's impacted?"

She thought for a second. "FBI, NSA, Department of Defense—everyone, right?" she asked Morgan, who nodded in agreement. "So, if failover happens immediately, you'd think we'd be back to normal by now. I just don't understand why everything's so slow. I get that the backup servers are on the West Coast, but I don't understand why it's causing our systems to lag so badly. We should be fully synced now."

"Actually, love, it takes a full hour for everything to be synced back up," said Morgan while keeping his eyes fixed on the laptop and continuing to type. "Yes, traffic for our surveillance programs and everything else would have moved already without any break in continuity, but it's the *syncing* of the East and West Coast servers that creates such a drag on the system."

Shapiro looked at his watch before turning to Jami. "So we have forty-five minutes until the failover is complete and the system lag is diminished. What could go wrong during that time? Is the system vulnerable in any way? Are we open to losing any of our data during the failover to the West Coast? I'm trying to understand the risk here, not just for DDC, but for all agencies" he said, getting frustrated.

"Data isn't an issue," Morgan said before Jami could answer. "There are safeguards for all of that, like the big data center the NSA has in Utah for long-term storage and backup purposes, so there's absolutely no risk of losing data. The problem, and it's a really big one, is with *responsiveness* during the traffic shift."

We sat silently, listening to the sound of Morgan typing. A forty-five-minute downtime in responsiveness could be disastrous. "Bloody hell," Morgan whispered, breaking the silence. "I've been sitting here for the last few minutes looking for the source of the breach." Morgan's eyes stayed fixed to his screen. "I think I've found it. It's an NSA IP address. And you won't believe it, but the connection is still open and active."

11

Jami and I stood and looked over Morgan's shoulder. Shapiro did the same. "Why would they leave the connection open?" I asked. "Won't that let us be able to trace their location and figure out who they are?"

Morgan shrugged. "Don't know," he replied. "They could have just left it open by mistake."

"Or maybe they're not done yet," said Jami as she walked back to the other side of the table and sat down.

"What do you mean by that?" asked Shapiro.

Jami held up her wrist and looked at her watch. "It's been a while since the cyberattack started. Maybe whoever is doing this wants to take advantage of our vulnerability and do more damage while they can."

"I don't think that's the case, love." Morgan sighed. "The connection was closed just now. They're gone."

"Damn it," I whispered to myself as I turned and started pacing. "Can you figure out where they entered the system from? Were they stateside or offshore?" I asked Morgan. "We know the Russians tried to interfere with the election last year. We also know that they've been trying to breach the

NSA since this past summer. If the connection's closed, can we confirm if it was them or where the breach was initiated?"

Before Morgan could answer, my cell rang. I pulled it from my back pocket and looked at the screen. "I need to take this," I said as I stepped out of JW7 and kept walking until I was just outside my old office.

"Hey, man," I said and rested my back against the wall. "How's the failover going for you guys?"

"No issues yet," replied Chris Reed, followed by a long pause. "But that's not why I'm calling."

I looked out over the center floor and nodded to an analyst as they walked past me. I decided to step into Shapiro's office to continue the conversation with Reed. I closed the door and took a seat behind my old desk.

"Morgan and Jami are with Shapiro right now. Morgan's trying to figure out where the system was breached from," I said and looked at the TV on the wall, still on the news station that Shapiro had it set to. A banner slowly scrolled across the screen. It read MAJOR INTERNET OUTAGE ON EAST COAST.

"Blake, have you talked to Keller?" Chris asked as I stood and searched for the volume button on the TV.

"No," I replied. "I'll give him a call in a bit. Unless you know something I don't, everything seems to be handled." I looked at my watch. "The failover is in progress, should be finished within forty minutes. By then all systems and traffic will be completely moved to the West Coast, so I think we're gonna be okay."

There was silence on the other end of the line. "Chris?" I said. More silence. "Am I missing something?"

"I'm not sure," he replied.

"Talk to me, Chris," I said and walked to the office

window and drew the blinds so I could see JW7. I saw the door open and Jami leave the joint workroom, headed for her desk. "What's wrong, Chris?" I pressed.

"It's about Claudia Nazir."

"Nazir? What about her?" I asked, not understanding what she had to do with the systems breach.

"Bill Landry stopped by my desk. He said he wants to meet with me and talk about her," he replied.

I slowly shook my head, sat back down, and leaned forward. I rested my elbows on the desk and massaged my temples with my left hand as I held my cell phone in my right. I thought about Claudia and all of the things that she and her husband, Aasaal Nazir, had done. Not just to my country, but also to me.

The Nazirs were behind the kidnapping of then-Senator James Keller. They had also worked with the outgoing administration's Defense Secretary, Ron Gibson, to try to take out not only Keller, but his entire cabinet during the presidential inauguration in January. They were also responsible for Maria's death.

"Blake? You okay?" asked Chris.

I raised my head and blinked a few times, trying to stay focused.

"Yeah," I replied and watched as Jami returned from her desk and walked back into JW7.

"It's probably nothing, Blake. You know how Landry is, always looking for someone to blame for everything. Don't worry about it. I'll call you back after I meet with him. If Morgan finds anything, let me know so I can communicate that out. If our people find something, we'll do the same."

"Fine," I said. "I'll head back to DC day after tomorrow, and we can figure out what happened."

There was a pause on the other end of the line. "You think she'll say yes?" Reed asked, ribbing me.

I smiled as I stood and walked out of Shapiro's office, heading back to JW7. I reflexively put my hand down to feel the ring in my pocket. That made me think about Jami's sister and what she had said about me. "I'll talk to you later," I said as my smile faded. I disconnected the call and slid my cell phone into my back pocket.

When I stepped back inside the joint workroom, Shapiro was gone and Jami was once again sitting across from Morgan with her laptop open. She said the director had to call his boss to give him an update.

"That was Chris Reed," I said. "Bill Landry's got everyone at the FBI working on this, too."

I turned to Morgan and remembered the call we had earlier while I stood outside Giordano's. "I forgot to ask him about the guy you called me about," I said. "What was his name again? Was it Beckman?"

Morgan stopped typing and looked up at me. "I didn't get a chance to call him about it, either," he said. "The breach happened and Shapiro's been all over me ever since. Don't worry about it right now, mate."

Jami lowered her screen and looked up at Morgan from across the table. "Who's Beckman?"

"Nothing," Morgan said and started typing again.

Jami turned to me and shrugged.

I leaned back in my chair and watched Morgan get back to work. Something about him was bothering me.

There was a wrinkle in the center of his forehead. I could see white showing in the upper part of his eyes. And his eyebrows were raised more than usual. I couldn't help but think about my training as a Navy SEAL years ago. I had become pretty good at reading people, and the skill had proven useful many times.

I didn't want to press Morgan while he was trying to figure out who had launched the attack on the East Coast, but I told myself that I'd need to find out more about this guy Beckman when I got back to DC.

Morgan turned to me and saw me watching him work. "Seriously, Blake, it's nothing that can't wait."

I nodded. But there was more to it than that. Morgan Lennox was scared. And he was lying to me.

12

AJ Lennox pushed his chair away from the table. "I'm done," he said and turned to his right to look at Wolf. "I went back through and checked everything."

Wolf nodded, satisfied with the work AJ had done.

To his left, AJ saw Ivanov standing at the factory door. It was open about an inch, and he was staring outside as if he was waiting for someone to arrive. A few seconds later, Ivanov pulled the door closed, pushed the locking bar to secure it shut, and headed back to the table where AJ and Wolf were seated.

"What is the status?" Ivanov asked, his sharp tone of voice making AJ sit up straight as he approached.

"The connection is closed. As far as I can tell, all bread crumbs were removed, making us untraceable," answered Wolf, who had taken the laptop and was navigating through a mainframe session to confirm.

Ivanov walked to the table and stood at the edge, looking over the men. "How much longer?"

"It's done," answered Wolf. "Fifteen more minutes until normal operations are restored. Now's the time."

Ivanov grabbed the chair at the head of the table, pushed it next to AJ, and took a seat. AJ kept his eyes fixed on the laptop, avoiding direct eye contact with Ivanov, as Wolf pushed it back in front of him.

"It appears as if you've passed the test," said Ivanov, who rested his hand on AJ's shoulder. "Now that the United States government is focused on stabilizing their systems, they're going to start looking into who may have done this and why. I need you to hit them again right now. Are you up for another assignment?"

AJ nodded cautiously.

"That's the spirit," said Ivanov with a laugh. "Mr. Wolf, I believe you've mapped out our next steps?"

Wolf reached inside his jacket and found a small notebook. He flipped through the pages until he found his notes on how the next attack would work. He set the notebook down in front of AJ. Ivanov watched him pick it up to take a look at it. AJ's eyes grew wide as he read through what was to be done.

"This is crazy. I'm not gonna do this," said AJ as he got to the bottom of the page. "Bringing a system offline is one thing, but what you've outlined here is completely different. People will *die* because of this."

"You can and you *will* do this, Mr. Lennox," pressed Ivanov.

"I won't," AJ insisted. "Do whatever you want to me; I'm not gonna kill innocent people." As soon as AJ finished speaking those words, he felt the rumble of a vehicle approaching the old factory. The walls began to vibrate. Ivanov stood and headed for the door. Wolf followed. AJ watched, praying he had left the connection open long enough for someone within one of the intelligence agencies to track his location.

Ivanov pushed the slide bar to unlock the door and opened it slightly to look outside. AJ held his breath.

But the vehicle wasn't there for AJ. He knew it the moment he saw Ivanov pull the door completely open and step outside, followed by Wolf. AJ listened and heard Ivanov speaking to someone in Russian.

A moment later, Ivanov reentered the factory, walked toward the large bay door, and pulled it open. A white van was parked at the end of the driveway. Ivanov barked an order in Russian, and the van's white reverse lights illuminated as it slowly started to back up with Wolf directing the driver inside.

Exhaust from the van billowed inside, causing AJ to start coughing. Ivanov slapped the back of the van twice, and the driver put the vehicle in park and turned off the ignition. Wolf grabbed a leather strap at the bottom of the bay door and pulled it closed before reappearing at the back of the van next to Ivanov.

The driver and another man in the passenger seat stepped out of the van. Wolf closed the passenger door and began speaking with the man at his side while Ivanov spoke with the driver. AJ listened closely.

Ivanov asked about AJ's apartment to confirm it was cleared out. The driver answered yes, but went on about something that AJ couldn't understand. A surprised look fell across Ivanov's face. He called for Wolf. AJ continued to listen, but the men spoke fast and whispered, making it impossible to understand.

Then there was silence. Wolf approached the table again as AJ watched Ivanov walk around to the back of the van. A smile began to form on Ivanov's face as he stared at AJ. "Open it," he ordered the two men.

They each pulled on the handles on the van's back

doors, and they swung open slowly. The first thing AJ saw were boxes on each side of the van. "We made a trip to your apartment," said Ivanov. "Had to get your belongings, a form of insurance in case anyone went there looking for you. We wouldn't want them thinking you were still in Washington," he added and turned to look inside the dark bed of the van. "It's a good thing we did. It seems there was something inside the apartment of great value to you."

AJ squinted as he looked inside the back of the van from across the large factory floor. It was too dark inside to see what Ivanov was looking at. All AJ could see were the few boxes at the edge of the van's bed.

"Get out," said Ivanov as he quickly reached for his gun. "I said get out!" he yelled, repeating himself.

AJ's heart was pounding inside his chest as Wolf took a few steps closer. AJ's eyes shifted from the van to the men standing all around it, then back to the van again.

Then he saw movement. Slowly, a leg appeared, followed by another, until it became clear what was happening. "Lisa!" AJ yelled, and Wolf grabbed him, putting an arm around his chest to restrain him.

Ivanov laughed. "Lock her up," he ordered, pointing to the room where AJ had spent the night. The two men who had brought Lisa to the factory each grabbed an arm and escorted her inside the makeshift cell. One stayed inside the room while the other stood outside the door, waiting to be given additional orders.

As Wolf continued to restrain AJ, Ivanov approached, slowly inspecting the gun in his hand. "Tell me now, Mr. Lennox," he said. "Have you had a change of heart? Will you execute the next step in the plan?"

AJ stopped struggling, so Wolf slowly let go and backed away.

The two men watched as AJ thought about what he wanted to do. AJ looked at the laptop and the notebook with instructions next to it. What Ivanov was asking him to do would kill hundreds of people.

But before AJ could refuse again, he heard Lisa scream from inside the cell.

"Okay! Please don't hurt her," he said. "I'll do it."

Ivanov smiled and barked an order in Russian to the man standing outside the cell. He banged on the door, and a moment later, it opened. AJ caught a glimpse of Lisa standing in the corner, visibly shaken.

"Get started," said Ivanov as he turned to AJ, and the man inside the room left Lisa alone.

After taking a deep breath, AJ sat back down at the table, unlocked the screen, and got to work.

13

THE THREE OF US WERE STILL SEATED IN THE ROOM WHEN Roger Shapiro finally returned. He stood at the head of the table opposite me, removed his jacket, and set it on the back of his chair. Then he paced the room, running his fingers through his graying hair out of what appeared to be nervousness. Then he rolled up his sleeves, stood next to his chair, and leaned both hands on the table to talk with us.

"I'm being asked to take a more hands-on approach to this," he said. "My counterparts at the FBI, DoD, and Homeland are reporting that they've made no progress in identifying the source of the data breach. Morgan, I need you to figure out exactly what happened and who did this, right now. Can you do that?"

Morgan sighed. "Mr. Shapiro, with all due respect, what the hell do you think I've been doing?"

I leaned in. "Morgan, can you at least explain to us what happened?" I asked. "How could someone bring down every government system on the East Coast, which is almost all of them? And why is the media reporting that retail websites where people shop are down. How are they all related?"

"Blake, all I can tell you is that someone with an incredible amount of privileged access went into our mainframe shortly before directing an onslaught of attacks against Dyn. That's what I'm seeing at least."

"What's Dyn?" asked Shapiro.

"Dyn is an internet service company that hosts dozens of major businesses and online retailers all along the East Coast. Most of them, actually. Dyn is also used by the federal government because it's so secure."

This prompted a sarcastic chuckle from Shapiro. "So that's why the online retailers are also down?"

"Right," replied Morgan. "I've been reviewing the chain of events from the past hour. It looks like there was a distributed denial-of-service attack directed at Dyn, which started an hour ago, and that DDoS attack is what caused us trouble." He rubbed his eyes and leaned in to look at the screen. "It's incredible, really. There's close to two terabits per second of data still being sent to Dyn-managed servers. It's just unreal."

"Morgan," said Jami as she lowered the lid to her laptop slightly to look across the desk at her colleague, "I'm familiar with DDoS attacks. There's no way this could have been done by one person, right?" she asked, tucking a lock of brown hair behind an ear. "Something this big would have to be coordinated."

"I'm not sure, love," Morgan replied. "It looks like after it was initiated, the attack grew in size and intensity over the last hour. It's growing exponentially; that's why those websites Blake referred to are still down. While the federal agencies have business-resumption plans to move data and traffic across the country to another server, most online retailers don't have anything like that set up. Why *would* they?"

"But how, Morgan?" I asked. "You said it's still growing in intensity. How is that even possible?"

Morgan shook his head. "One hell of a hacker is all I can say, mate."

"If *you* were doing this," Shapiro interjected, "how would you pull it off?"

Morgan thought for a second. "I'm not sure, really." He leaned back in his chair. We watched his eyes look up to the ceiling as he thought about it some more. "I guess I'd try to use everyday devices as weapons to help me. Smart TVs, DVRs, security cameras, I'd use anything I could and leverage them by bombarding Dyn with requests to overload them and shut it down." Morgan thought some more and nodded to himself. "Yes, I think that would work. It would cause the most damage with the least amount of effort."

"And is that what's happening here? I need to give Base an update by the top of the hour," said Shapiro.

"One thing at a time," replied Morgan. "Do you want me to work on who did this or how it was done?"

Jami turned to Shapiro. "I'll get on that to confirm Morgan's theory on how this was executed."

"Good," the director replied. "Base wants answers and so do I." Shapiro turned to Morgan. "And as soon as you're done, I need you to help Jami and confirm your theory. Got it?"

Morgan stared at his screen, ignoring his boss.

"Understand?" Shapiro asked, slapping the table twice to get his analyst's attention.

"I understand," Morgan replied. "Now give me some space. I can't think with you people here."

Shapiro stood, grabbed his jacket, and left. He slammed the door, causing the entire room to shake. "He's so worried about his reputation that he's overlooking the real issue here," I said. "Morgan, earlier you told us the main problem from the failover is with system responsiveness should there be another attack or something requiring quick access to the system. Do what you can to minimize that risk to us, okay?"

Morgan nodded. "Give me a few minutes, guys."

I watched as Jami grabbed her laptop and left.

As I started to get up, Morgan leaned back in his chair. "Blake, wait," he said. I turned to face my friend. "It hasn't been the same since you left. Nobody likes Shapiro. This is what we have to deal with every day."

"Trust me, I understand," I said, remembering how difficult it was to work for the man. I knew his endgame. Shapiro was trying to show his superiors at Base that he was better than his peers at the other agencies. But what he didn't understand was that people always come first if you want results.

I looked up and noticed the wrinkle on Morgan's forehead. It again reminded me of our conversation from earlier. "Don't worry about Shapiro," I said. "He needs people like you to keep him looking good."

Morgan forced a smile. "I'll let you know when I have something," he said with a wink.

I watched him start typing again, determined to figure out who had initiated the DDoS attack. I hesitated, knowing this wasn't the time or the place to ask what I needed to ask, but it was bothering me so much, I just couldn't help myself. "Morgan," I finally said, "I'm sorry to ask, but I need to know. Who's Beckman?"

Lennox turned to me and I studied his face. What I had read earlier as lying I now recognized as nothing more than worry. He was truly concerned about the guy, whoever he was. "A friend of a friend that I care about. Just trying to keep a promise, that's all," he said. And I believed him. Morgan was a loyal man.

I leaned against the door and thought about how I had brushed him off when he called, telling him to call Chris Reed instead. I felt guilty about it. "I'll look into it as soon as I get back to Washington."

"Thanks, mate."

I walked out of JW7 and pulled the door to the conference room closed behind me to give him some space. Whoever Beckman was, it seemed it could wait a few more days. I was satisfied with Morgan's answer and decided to deal with it later. We had a lot of work to do to try to figure out who initiated the cyberattack, how they did it, and make sure our many government systems were stable after the failover.

As I walked to Shapiro's office, Jami saw me and motioned for me to join her. She was standing at the desk of one of DDC's employees, a woman I hadn't met before. I figured she was new, someone who Shapiro had hired over the last year. "Blake Jordan," I said, introducing myself to the woman. "What's going on?" I asked her and Jami. I wasn't prepared for what they had to tell me.

14

When Morgan Lennox was finally alone and sure he had a few minutes to himself, he minimized the programs on his screen that he'd been using to investigate the cyberattack and reached for his notepad. He flipped through until he got to the page where he had written down Lisa's number.

It had been over an hour since he last spoke with her, explaining that she needed to get somewhere safe. Unable to locate AJ, he had worried that his nephew might be in some kind of trouble. So far, he'd been able to hide the issue from his boss, but knew he was probably coming off as extremely stressed out. The last thing he wanted was for Shapiro to think he was unfocused and dealing with a personal issue at work.

But Morgan needed to deal with this. He reached for his cell and stared at Lisa's number on the notepad.

Morgan thought about AJ. He had only mentioned Lisa a few times. Morgan knew his nephew had dated the woman, but didn't know much more than that. After moving to Chicago, he and AJ had begun to grow apart. AJ had graduated from college and landed the job at the Department of Defense, and Morgan was busy, too. They stayed in contact, usually through texts, mostly surface-level conversations.

He tried to focus, holding onto the yellow notepad while calling Lisa, expecting to hear her voice again.

But she didn't answer.

Instead, the call went straight to voicemail. "Lisa, this is Morgan Lennox," he said, trying to gauge how much he should share. "Listen, I'm still unable to locate AJ. I've got a few things going on, but I haven't forgotten about you. Please give me a ring at this number as soon as you can so I know you're okay."

Morgan disconnected the call and set his cell phone down on the table. He decided that the call went to voicemail because Lisa must have been on the phone or in a spot inside the DoD with poor reception.

Toggling his screen to get back to work before his boss returned, Morgan inadvertently brought up the tracking software he had used earlier to locate AJ. His nephew's cell number was still in the search field.

Looking out the window of the joint workroom, he saw Shapiro still in his office. He had time to spare.

Morgan clicked on the button to search for AJ's cell again, hoping to get a different result this time. Maybe there was some kind of explanation for why the cell couldn't be located earlier. Maybe AJ lost it and the battery was completely drained somehow. Maybe the phone was broken. Maybe AJ was safe after all.

If so, where was he? It was possible, Morgan reasoned, that he had already driven up to Fort Meade. But Lisa said there were boxes left in the apartment. AJ wouldn't have left behind the computer equipment and other electronics that

Morgan knew AJ had. He would have stayed to make sure they were secure.

The blinking status that read LOCATING made Morgan anxious, so he switched screens to continue looking into the cyberattack. Knowing Shapiro, he'd be back soon enough to check up on him and ask for another status update. If he didn't have a substantive update to offer, there'd be hell to pay for sure.

A minute later, Morgan heard the familiar chime from his laptop. The search had completed.

After hearing the sound, Morgan stopped typing. He desperately wanted to see if there was a different result. At the same time, he was afraid of what he might find. After taking a deep breath, Morgan toggled through the programs, bringing the tracking software interface back to the forefront. The status read DEVICE INACTIVE. Same result. "Where are you?" Morgan said to himself as he stared at the screen.

Thinking through his options, Morgan considered trying to find the moving company in DC that AJ might have been using. He searched online and found there were seven movers in the Washington metro.

Calling each of them would take some time, but he could do it if he had to. He could just ask if they had an appointment for The Bartlett on Twelfth Street. If anyone gave him a hard time sharing the information, he'd just say he was AJ's father, wanting to make sure his son was okay. *That just might work*, he thought.

Before he started making the calls, Morgan's eyes drifted to his right and landed on the small yellow notepad he had set back down on the desk next to him, with Lisa's cell number written on it. *She was probably just on the phone*, he thought, trying to calm himself down as to why she didn't answer her cell.

Morgan continued researching the DC moving companies and wrote each of their numbers down on the yellow notepad right underneath Lisa's number so he could keep track of which ones he needed to call.

But after the list was made, Lisa's number at the top of the page kept distracting him.

He decided to try calling her one more time to ease his mind. Just as before, Lisa didn't answer her phone.

Morgan set his cell down on the table and exited the websites he had visited to look up DC moving companies, in case Shapiro walked in. When he did, the tracking program was once again on his screen.

"Fine." He sighed. Morgan deleted AJ's number from the search field and replaced it with Lisa's number.

He clicked on the button to start the search. But instead of going back to his work, this time, he waited.

Staring at the screen, Morgan thought about the path that Lisa would have taken to get to work. He was familiar with DC and knew that his nephew's apartment was close to the DoD, just across from the Potomac River, a fifteen-minute drive away. Lisa surely would have made it to the office by now. Morgan continued to stare at the blinking LOCATING status message, trying to make sense of what was going on.

Then he heard the chime. Morgan leaned forward and stared at the status that read DEVICE INACTIVE.

Now both phones, AJ's and Lisa's, were off the grid. Panic began to overtake Morgan as he felt his heart start to beat even faster in his chest. *There has to be some kind of explanation*, he thought to himself and considered what options he might have to track down not only AJ, but now Lisa, too. Morgan placed his fingers on the sides of his head and massaged his temples as he thought through possible next steps.

There would be cell tower data he could try to access. He could find the precise location where both cell phones last pinged the closest tower. That would give him an idea of their last known locations. He could—

The door to JW7 swung open fast. Morgan jumped, startled by the appearance of Roger Shapiro.

"Lennox, I need you out here now!" yelled Shapiro, who then turned and quickly walked away from JW7.

Morgan sat up straight. With wide eyes, he looked out the joint workroom's window onto the center floor.

He had been so caught up in the situation with AJ and Lisa that he hadn't noticed the entire DDC operations center's staffers were standing and staring at a video playing on the large screen on the wall.

Morgan grabbed his laptop and left the room. He pushed his way past his colleagues until he got to Jami, who was standing at the center console, frantically switching channels, searching for a live feed to project onto the screen. Shapiro stood at the front of the room, cleared his throat, and raised both hands to quiet everyone down. He was about to make an announcement. Something very bad had happened.

15

I WAS STANDING NEXT TO JAMI WHEN MORGAN JOINED US IN the middle of the operations floor and set his laptop down on the desk in front of him. Jami continued to search for a live feed of the incident that she had just made me aware of a few minutes earlier. Shapiro got a call about it at the same time.

I needed to call Chris Reed as soon as I could. But first, I wanted to hear what Shapiro had to say.

"Listen up!" he yelled from the front of the room, waving two hands in the air. The voices started to lower. "I just received a call from Bill Landry at the FBI. Approximately ten minutes ago, a northbound train crashed at Union Station in Washington, DC. First responders are on their way to the scene right now."

"Mr. Shapiro, do we think it's related in any way to the cyberattack from earlier?" asked Morgan.

He held both hands out in front of him. "We don't know yet, Morgan. That's why we need anyone not working on a critical task for the earlier attack to look into this immediately." Shapiro looked around and pointed to some of the analysts huddled up. "Beltran, Robinson, and of course, Lennox," he said, looking at Morgan, "I need you all on this *now.*" Then he looked over his shoulder at the screen behind him and shot Jami a look. "Davis, can you get us a decent video feed? We don't need to be watching talking heads."

"I'm trying," said Jami, still flipping through different news stations and looking for live coverage. "I'll have to try social media," she added and switched the projector's input. Jami then plugged her laptop into the console and accessed one of the agency's proprietary systems created by Morgan to search for a live stream coming from a specific location. She needed to program it to search inside Union Station. But the system was very slow, and Jami became frustrated. The program was frozen and stuck on the log-in screen.

I heard my cell phone ring. I grabbed it out of my back pocket and looked at the screen. It was Chris Reed.

"Chris, what do you know about this?" I asked as I answered the call and headed for the back of the room. There was a lot of road noise on the line. I could hear the voice of another man talking in the background.

"We just got here," Chris said as I thought about the close proximity to the J. Edgar Hoover Building.

I leaned against the back wall and watched as Jami finally found a feed from someone live-streaming the scene from their phone. Dark smoke billowed from the wreckage. People were walking around confused. Some were crying. Others were guiding the first responders as they arrived.

"I need to tell you something," Reed said as the road noise lowered, and I heard him get out of the car and start running. Chris said to hang on and asked Mark Reynolds, his partner at the FBI, something before coming back on the line. "Before this happened, I got to talk to Landry about Nazir. It's not good, man."

"What did he say?" I asked, keeping my eyes on the live stream being projected in front of me and using my other hand to cover my ear as Jami raised the volume and I tried to hear what Chris had to tell me.

"Landry said that Claudia Nazir predicted this," Chris replied.

I slowly shook my head, trying to make sense of the news. "What do you mean she predicted this, Chris?"

"He pulled me into his office, told me he got a call from someone over at the correctional facility where Nazir's being held while she awaits trial. She apparently told someone there would be an attack today. Nobody took her seriously. When Landry got the call, he thought she was referring to the cyberattack. Before I could call you, *this* happened. Hang on," he said, and I heard a muffled voice.

It sounded like Chris was talking to Reynolds, who I guessed was having a separate phone conversation with someone while Chris spoke with me. "You're kidding me!" Chris said. "*Right now?*" he asked, with a voice still muffled, and brought the phone back to his face. "Blake, we have a problem."

"What is it?" I asked and kept my eyes fixed on the footage being streamed in front of me in real time.

"Mark got a call. There's another train headed to the station, right behind the northbound that crashed fifteen minutes ago. The operator says it's not responding. He's lost control, Blake. He can't stop it."

I ran to the front of the room, keeping the cell to my ear and raising my left hand to get the team's attention. "I have the FBI on the line," I said as I approached Morgan and

Jami. "There's another train, and it's headed for the same terminal. The operator lost control and can't stop it."

"Morgan, can you do anything?" Shapiro yelled to his analyst. "Can you try to take control of it?"

Lennox took a step back from his laptop and put his hands on the back of his head. He looked overwhelmed. Morgan stared at Shapiro, then fixed his eyes on the screen. "I don't know, let me try."

"It's the Washington Metropolitan Area Transit Authority. Access the system, find the train, and stop it," Shapiro barked as Morgan began typing into his laptop as he stood next to Jami. I stayed behind Morgan, watching his monitor as Roger Shapiro turned to watch the live stream being projected on the wall.

"Morgan, just divert it. Buy us time if you can't stop it," I said calmly, trying to ease the pressure.

"Blake, please. You people need to give me a minute. I haven't even accessed their system yet."

Shapiro and I looked at each other. I turned to Jami; her face was pale. I felt helpless. We all did.

"Okay, I'm in," Morgan said and started to type. "But the system's slow as molasses. I can't work like this."

I was thinking about what Morgan had said earlier, the warning he'd given us about system responsiveness, when I heard Reed starting to talk. "Is that it?" he asked Agent Reynolds. "Is that the northbound?"

"Get out of there, Chris!" I yelled. "Get everyone out!" I looked up at the video being projected on the wall. The person at the station who was streaming the video panned the camera to their left. We watched as the dark tunnel was slowly illuminated until the light turned the corner and started to approach the platform.

Morgan turned to me. "I think I have it, but there's too

much lag! I need more time!" he yelled and used his sleeve to wipe sweat from his forehead and dried his hands on his jeans, waiting for the system to respond. I turned my attention back to the shaky video on the wall as the train's headlight grew brighter.

The person filming started running. The video feed showed the station's floor and rocked back and forth as the person holding the cell phone ran away from the platform and climbed the stairs to safety.

"There," said Morgan. We heard a loud screech from the video feed. I heard the same sound on the phone.

The video continued to rock as the person broadcasting the stream climbed the stairs. We heard more screams and shouts on the feed. I asked Chris if he and Reynolds made it out. There was no response.

When the person with the cell phone reached the top of the stairs, they turned the camera around. The screeching grew louder as they filmed the train rapidly approaching. The sound of the impact caused the audio portion of the feed to cut out. The bright light from the explosion caused an overexposure of the video. Then it faded to black. Morgan put his hands behind his head and walked away.

We were too late.

16

At two in the morning, Jami, Morgan, and I arrived at Washington Dulles International Airport. Convincing Shapiro to let me bring Jami wasn't a hard sell. He needed her in DC to be his eyes and ears.

Morgan was a different story. I didn't plan on him coming with us. I thought he should stay in Chicago.

But Morgan insisted on joining me. Shapiro rejected the idea immediately and told Morgan he needed to stay at DDC and focus on the system breach and figuring out who had unleashed the cyberattack from earlier.

But once Morgan got something in his head, he wouldn't let it go. He could be stubborn like that. Morgan explained that Beltran and Robinson could stay behind, and if he joined me, he could just work from FBI headquarters at the Hoover Building. He said there'd be synergy with their analysts.

Plus, Bill Landry, Roger Shapiro's friend and FBI counterpart, would be there to oversee everything, anyway. It wasn't until Morgan said he'd relay the FBI's progress or lack thereof to Shapiro that the director agreed to the idea.

Morgan knew how to get what he wanted. I was glad to have him on my side. I needed his help.

While in Chicago, I had tried to get a hold of the president, but Keller wasn't available, so I spoke with Chief of Staff Emma Ross instead. She was aware of the situation and explained that Keller was in a meeting with Vice President Mike Billings and would call me back as soon as he could. I let her know that I needed to get back ASAP. Ross made some calls and had us on a chartered flight within the hour.

After we hit the tarmac, Shapiro called Jami. He said he had spoken with Bill Landry and he'd be expecting our arrival. The new DDC field office in Washington was still under construction, so our only real option was to work from FBI headquarters. I couldn't help but think about last January, when Landry gave Jami a hard time for wanting to work there alongside Chris while they tried to search for me during the terrorist threat on Inauguration Day. That was why I didn't like Landry. He liked to complicate things.

But I guess it was different when a friend like Roger Shapiro called in a favor.

After we landed, we followed the signs for GROUND TRANSPORTATION and hailed two taxis. I let Jami and Morgan take the first one and watched as the sedan disappeared down the stretch of road that ran alongside the edge of the building until it turned a corner and disappeared. I watched my driver step out.

"Where we goin'?" he asked as he opened the trunk and held out two hands to take my messenger bag.

"I need to get to Union Station," I replied. "And I'll keep my bag," I said and tugged the handle to open the door to the backseat. I climbed inside and pulled the door shut. The car bounced as the man pushed the trunk closed. I latched my seatbelt into place as the driver climbed into the front seat.

"Don't think that's such a good idea," he said, turning around to look at me. "Big train crash a few hours ago. Two of them, in fact," he added and coughed a smoker's cough. "Everything's shut down; it's all over the news. So if you were planning on taking a train out of DC, I don't think you'll get very far, my friend."

I found my credentials and showed them to the man. He reached inside a shirt pocket to get his reading glasses, put them on, and turned on an overhead light. The man grabbed the badge with my picture on it.

"I work for the president," I said. "I need to get down there now. Just get me as close as you can."

The driver looked up at me over his glasses, still holding onto my credentials. He handed them back and took the readers off, setting them on the dash, and reached for his seatbelt. "Now *that*, I can do."

The driver was cautious as we left the airport, but picked up speed once we got out onto the Dulles Access Road and headed toward Washington. I told the man to drive faster, assuring him that we'd be okay if we got pulled over and that I'd handle it. We made the forty-minute drive in under half an hour.

It was almost three in the morning. I noticed Christmas lights from the suburbs we passed as we made our way into DC. Lights that would start to be taken down in another day or two. It made me think about New Year's Eve and the plans I had made at Navy Pier with Jami in less than twenty-four hours.

I tried calling President Keller again, but he was still unavailable. Ross said she'd make sure to have him call and said it'd be within the hour. She assured me that Keller wanted to talk to me, too.

As we approached, the driver entered the Third Street Tunnel. The ceiling was lined with yellow fluorescent lights that whizzed by us as I told him to go even faster. He crossed over two lanes and got over to the right to take exit 9 for D Street as we raced toward the exit.

When we emerged at D Street, there was a barricade blocking the road. The taxi driver was forced to go straight, and I told him to stop when he got to E Street. I released my seatbelt and reached for my wallet to pay, but he refused to accept my money. "You just get the son of a bitch that killed those people. Okay?"

I grabbed my bag, lifted the strap over my head, and nodded. "Thanks for the lift," I replied and got out.

I jogged four blocks east, toward Columbus Circle. The large off-white structure appeared as I walked alongside Lower Senate Park. Snow covered the lawn and the sides of the street, much like in Chicago. I noticed the dirty snow at the edge of the road as I walked closer to Union Station, and I couldn't help but think about Giordano's as I crossed the street and how different things were just four hours ago.

As I picked up the pace and started jogging again, I headed for the center of the three large archway entrances. Two officers approached to intercept me. "Sir, the station is closed at this time," one of them said as I slowed my pace and noticed the other cop was walking toward my right as a flanking maneuver.

"My name's Blake Jordan. I work for President Keller," I said and presented my credentials.

But the cop refused to take the badge from me or even look at it. Instead, the officer just kept his eyes fixed intensely on mine. "I don't care *who* you are or *who* you work for. I told you, the station is closed."

"Fine," I said and reached for my phone in my back pocket. Chris didn't answer, so I tried Reynolds.

Two minutes later, Agent Reynolds emerged and told the officers it was fine, saying that I was with him. Sweat dripped from his forehead and he wiped it away. He had his signature thin mustache, but hadn't shaved the rest of his face. I figured he must have had the day off and got called into work a few hours ago.

I followed Reynolds inside. Black and white tile stretched as far as I could see as we walked closer to the crash site. I was glad he and Reed were okay. "How bad is it, Mark?" I asked as we took an escalator down one floor and then descended a set of stairs, hearing shouts in front of us, directing our path.

"It's *real* bad, man. You never seen nothin' like this before, Blake," he said.

I walked with Reynolds and descended another level, taking a set of stairs down to ground zero. A dark haze hung in the air, lingering far longer than I thought it would. It burned my eyes as we approached the crash site. When we arrived, I saw why the smoke wasn't clearing—two areas were still smoldering.

The first was all the way to my right from the initial crash. The second was to my left, when train number two hit number one. I looked up and saw Chris Reed talking to one of the first responders. He noticed me, ended his conversation, and walked over. "Need to talk with you," he said out of breath.

17

I FOLLOWED REED UP ONE OF THE STAIRS, STILL OVERLOOKING the platform where the first responders and emergency crews were rushing up and down the strip of concrete, helping the injured stay calm while a continual rotation of ambulances arrived outside to take people to the two closest hospitals in DC.

"What are we dealing with?" I asked when we got to the top.

Chris looked down and shook his head.

"Not really sure," he said, putting his hands on his sides. "They've pulled out everyone they could find. It's been three hours now. If they're not at the hospital and if they're not sitting on the side over there," he said, pointing to a group of people being attended to, "then we're assuming they're buried in the rubble."

"How many casualties?"

Chris looked to his right where the first train crashed. "At least fifty from the first one," he replied and then turned to his left to gesture behind me. "And two for sure from that one. We found both of them."

"Only two? How's that possible?"

Chris shrugged. "Whatever Morgan did, he slowed it down enough to save a few lives."

I turned back to Chris, trying to stay focused. It was hard to hear him with the shouts down below from the first responders walking up and down the strip, using flashlights to search the mangled wreckage. I noticed a man on the platform, one of the victims, repeatedly shouting a name. Someone tried to get him to take a seat with the other survivors who were awaiting an ambulance to take him away, but he refused.

"You wanted to tell me something," I asked, turning back to Reed. "Is it about Claudia Nazir?"

He nodded. "Reynolds just got off the phone with Bill Landry. He said she's being moved."

"What do you mean she's being moved?" I asked, crossing my arms and moving a step closer to my friend. "Isn't she still being held at the DC Central Detention Facility while she awaits trial?"

"Yeah, Blake. She's been there since earlier this year."

"And that's where she needs to stay," I said. "That woman is the last person alive responsible for Maria's death, President Keller's kidnapping, and the attempted inauguration bombing. What's Landry thinking?"

"It's not Landry doing this," Chris replied. "He doesn't have the authority to make that call. If Claudia's being moved to another correctional facility, it's because someone's worried she's not going to make it through the night. I heard there were six stabbings there this year. You know how rough that place is."

I thought about that for a second and looked to my left, back down at the smoldering mass of bent steel. "How'd she know about this?" I asked Reed in a low voice, keeping my eyes fixed below. "She's been locked up for months with no contact with anyone on the outside. How'd she know this would happen?"

Chris didn't answer. I didn't expect him to. None of this made sense, but I needed to figure it out, fast.

"I need to talk with her," I said finally.

"What?" Chris asked. "With Nazir? Yeah, good luck, man. They're not gonna let you anywhere near her."

I turned back to my left, keeping my eyes fixed on the wreckage next to the platform, when I noticed something. I squinted and pointed at it. Chris turned and looked with me. "Do you see that?" I asked.

Before Chris could respond, I turned and jogged down the stairs to get back down to the main platform.

I walked over to the spot where I thought I saw some movement and was shocked at what I found: it was a hand moving. It was small and covered in blood, but it was moving. "Medic!" I yelled. "I need some help!"

As soon as I said those words, a memory flashed across my mind. I was standing over my father, yelling for a medic and watching blood starting to puddle on the ground around his body.

I shook my head to clear the thought and lowered myself into the sea of scattered steel and carefully crawled a few feet to the area I had spotted from the top of the stairs. A group of men followed me in. One of them held me back while three other men wearing black protective gloves crawled to the spot where I pointed and started removing the debris surrounding the young child. A minute later, they were done.

With the noise surrounding the crash site and echoes from law enforcement vehicles up above reverberating throughout the train station, it had been hard to hear the little boy's cries for help.

The boy was lifted out and handed to the second man standing behind the first, helping to peel back the debris. He handed the boy to the third man. I climbed out and stood on the platform. The third man lifted him up to me, and I bent down to grab the boy, who looked like he was three, maybe four years old.

He had a small gash on his forehead. Dried blood stained the side of his face and his long-sleeve shirt.

I stood and turned. The man I had seen shouting earlier stood behind me. I extended my arms and he took the boy from me and held him tight. The man cried and repeated the boy's name over and over again.

An EMT grabbed the child from his father, rested him on the ground to check for injuries, and reassured the man that his son would be part of the next group transported to the hospital three miles north of us.

I turned and bent down to help pull the rest of the men back onto the platform. I tried to keep it together.

I didn't know if it was seeing the father reunited with his son, or the memory of my own father and how helpless I felt at the time he was shot while I desperately called for help, but I was overcome with emotion.

I climbed the stairs and Chris followed. "Blake," he said, and I held two hands up as I passed him.

"Give me a minute, Chris," I replied and kept climbing the stairs until I made it two levels up where I had entered a few minutes earlier. Just outside the large stairwell, I leaned against the wall. My legs started to buckle. I slid to the ground and sat there, listening to the loud, frantic shouts coming from down below.

Before I could catch my breath, I heard the muffled sound of my cell phone ringing.

I leaned forward, dug into my back pocket, and grabbed my phone. "This is Jordan," I said, answering it. I could feel the cold floor through my jeans as I sat, waiting for a response. "This is Jordan. Go ahead."

"Please hold for the president," a woman's voice replied in a monotone, followed by a long, silent pause.

"Blake, Emma said she chartered a flight to bring you back. Are you on top of this situation?" Keller asked.

I pushed myself off the floor and stood. "Yes, Mr. President. But I need you to do something for me."

18

THE CONFERENCE ROOM THAT BILL LANDRY SET UP FOR Morgan and Jami to work from was on the south side of FBI headquarters at the Hoover Building. The room overlooked Pennsylvania Avenue and was just down the hall from Landry's office. Close enough for him to keep an eye on what they were up to, but far enough from his team of analysts working out on the floor so the visitors couldn't interfere too easily.

Lennox and Davis had interfered enough over the past year. When Senator Keller was kidnapped the night he was set to accept his party's nomination for president, Morgan had kept Landry and the FBI from interfering with DDC's recovery efforts. And during the inauguration back in January, Jami had worked with Chris Reed and played a vital role while investigating the credible threat. So although he was doing a favor for his friend Roger, from Bill Landry's point of view, neither Davis nor Lennox could be trusted.

But if the two were here, under Landry's watch, they couldn't be out in the field undermining his team.

Landry lifted his arm and pulled back his sleeve to

check the time. "I need to jump on a call," he said. "Need anything, just come and get me. Agent Davis, I believe you know where my office is located?"

Jami nodded knowingly and watched the special agent in charge of the FBI's DC field office step away.

Once he was gone, Morgan unzipped the laptop bag in the chair next to him. He kept it there, hoping that Jami would choose a seat across the table so Morgan could continue searching for AJ and Lisa without his coworker looking over his shoulder. And she did. Morgan pulled out his laptop, set it in front of him, and opened the lid. He unzipped another compartment in his bag, found the power supply, and attached one end to the back of the laptop and the other to a power strip in the middle of the table in front of him.

"You gonna log in, love?" he asked, eyes flicking back and forth from Jami to her bag resting on the table.

She unzipped the bag, grabbed her laptop, and set it down but didn't log in. Instead, Jami walked to the window and stared out onto Pennsylvania Avenue. "So let me make sure I understand," she said as she looked out onto the dark street. "Someone hacked into Dyn and redirected an incredible amount of data to their servers using smart devices, bringing every government system on the East Coast down. Failover for these agencies happened immediately to servers in other locations, mostly on the West Coast. But because of the huge amount of data being recovered, it made the system slow, almost unresponsive. Right?"

"Mostly," answered Morgan. "They didn't hack into Dyn, really. Dyn was just the service they targeted."

"So that happened, and we were all trying to figure out why the cyberattack was carried out and who did it. Meanwhile, they used the slow response time to their advantage by hacking into the Washington Metropolitan Area Transit Authority and taking control of the two trains that crashed at Union Station."

"It all happened so fast," said Morgan. "By the time Chris Reed called about the second train and we realized what was happening, I just didn't have enough time to stop it because of the system lag."

"So what are they planning now?" asked Jami. "What's their next move? Are we still vulnerable?"

Morgan shook his head. "No, all systems are running normally, albeit from West Coast servers. I'm seeing absolutely no lag on the Bureau's network." Morgan pulled an RSA SecurID token from his bag, entered his four-digit password, and typed the response code into his laptop to connect to DDC's VPN. He set the hard token down on the table and started typing again. "Even with the FBI watching everything I'm doing right now, system's running fast." Morgan gave Jami an annoyed look and shrugged. "They must have enabled monitoring, I guess. I see spyware running right now, watching me."

"Unbelievable." Jami sighed and returned to the table to pick up her laptop. She walked to the other side where Morgan was sitting and saw that he had set his laptop bag in the seat to his right. So she pulled out the chair to the left of him and pressed the power button while looking over at the spyware on his screen.

Morgan's pulse started to race. The whole point of coming to DC wasn't to work alongside Landry's analysts, as he had suggested to Shapiro. Landry would never allow that to happen. No, Morgan needed to get to Washington so he could get closer to where AJ and Lisa might be and try to ping the cell towers from a closer location. He'd try to access archived cell tower data to figure out the precise location of the closest tower both cell phones were last connected to so he'd know where to start looking.

"Morgan?" said Jami. "You're acting weird."

Wiping sweat from his brow with a sleeve, Morgan leaned back in his chair again. "It's nothing, love."

"Listen, you did everything you could to stop that second train. And we think you slowed it down. That saved lives, Morgan. You did the best you could with what you had. That's all any of us can do. Right?"

Morgan thought about Jami's words. He was in Washington. He could access the cell tower data if he could just be left alone for a few minutes. That would be the best he could do right now.

"*Right?*" Jami said again.

"Right," he answered and lowered his gaze back to his screen.

A knock from behind startled Morgan. He and Jami turned around and saw Landry standing at the door. "Davis, come with me. Shapiro's on this call and he has some questions for you." Landry crossed his arms. "Come on," he added, quickly growing impatient as Jami picked up her laptop and joined him at the door.

"I'll be back," she said to Morgan. "Try to locate the source of the cyberattack, okay? That's the priority."

Morgan nodded. "On it." He watched Jami and Bill Landry disappear down the dark corridor, and turned back to his laptop. The FBI would see him pinging the cell towers. But it would only take a minute, maybe two. If anyone questioned what he was doing, he'd just explain it away somehow. Besides, this might be his only chance to do something before Jami returned and would be able to see everything on his screen.

Morgan accessed DDC's location-tracking software. He

typed AJ's number and hit enter. He immediately heard the chime of the program indicating that it was done. The screen displayed DEVICE INACTIVE. He reached into his bag to find the yellow pad and tried to locate Lisa's device. The results were the same.

"Damn," he whispered and shook his head. Morgan took a deep breath and accessed the Stingray program. Initially used by the NSA and rolled out to the other agencies, Stingray let the FBI and DDC access cell tower data through an application that connected with physical devices located in major cities. Morgan thought about the two things that had been holding him back from using it before now. First, he needed to be connected to the FBI's system to use the DC Stingray. Second, the DOJ had a new rule that required a warrant to use the system. Morgan didn't have a warrant. But he had access. And he was in DC.

Morgan searched AJ's number first. Thirty seconds later, it returned latitude 38.862456, longitude -77.054843. Morgan turned and looked down the dark corridor. Nobody was there. He quickly entered Lisa's number and searched again. Thirty more seconds passed and he received the results. The latitude and longitude were nearly identical. Morgan clicked on a panel inside the program to bring up DDC's Maps application.

It displayed the closest address related to the coordinates: 520 Twelfth Street in Arlington, the address for AJ's apartment building. He checked the distance from the Hoover Building and saw that it was 3.4 miles away. Morgan locked his computer and took a pen from the table. He ripped a sheet of paper from the yellow legal pad, jotted down a message, and left it on his keyboard as he stood to put on his coat.

19

The drive to the Department of Corrections Central Detention Facility was quick. Reed drove his SUV two miles southeast down Massachusetts Avenue and slowed as we approached D Street and parked across the street from the reddish building at the corner of D and Nineteenth Street. I stared at the building out the passenger window. Somewhere inside was Claudia Nazir. The woman who stabbed me a year earlier. A woman involved in my wife's murder. A woman who would spend the rest of her life behind bars.

I'd make sure of that.

"How'd you do it?" Chris asked as he turned the ignition off. "They're really going to let you see her?"

"The president is friends with the warden. Keller told me after she was captured that he made a few phone calls to make sure she'd be kept at this facility. He wanted her kept safe."

"Kept safe? *Here?* Blake, this is one of the most dangerous prisons she could have been sent to."

"Yes, but the warden promised to keep her safe. He said he'd keep her in a cell far away from anyone who could hurt her. And he'd make sure that she couldn't hurt herself, either. The president wanted to make sure that Claudia made it to her trial. He did it for me. And he did it for Maria," I said and looked away.

"And just like that, one phone call and you get access to talk to her," said Reed as we stepped out.

I stood on the sidewalk and closed the door, still staring at the large, six-story building. "Two phone calls." I turned to my left and nodded to Chris. "Let's go meet the warden," I said and walked across the street.

We followed the long and winding sidewalk around to the north side of the building. As it curved to the right, we saw the main entrance into the facility. We entered, and a middle-aged woman approached us.

"Can I help you?" the uniformed woman asked, dropping a stack of papers onto a desk in front of her.

"We're here to see Warden Wagner," I replied.

"Name?"

"Blake Jordan," I said and turned to my left. "This is Agent Reed, FBI."

Chris handed the woman his credentials, and I showed her mine. She stared at my badge for a few seconds. "Executive Office of the President?" she said and shook her head slowly before looking back at me. "I don't know what this is all about, but I do know that Wagner's expecting you. I'll go get him now."

The woman disappeared around the back, and Chris turned to me. "What are you going to do to her?" he asked.

I didn't respond. Instead, I looked around the room, taking in my surroundings and trying to get my bearings.

"Blake—what are you going to do to her?" he asked again, putting a hand on my shoulder.

"I don't know yet, Chris," I replied.

"One wrong move and Bill Landry will be all over you. And Keller can't stop him. You know that, *right?*"

Before I could respond, we heard the sound of the woman's footsteps as she returned. She reappeared around the corner, carrying a small gray basket in one hand and a black metal detector wand in the other.

"Need you boys to empty out your pockets for me, okay?" she asked, holding out the basket for us. I pulled my cell phone from my back pocket and dropped it in, followed by my badge. Chris did the same. "I know this might seem a little Mayberry-like to you, but this is an exception. We don't allow visitors here. *Ever.*"

The woman pressed a square green button, and I heard a clicking sound as the metal gate in front of us slowly detached from the magnet holding it in place and it swayed open. I walked through as she held the black wand up to my body. "Spread your arms and legs for me," she said in a matter-of-fact tone of voice.

At the last minute, I decided to remove the small box in my pocket with Jami's ring in it. I reached over and placed it in the basket as the woman slowly ran the wand across my body.

"Ring?" she asked.

I nodded.

"Not enough metal in gold to set this thing off, but it'll be here when you get back," she said.

When she was done, she motioned for me to walk through. Chris followed, and the woman waved the wand over him as well. We heard a loud beep. "Just your belt buckle," she said and motioned for him to follow me inside. She tucked the basket under the desk and dropped the wand on the counter.

Chris and I followed the woman into a dark hallway. We

turned a corner and I saw an older man with thinning gray hair, rimmed glasses, and a gray mustache waiting for us at the other end as we approached. He wore a light blue dress shirt with rolled-up sleeves and black dress pants with a gold badge clipped onto his belt. He extended a hand.

"Bob Wagner, you must be Blake Jordan," he said, and I nodded as our hands met and we shook twice.

"Warden, this is Chris Reed, FBI," I said, turning to face my friend.

"Pleasure to meet you," said Wagner. "Jim called me a little while ago, said you could use some help."

I nodded again. "Warden, as I'm sure you know by now, there was a terrorist attack at midnight."

"The entire country knows," replied Wagner. "And I hate to say it, but I think we knew before it even happened," he added and stared at me. The warden furrowed his brow before he continued. "But something tells me you already knew that."

"Yes, sir," I replied.

"So you're here to see Nazir. You know she's not talking to anyone. She says she wants immunity."

I turned to my left to look at Chris, then back at Wagner. "That's not gonna happen. But if you give me five minutes with her, I promise I'll get her to talk."

The warden didn't answer; instead he just looked me over.

"Listen," I continued, "I hear she's going to be transported to another facility in a few hours. Please, let me try to talk to her before it's too late and she's under somebody else's authority. Let me get some answers."

Wagner kept a hand inside his pocket. With the other, he stroked his mustache, thinking about it. "Not sure when they'll pick her up. They like to come early and try to avoid the media if they can," he said and motioned for us to follow. We walked inside an elevator and Wagner pushed the button for the sixth floor.

When the elevator doors opened, we followed the warden down to an unmarked door. He inserted a key and let us in. I followed the man inside. Chris entered after me. In the small room was an armed guard waiting for us. I looked through the two-way mirror and saw a large dark room, with a table and two chairs. I saw another door on the other side of the room and decided it must lead to the inmate area.

Then I saw her.

Seated to the left was a woman wearing a white, long-sleeved shirt underneath an orange jumpsuit. A woman I hadn't seen in over a year. She stared into the two-way mirror, and it felt like she was staring right through me. A cold chill ran over me. I was about to come face-to-face with Claudia Nazir.

20

I CLENCHED MY HANDS INTO FISTS AS I FELT SOMEONE SLAP MY back. It was the warden. "Jim's a good friend. Any friend of his is a friend of mine. Do what you need to do, but she's not gonna talk to you." Wagner nodded at the guard, who proceeded to enter the code to unlock the door for me. He pushed it open and gestured for me to enter first so he could close and secure the door behind us once we got inside.

After taking a deep breath, I entered the interrogation room. Claudia Nazir looked up, studying my face.

"Remember me?" I asked in a low, gruff voice, keeping my volume down, trying to intimidate her. I saw a smile start to spread across her face. "Yeah. Of course you do," I added and walked to the table and pulled out a chair, turned it backwards, and sat down. I rested my arms on the back of it and forced a smile.

"Last time I saw you, you stabbed me. Right about here," I said, lifting my shirt up slightly with one hand and touching the healed wound with the other. "Then you ran and hid in a bedroom so your husband could deal with me.

Just like you ran from me at Dupont Circle back in January. You know what that makes you?"

Claudia didn't respond. She just kept her eyes fixed on mine.

"It makes you a coward."

Nazir's eyes flicked left at the guard who was standing behind me. He walked to the opposite side of the room and stopped when he got behind Claudia. I might have had the warden's support, but I could sense that I didn't have the guard's. I stood and grabbed the back of the chair and dragged it to the door I had entered to get it out of the way. Then I turned to Claudia. I walked back, rested both arms on the table, and got in her face. "How'd you know about the attack?" I asked as she leaned back in her chair.

She took a deep breath and said, "I want full immunity from President Keller. Only then will I talk."

"That's not gonna happen, Claudia. I will do everything in my power to make sure you live out the rest of your life in a place like this," I said, looking around the room. "Now tell me, how'd you know about it?"

"If you want to prevent the next attack, you'll need to make it happen, Mr. Jordan."

I looked at the guard. He began to pace the room and took a stance closer to me. My eyes returned to Claudia. "What do you mean next attack?"

She didn't respond.

"Where? What's the target?" I pressed.

Claudia shook her head. "I want full immunity first and safe passage out of the country with my children."

I walked to the left side of the table and, with a quick motion, lifted it and slammed it against the wall. "Tell me what the target is!" I yelled in her face, and she recoiled as the guard ran over to restrain me.

"You're done here," he said, and I pulled my arm to break free of his grasp. I watched the guard unbutton the strap on his holster and set a hand on his gun before pointing to the door. I heard the muffled sound of the code being entered from outside the interrogation room to unlock the door and get me out of there.

"You can't touch me in here," Claudia said smugly, and I turned back to see her smile slowly widen.

I took a step closer, fully expecting the guard to grab me again, but he didn't. Claudia stared at me, enjoying the moment. She was right. I was powerless. I couldn't make her talk. And she knew it.

I turned to face the guard, looked at the door, and nodded as I walked up behind him to follow him out.

But instead of making me exit in front of him, he walked ahead of me. That was his first mistake.

His second was leaving the strap securing the gun in his holster unbuttoned.

As soon as the guard started to walk into the room where Wagner and Chris Reed were waiting for me, I grabbed his gun with my right hand and shoved the man into the room with my left. Quickly, I slammed the door closed and jammed the chair I had placed there a few seconds earlier against the handle to hold the door shut.

I turned around, and Claudia Nazir stood, holding her hands in the air. I heard the sound of muffled shouts coming from the other side of the two-way mirror and someone pounded their fist against it.

I approached Claudia and grabbed her neck with my left hand and walked her backwards, slamming her head against the wall as I shoved the gun against her throat. "Tell me what you know!" I yelled as the shouts coming from the next room stopped. She was struggling to breathe, so I loosened my grip. "Start talking!"

"Soon," she said. "It's happening within forty-eight hours of the first attack."

"What's happening?" I asked, shoving the barrel of the gun deeper against her throat. "Tell me."

Claudia was shaking and breathing hard. "I won't tell you more without immunity," she whispered.

"You're not getting immunity!" I yelled as I once again heard the sound of an access code being punched in. I remembered that there was another entrance into the interrogation room. I was running out of time. "Tell me what's happening so I can stop this!" I yelled as the door flew open.

"Stand down!" the guard yelled from behind me.

I looked over my shoulder and saw another guard with the man whose weapon I had taken, aiming his gun at me as Chris Reed followed them into the room. I couldn't see the warden from where I stood against the wall with my hand still wrapped around Claudia's throat. I turned back to Claudia and saw sweat dripping from her forehead. I leaned in closer. "If you know something, then tell me now."

"I repeat, stand down! Last warning!" the guard standing behind me yelled and took a step closer.

Chris approached and stood between the two guards and me. "Blake, stand down, man."

"You don't know what the target is, do you?" I asked and watched her reaction carefully.

Her eyes jumped from Chris back to me. "I do," she replied in a whisper once again, her voice quivering.

I had already established a baseline with Claudia when I first entered the interrogation room. I watched how she acted when telling me the truth. I paid attention to her body language and her facial expressions. I wanted her to be lying to me about the next attack to try to get an immunity deal out of the false claim.

But she wasn't lying. Somehow, she knew about another attack that would be taking place soon.

"Damn you," I whispered, slowly letting go of her throat. She dropped to her knees, gasping for air.

I turned the gun around and walked to the door, extending my arm to hand the weapon over to the first guard. He grabbed it and walked past me, heading for Claudia to attend to her and take her back to her cell. The second guard directed Chris and me out of the interrogation room to where Wagner was waiting.

"I want full immunity from the president!" Claudia yelled from the room. "That's the deal. I told you *when*. Get that and I'll tell you *where*. You're running out of time! Your move, Mr. Jordan. Your move!"

21

Chris and I left in a hurry. Both Wagner and Reed had missed most of the conversation between Claudia and me as they worked their way to the other door to get inside the interrogation room. But they had heard enough as Claudia yelled her confession from the room, saying what she knew about the attack.

The warden escorted us back to the elevator and took us to the first floor. The uniformed woman who we had spoken with earlier handed our things back to us. Wagner stood with her and watched us leave.

We jogged across the street. Reed unlocked the SUV as I climbed inside and dialed the White House.

"We need to figure out where this attack is happening," I said to Chris as I heard the line start to ring.

"You believe her?" he asked as he pulled the vehicle out onto Pennsylvania Avenue and headed northwest.

"I do. Chris, where are we going?" I asked, the line still ringing as I pressed the cell against my ear.

"Hoover Building," he replied, and I nodded.

There was no answer, so I disconnected the call and

tried contacting someone who I knew would answer. She picked up on the first ring. "Blake?" Keller's chief of staff said with a concerned tone to her voice.

"I need to talk to the president, Emma."

"Yeah, he wants to speak with you, too," replied Ross. "Here he comes now. Hang on a second."

I heard a shuffling sound as her cell was passed to the president. Even though the drive was less than three miles, Chris had his overhead lights on and was weaving in and out of traffic to get us to FBI headquarters as fast as he could. I held my left hand to my ear to help me hear the phone conversation over the road noise.

"Damn it, Blake. I just got off the phone with Bob Wagner. *What the hell happened over there?*"

"Mr. President, your contact at the correctional facility agreed to meet with me. He let me in to talk with Nazir, but she was uncooperative and immediately asked for immunity before she'd agree to talk to me."

"Did you *think* she was going to cooperate?"

"No, but—"

"Blake, you called, asking if I could pull some strings to get you a meeting with Claudia Nazir. You said you were going to ask about today's attacks. Bob said you pulled a gun on her. *What were you thinking?*"

I shook my head and looked to my right. Out the passenger window, the Capitol Building came into view. The large white dome was illuminated for a brief moment before it disappeared behind some trees. "Mr. President, I'm sorry if this puts you in a bad situation, but I had to get her to talk. And I did."

There was a pause on the other end of the line. "What do you mean you got her to talk? What did she say?"

"A second attack. She said there's something else planned, taking place within forty-eight hours."

There was another pause from the president. "What *kind* of attack? Where is this happening?" asked Keller, his voice lowered. I could imagine him stepping away to get some privacy as we continued to talk.

"I don't know," I replied. "She said she'll only tell me what the target is if you grant her immunity."

"And you believe her?"

I kept my gaze on the dark street, reflecting blue and red as we drove.

"Blake?"

I took a deep breath and let it out slowly as Chris approached the guardhouse at the Hoover Building. "Yes, Mr. President. I believe her," I answered as I handed my credentials over to Chris. I watched him give both his and mine to the guard to inspect. A few seconds later, the guard let us through to park.

"The vice president will be here shortly. I'll bring him up to speed with the situation along with Emma."

Chris pulled into a spot, and we stepped out of the SUV and approached security at the back entrance to the building.

"You're not seriously considering granting her clemency, are you?" I asked as we walked.

Keller didn't reply.

"Sir, you told me yourself that the very reason she was being held at that specific correctional facility was to keep her safe until she could stand trial. She needs to pay for her crimes. For Maria. For my father."

Once again, Keller didn't respond.

"Mr. President, please."

"Blake, I want to see justice for your wife's murder and for Ben's death. But I can't make any promises."

Chris and I got to the back of the building and approached another guard. Chris worked out of the office and had his keycard to enter, but waited for me to show my credentials to the man. I visited enough on matters of domestic counterterrorism on behalf of the president that he knew who I was and let me in.

"Where do we go from here?" asked Keller as we got to the elevators, where I knew I'd lose the cell signal.

"I'm with Chris Reed, just arrived at the Hoover Building. We're heading upstairs now and Jami's waiting for me. We're going to figure out what's being planned by these guys. Then I'm going to try to stop it." The doors to one of the elevators opened and we stepped inside. "We're heading in. I need to go."

Chris pressed the button to get to his floor. I held the elevator door open by keeping my arm extended past the sensor so it wouldn't close so I could finish the conversation with Keller. Memories of Maria and my father rushed in as I realized that President Keller was putting Claudia's request on the table.

"Blake, I've known you for a long time. I know how you think. And I know how you act. Tonight is New Year's Eve. A lot can go wrong on a night like this, Blake. Lots of crowds. Lots of people gathered together. If you truly believe she knows something, then I have to consider every option. Do you understand that?"

I didn't respond. I just stood in silence, listening to the sound of his voice coming through the phone.

"I know you do, Blake. I'm going to meet with Mike Billings and figure out where to go from here."

"Mr. President, I want nothing more right now than to

see Claudia Nazir stand trial and pay for her crimes. I don't have to tell you the significance of seeing that part of my past resolved. If you and Vice President Billings are going to seriously consider a deal to prevent the attack, then I have to do everything in my power to find out what's happening first, because I simply cannot let that happen."

"Fine. Try to figure out what the target is. But I need you to play it straight from here on out. I don't want a repeat of what Bob Wagner said you did to Nazir, or someone like Bill Landry is going to take you out."

I dropped my arm and stepped to the back of the elevator and leaned against the wall next to Chris.

"Blake? Can you do that for me, son?" Keller asked.

"I'll try," I said and watched the elevator doors close in front of me. "But I can't make any promises."

22

The elevator stopped at the third floor. Chris and I stepped out and walked down the familiar, dark hallway. When I joined the president's team as an advisor back in January, I started making frequent visits to the Bureau to meet with Chris, much to Bill Landry's frustration.

Bill and I had a rough history together. As the special agent in charge of the DC field office, Landry was in charge. And Chris Reed reported to him. But when the president asked me to put together a special task force to identify and stop terrorist threats against the homeland, I asked Chris to join me, and he accepted.

That made things interesting, because Landry and I didn't seem to agree on much of anything except that Chris Reed was a damn good agent and we both wanted him on our teams. Few people knew my job as one of Keller's advisors was just a cover. Agent Reynolds was one of them. Bill Landry was another one.

Chris and I walked to another security checkpoint, and he swiped his keycard against the card reader. The entry system beeped and Chris pulled the door open. We continued down another hallway, and after passing a long row of offices, I stopped at the conference room we occasionally worked from and looked inside. Except for a single laptop at the far end of the table, the room was empty.

"They have to be here somewhere," said Chris, looking around, wondering where Jami and Morgan were.

I heard a door open behind us and the sound of Landry's deep voice echoing down the long, dark hallway. Chris and I turned around and saw Jami step out of his office, holding her laptop and heading our way.

"Glad to see you two," she finally said as she got to the conference room. Jami smiled at me, then turned to Chris. "I just spent an hour in your boss's office on a call with Roger Shapiro and a couple of guys from Homeland. They have no idea who's behind today's attacks. Shapiro's trying to get the CIA on the bridge line now. They're back to thinking that Russia's involved in this." Jami rolled her eyes and walked past us.

Chris and I followed her into the conference room. "Where's Morgan?" she asked, looking around and setting her laptop down opposite the one on the table, which I then realized must have been his.

I looked at Chris then turned back to Jami and shrugged. "Don't know. We just got here."

I walked over to Morgan's laptop and found a handwritten note resting on the keyboard. I held up the small sheet of yellow paper. "Went out for a smoke. Be back soon," I said, reading the note out loud.

"Thought he quit," Jami said, pulling her chair out and taking a seat. Chris sat down to the right of her.

Dropping the note back on Morgan's keyboard, I looked up and noticed a red light on the coffeemaker and walked over to pour myself a cup. I looked over my shoulder and watched as Jami logged back in to the DDC network. Chris was leaned in, watching her work. "I wonder how much progress he made," I said.

"Checking to see if he sent me anything," Jami replied as I turned around and watched, standing behind her. "Nothing yet," she added as I walked to the other side of the table to take a seat across from Chris.

But before I could sit down, I heard the muffled sound of my cell phone ringing in my back pocket. I reached for it and set my coffee down on the table. "Here he is now," I said, answering the call and placing it on speakerphone. I placed my cell in the center of the table in front of me so Chris and Jami could hear the conversation. "Morgan, where are you?" I asked and waited for an answer, but there was no response.

I rested my arms on the table and looked up at Chris and Jami. "Morgan? You there?" I asked and waited.

Then something happened on the other end of the line. A loud bang caused the sound coming from my phone to overmodulate. The sound echoed in the conference room, causing Jami to jump in her chair.

"Was that a gun?" Chris asked, turning to Jami, and she nodded in response. Then they both turned to me.

"Move," we heard a muffled voice demand. A second later, we heard the rhythmic sound of a cell phone being jostled inside a pocket as the caller, who I assumed to be Morgan, obeyed the order they were given.

"What's happening?" I asked. But before Jami and Chris could answer, the jostling sound stopped.

"Where are you taking me?" we heard Morgan ask, his voice distant, and I raised the volume on my phone.

I muted the line and looked up to Jami. "Can you trace this?"

"Yeah," she replied and turned my phone around on the table so she could better see Morgan's number. "There's an NSA program we now have access to called Stingray, but we need a warrant to use it."

"Forget the warrant, Jami," I said. "Just do it."

She started typing again when we heard the voice come back on the line.

"Move," the man ordered, and the jostling sound started back up again. Morgan asked another question, but because of the noise being made by his walking, it was impossible to understand what he had asked.

Chris and I stared at the phone as Jami looked up in frustration. "Blake, I haven't really used this before," she said and turned back to her laptop. "We had training on Stingray, but that was months ago."

"Just try to figure it out. Hurry," I said and noticed that the sound of Morgan walking stopped again.

A voice ordered him to do something, but it was too distant to make out what they had said. We waited for Morgan to reply, but all we heard was silence. "I said get in the back!" we heard a man yell at Morgan.

I held up my hand. Jami stopped typing. The room was perfectly quiet as the three of us held our breath.

"Ninety-one fifty-two!" Morgan yelled, his voice still muffled, but louder than it was earlier.

"Shut up!" the other voice yelled, farther away from the receiver.

"Ninety-one fifty—" Morgan tried to say it again, but was stopped before he could finish. We heard what sounded like the wind getting knocked out of him. Then we heard a struggle. "Let go of me," he managed to get out, and we once again heard the sound of large thuds as if Morgan was being beaten on the ground.

"Where are you?" I yelled into the phone after turning it back around to face me and taking it off mute.

He didn't respond. Instead, we heard the muffled sound disappear and a voice clearly say, "Start it up!" Morgan's phone was in the hands of his attacker. The three of us heard Morgan try to yell something, but he was too far away for us to make out what he was saying. We heard a loud thud.

Then the line went dead.

I looked down at my phone and saw the screen brighten and display a message that the call had ended.

23

THE THREE OF US STARED AT EACH OTHER IN COMPLETE silence. The screen on my phone faded to black as I took a step backwards and clasped my hands together, wringing them, trying to figure out what to do next.

"What's ninety-one fifty-two?" I asked Chris. "You think it's a plate number?"

He shrugged. "Could be anything, Blake. Maybe it's a building number and he was trying to tell us where he was. We need to get that trace and get over there. It can't be that far from us, right?"

I nodded. "Jami, how you doing on that trace?" I asked and walked around the table and stood behind her. Chris moved his chair over to the left to get closer and watch her screen, as well.

"Just got access to the program," she said and clicked on something. We watched a dialogue box open, prompting her to enter a number. Jami reached for her cell to reference Morgan's number and typed it in.

She hit enter and the interface connected to a Stingray device located somewhere in the Hoover Building.

Less than five seconds later, we heard a chime. Reed leaned in. "That's it?" he asked. "It's done already?"

Jami nodded. "I think so," she replied. "His phone's on, but the location is stationary. It's not on him."

"That was fast," I said. "Looks like it gave us some coordinates. Know how to get an address from that?"

Jami nodded again. "I think I remember," she replied and clicked on a panel inside the program to view the results in DDC's Maps application. "Okay," Jami continued. "The address is 520 Twelfth Street in Arlington."

"How far away is that?" I asked.

"Looking," she replied and clicked on something to calculate the distance between the addresses. It took a second for the application to access our current location before it gave the results. "Just over three miles."

"It checks out," said Reed, leaning back in his chair, which he turned slightly so he could look at me. "About how long did you say you were in that meeting with Landry and Shapiro?" he asked Jami.

She turned to face Chris and thought about it. "I don't know. An hour, maybe a little longer, I guess."

"Plenty of time for him to leave the building and get over to Twelfth Street if it's that close," he said.

"What's at that address, Jami?" I asked.

She started typing and brought up the location in Maps and showed us a street view on her screen. "Looks like an apartment building, about twenty-plus stories high. Let me cross-reference the name," she said and clicked on something to apply a filter to show more information. "Got it. It's called The Bartlett."

"We need to go," I said to Chris. He stood and followed me to the door. "Jami, try to figure out what ninety-one fifty-two is, okay? See if it's an address close to the apartment building. Find the connection."

"I'll do my best, Blake," she replied.

I turned and headed back down the long, dark hallway with Reed. We jogged down the corridor and rushed through the security checkpoint. But instead of taking the elevators, we took the stairs and picked up speed as we ran down the three flights, and Chris pushed the doors open.

We were in the lobby and ran toward the back entrance. Security didn't stop us. They knew who we were. They just watched as we got to the back of the building and quickly passed through the last checkpoint.

As we approached the SUV, Chris threw me the keys.

We climbed in and I started the SUV, put it in gear, and floored it, only slowing as we approached the guardhouse. The man nodded at me as he pressed a button to open the gate for us. Chris typed in the Arlington address for The Bartlett, and his GPS began navigating us to the apartment complex.

But when we got to Pennsylvania Avenue, I was reminded of something and reached for my cell phone.

"What's wrong?" asked Reed. I didn't have time to reply because Jami answered on the first ring.

"Hey, everything okay?" she asked.

"Jami, hold off on what you're doing right now. I just remembered something that Morgan told me."

"What is it?"

"When we were at Giordano's, Morgan called me. He said there was a murder in DC and asked if I could look into it. I told him I couldn't. I said I was in Chicago, but I could ask Chris to help him instead."

Chris turned to look at me. It was the first he had heard of it.

"Then the cyberattack happened," I continued. "We headed over to DDC, and just before the train crashed at Union Station, I remembered his phone call."

"Turn here," Chris said, tapping the passenger window twice, and I made a right onto Ninth Street.

"Why are you telling me this?" Jami asked. "Do you think it's related?"

I turned on the overhead lights and sped down a long ramp that took us directly underneath a large building. Five seconds later, we were back above ground again and merged onto the freeway, headed west.

"Blake?"

"Yes," I said. "It has to be. I didn't really think about it before, but why would Morgan insist on coming to DC with us?" I cut across two lanes of traffic and accelerated. "I'm gonna give you a name, you ready?"

"Hang on," she replied and paused for a moment before telling me to proceed.

"Shawn Beckman."

"Beckman. Got it. Who is he?"

"Don't know. Morgan said it was a friend of someone he cared about."

"I'll try to find him."

"You won't," I replied. "He's dead. Morgan said he was murdered two blocks south of H Street in DC."

There was a pause on the line. "I don't understand, Blake."

"I don't either. Just look into Beckman, okay? Figure out who he is and why Morgan asked about him."

24

JAMI SET HER CELL PHONE DOWN NEXT TO HER AND STARED AT the name she had written down moments earlier on the legal pad from the center of the conference room table. It made her think about Morgan. She cocked her head to the right and looked at the single sheet of paper on his keyboard. *Why did he leave that note saying he was going out for a smoke? Why did he lie to us?*

Her eyes shifted back to the legal pad in front of her and the name written on it.

"Shawn Beckman," she whispered to herself, playing with the pen while staring at the name.

She turned the pen around and tapped the end of it on the pad of paper, thinking through the last conversation she'd had with Morgan before she left to go to Bill Landry's office for the conference call with Shapiro. She closed her eyes, trying to remember if Morgan had said anything that might explain the situation. She shook her head and opened her eyes. "Okay," she whispered. "Let's start with Beckman."

Knowing that the man had been murdered in DC less

than twenty-four hours earlier, Jami knew there wouldn't be much to learn about his death just yet. But she decided to access the Metro Police Department records anyway to review what they had documented. Five minutes later, she found his newly created file.

"Shawn Beckman," she whispered. "Age twenty-seven, two shots to the back, his body found at three forty-seven in the morning at the corner of Morris and Sixth, behind an elementary school."

Scrolling further through the report, she looked for more details and stopped when something caught her eye. "Found with a cell phone in his jacket, Bulova watch on his left wrist." Jami kept scrolling. "Wallet in a back pocket, seventy-five dollars cash," she said and scrolled back to the top of the report. "This doesn't make any sense. Why was this tagged as a robbery? Who *was* this guy?"

Jami decided she would try to find out. She located the driver's license number from the images of the contents of the wallet that were photographed, and did a reverse lookup to get his Social Security number.

From there, she accessed another program to perform a background check. "Employer is Department of Defense?" she said, reviewing the results, and wrote 'DoD' underneath Beckman's name on the legal pad.

Jami minimized the web browser. This left the Stingray program up on her screen, front and center. She was still logged in and viewed the results she had received earlier when trying to locate Morgan's cell. She'd have to come up with something to tell Shapiro if he asked why she was using the program without a warrant. Jami closed out of the search results and noticed another button at the top of the application.

It read SEARCH HISTORY. Jami hadn't noticed that button before and slowly moved the cursor over it and clicked. Results displayed on her screen immediately. Jami saw the last entry as CIJD23, her RACF ID that she used to log in to the DDC system. To the right of her RACF was the number she had searched for earlier, which she knew was Morgan's cell number, and next to that was a time stamp from the search.

But just under that record was a series of several searches, all marked with the RACF ID of CIML74.

"That's Morgan's ID," she whispered and felt adrenaline shoot through her veins as she realized that Morgan had used the Stingray search several times. Jami scrolled through the search history, seeing location searches on the same two cell numbers. "Who was he searching for?"

Jami grabbed her pen and circled Beckman's name. Below that, in the middle of the page, she wrote down the two numbers that Morgan had been searching for. One at the middle left of the page, one to the right, and both directly underneath Shawn Beckman's circled name. She stared at the legal pad, wondering what the relationship of the two numbers were to Beckman and how all of them were connected to Morgan.

Jami sighed, trying to think through what she'd need to do to get the names that the other two cell phone numbers belonged to. She'd have to access one more program that she had seen Morgan use often at DDC. It was an interagency program that had a backdoor to every cell phone provider in the United States.

But like Stingray, it would create a record on a database somewhere showing that she had accessed it.

As Jami was thinking it over, she heard a man clearing his throat and approaching quickly. She minimized the screen and accessed her DDC email. Bill Landry walked in, and Jami looked up, trying to remain calm.

"Where's Morgan?" Landry asked at the door and turned his head to take a look inside the room.

Jami offered a smile and dropped her gaze back to her laptop. "He stepped out for a second."

Landry leaned against the door. "He stepped out for a second?" he repeated.

"Yeah," Jami said and pointed at Morgan's laptop. "I went to the lady's room, came back, and found that."

Landry walked over and grabbed the note resting on Morgan's laptop and read it. "When he returns, I need both of you in my office. We have that bridge line still open. Shapiro wants an update from you two."

Jami looked up from her screen and made eye contact with Landry. "As soon as he's back, we'll stop in."

Landry's eyes shifted to Morgan's laptop, then back to Jami. He nodded. "You haven't heard from Reed, have you? He was supposed to check in with me half an hour ago," he asked, looking at his watch.

"Haven't seen him yet, but I'll send him your way if I do."

Landry's eyes narrowed. After what felt like an eternity to Jami, he nodded again. "Okay," he said and left.

Jami waited a few seconds and listened to the sound of Bill Landry walking back to his office. She felt her heart still beating hard in her chest. When Jami finally heard the sound of Landry's office door closing, she navigated back to the interagency program, took a deep breath, and logged in.

Quickly, Jami entered the first cell number, looking at the left side of the page on the legal pad as she typed it in. She did the search, and it came back with results showing that the number belonged to a woman named Lisa Evans.

The SSN tied to the cellular account was on the results, and Jami wrote it down underneath Lisa's name.

She cleared the results and performed a second search on the other cell number that Morgan had searched earlier. Again, the results came quickly, and Jami moved her hand to the right of the page so she could jot down the SSN tied to the name that the cell phone was registered to. Jami turned to her left to look at the screen. She squinted her eyes as she read the results. She couldn't believe what she was seeing.

"Anthony *Lennox?*" she whispered and continued staring at the name. She looked away and blinked several times as she realized there was a connection. Jami briefly glanced at Morgan's empty seat. Then she wrote the name down and stared at it before looking back at the screen to get the SSN. Then she set the pen down, still confused about who Anthony was and his relation to Morgan.

After taking a moment to collect her thoughts, she performed a background check on Anthony. The results came back Department of Defense. Jami felt sick to her stomach, but continued. She performed the check on Lisa Evans, somehow knowing what the results would be. A minute later, she had them. Jami wrote DoD underneath both names and circled them before drawing a triangle around all three names.

25

I PARKED IN FRONT OF THE BARTLETT AT 5:32 A.M. WE GOT out and walked to the back. Chris lifted the hatch and unlocked a drawer that came preinstalled in government vehicles like this one. He slid it open and handed me a Glock 22. Then he gave me a mag and I pushed it into the gun and checked the chamber.

"That's a lot of explosives," I said, noticing the material in one of the compartments of the drawer as I concealed the Glock inside my jacket and Chris handed me another magazine with extra ammunition.

I shoved it inside a pocket. Chris closed the drawer, pulled down the hatch, and we stepped back and looked up at the tall apartment complex. "How do we get in this place?" I asked, unable to see the entrance. Directly in front of us was a grocery store occupying the first-floor corner of the building.

"Maybe around the side," Chris replied, and we walked along the sidewalk until we saw the marquee with THE BARTLETT above a set of double glass doors. But before we went inside, I heard my cell ring.

"Find anything?" I asked Jami, stepping to the side of the building and resting my back against a wall that jutted out five feet. Chris joined me. The wall helped shield us from the brutally cold December wind.

"Shawn Beckman worked for the DoD. He listed his occupation as analyst on his last tax return."

"I think Morgan told me that before," I said, turning to Chris after putting the call on speakerphone. "Anything else?" I asked, waiting for Jami to respond. But there was only silence on the line. "Jami?"

"Yeah," she finally said. "When I was clearing the search results from looking for Morgan's cell phone, I noticed that the Stingray program has a panel that shows recent search results. Blake, Morgan performed a search on two cell numbers."

"What two numbers?" asked Chris, furrowing his brow as we waited for Jami's response.

"A woman named Lisa Evans, also DoD."

"And the other one?" I asked.

After a brief pause, she answered, "Anthony Lennox."

I shook my head slowly and stared at Chris. "Lennox?" I asked. "Any relation to Morgan?"

"I didn't get that far," replied Jami. "But it looks like the three of them worked together at the DoD. And that's not all. I found Anthony's home address, reported on his tax return. He lives at 520 Twelfth Street."

"The Bartlett," Chris said, looking up at the tall building next to us. "What apartment number?"

"Eight fourteen."

Chris nodded. That was all he needed to know, and I agreed. "Thanks, call me back when you learn more."

I stuffed my cell in my back pocket and looked over my shoulder at the double doors. "Let's figure out what happened here," I said. Chris asked if we should look for Morgan's phone to pinpoint where the struggle happened. I told him no. It didn't matter. It was on the perimeter of the building somewhere. Besides, I had a better plan to try to figure out what had happened and what ninety-one fifty-two meant.

"Good morning," a redheaded woman in her late fifties wearing an old green blazer said as we entered.

"We need to speak with the manager for the apartment building," I replied as the door closed behind us.

"You're looking at her," she said, pointing to the fading gold, rectangular name tag pinned to her blazer.

I reached for my credentials and showed my badge to her, as did Chris. "Ma'am, we need your help."

"Well, make it quick, because I'm very busy here," she replied sharply, her voice cracking as she spoke.

"You're busy at five thirty in the morning?" I asked, and she shrugged in response. "Okay," I continued, "you have surveillance cameras outside the building. We need to see the footage. And we need access to the residence of a man named Anthony Lennox, apartment eight fourteen. Can you help us?"

"That depends," she replied as her voice cracked again. "You fellas got a warrant to do all of this?"

I took a deep breath, trying to keep my cool. "No, ma'am, we don't have a warrant. But something happened here just outside your building," I said, gesturing behind me. "We have reason to believe that a federal agent was assaulted here, and we need access to your security footage to confirm what happened."

"I wish I could help," she said. "But you can go through the proper channels, tell me the date and time, and I'll send in the request to pull the tape and have it ready by the time you get back with that warrant."

"It happened thirty minutes ago," said Chris. "We don't have time to go through the proper channels."

I stepped closer and added, "And if we miss our chance to save his life because of your bureaucracy—"

"Fine," she said, interrupting me and holding two hands out in front of her. "But I can't rewind the tape from here. We don't even control the cameras. The feed goes straight to the company that installed them for us, and they're closed on weekends. I can't even submit the archive request until Monday morning."

The woman's eyes flicked back and forth between Chris and me. She was telling us the truth.

"Can you tell me anything about the numbers ninety-one fifty-two?" I asked. "Do those numbers mean anything to you?"

The woman looked up and to the left. She was thinking about it.

"Please," I added.

The manager nodded and turned around, reaching to grab the handle of an overhead cabinet. She pulled it open, took out a three-ring binder, and turned back around, setting it on the counter in front of her. "I'm bad at names, but I do remember numbers," she said as she slowly flipped through the pages.

"What *is* that?" Chris asked.

"We keep a record of every vehicle that's kept on the premises. I take a picture and keep it here along with a photo of the resident," she said, continuing to flip the pages and staring at each sheet intensely. "It can get slow during the day, so anyone working the front desk is asked to spend some time getting familiar with the renters so they can greet them by name. We want The Bartlett to feel like home to our residents."

At that, the woman stopped flipping through the pages and pulled the metal tabs at the top and bottom of the binder. She carefully lifted out a laminated page and held it up. "There it is. Sergeant Doug Anderson."

She turned the page around and handed it to me. I held it out so Chris could see it. A picture of the back of a Metropolitan PD vehicle was stapled to the resident information.

Car number ninety-one fifty-two.

26

AJ AND LISA HELD EACH OTHER CLOSE AS THE ROOM GREW colder. AJ thought the temperature outside had to be in the thirties, if not colder. Lisa wouldn't stop shivering, which made AJ hold onto her even tighter.

He again thought through the events that had taken place over the past day. Lisa had explained how she went looking for him to share the news about Shawn, and she told him about the phone call with Morgan. AJ was determined to keep her safe, but all he could do now was keep Lisa warm.

When it was clear that they were going to be in the room for a while, maybe even another day, AJ decided to turn off the overhead fluorescent light on the ceiling that had been flickering off and on every few seconds. That would help Lisa rest. AJ wanted the light off, anyway. Plenty of light was entering the room through the large crack underneath the door, and it helped him see movement outside the room.

From the couch where he and Lisa rested along the wall opposite the door, the spot was perfect for seeing out onto the factory floor, where a small team of men worked. AJ knew it would at least help him see when the men approached to open the door again. And he could be ready for them.

"We've been in here a long time," Lisa whispered, getting closer to AJ and wrapping her arms around him.

AJ remained facing the doorway and pulled back his sleeve to press a button to illuminate his watch. "It's almost six in the morning," he said. "I don't know what they're doing out there. Did I fail the last task they gave me? Are they preparing another assignment for me? It just doesn't make any sense to me, Lisa." AJ took a deep breath. "We have to find a way to get out of here. I hope Morgan realizes we're in trouble."

Lisa squeezed him tighter, and AJ closed his eyes. He missed her. And he loved her. Lisa's embrace was all he ever wanted. Just not here, and not like this. AJ listened to the sound of Lisa breathing. It calmed him.

A rumbling of the building caused AJ's eyes to open. They grew wide as he let go of her. "Someone's here."

"Are you sure?" Lisa asked as the two of them sat up straight.

"I think so," he replied and stood before walking cautiously to the door and pressing his ear against it.

Low voices could be heard from the large main room. AJ turned around and looked at Lisa. Although it was dark, his eyes had long since adjusted, and he could make out her face as she stood from the couch and came to the door to listen with him. They heard the sound of one of the bay doors being lifted, and loud shouts in Russian began echoing throughout the old building. It caused AJ's heart to beat faster.

"What are they saying?" whispered Lisa.

AJ didn't answer. Instead, he closed his eyes, trying to stay still and listen as carefully as he could.

Then he heard a word that the men had used several other times. *Avstraliyets*. The Australian.

"I think they're coming for me," he said and backed away from the door, pulling Lisa along with him.

The sound of the engine grew louder before the ignition was finally turned off, followed by the rattle of the bay door being shut. Seconds later, AJ and Lisa heard the sound of footsteps as they sat down. AJ held his arm out in front of Lisa as they watched a shadow appear on the floor from someone approaching their room. The door was unlocked and slowly opened as a figure appeared, and the bright light blinded them.

Wolf stepped inside. "On your feet," he ordered sharply as AJ and Lisa obeyed his command. "Step out," he added, walking backwards out of the room, and raised his arm to aim his gun in their direction.

AJ walked out first, holding onto Lisa's hand behind his back, trying to protect her any way he could.

When AJ stepped out into the main room, the bright light caused him to squint his eyes. After being in the dark, he needed a moment to fully adjust to the bright fluorescent lights inside the large main room.

"That's good. Stop right there," said Wolf.

AJ heard footsteps in the distance, thirty, maybe forty feet away from him. "Get him out," he heard the man with a thick Russian accent say. AJ knew it was Ivanov. AJ's right hand squeezed Lisa's. He lifted his left hand to shield his eyes from the bright light to see what was happening while his eyes adjusted.

Nikolai Ivanov nodded to one of his men, who walked to the rear driver's side door and opened it.

"You heard him. Step out," one of Ivanov's men said.

Slowly, the man in the backseat climbed out and stood. AJ blinked repeatedly, not believing his eyes.

"Morgan?" he said as he realized that *Avstraliyets* had been a reference to his uncle, not to him.

Ivanov laughed. "Go on," he said to Morgan. "Go see your nephew, Mr. Lennox. My associate," he said, nodding at Wolf, "has been taking very good care of him as well as the woman until you could get here."

Morgan kept his eyes fixed on Ivanov as he walked past the madman and approached AJ and Lisa. He stared down Wolf before turning to speak. "Are you okay?" Morgan asked his nephew and gave him a quick embrace. "And you, love. You must be Lisa," he added and embraced her, too, as her eyes teared up.

"Morgan, what the hell is happening?" AJ whispered before his eyes moved back to Ivanov and Wolf.

"That's enough," Ivanov barked, stepping closer. "Let us have a little chat, just you and me."

Morgan turned around to face Ivanov. "Why are you doing this? What do you want from me?"

Ivanov put his hand on Morgan's back, ushering him back toward the direction from which he had entered. "You're a very predictable man, Mr. Lennox. *Very* predictable. Claudia warned me about you."

Morgan turned and backed away from Ivanov. "Claudia Nazir? What does *she* have to do with this?"

Ivanov put his hands behind his back and began pacing, circling Morgan as he thought about how to respond. "Mr. Lennox, for ten years now, your government has been spying on the people of Russia. But you already knew this, didn't you?" he asked as he continued pacing and raised an eyebrow briefly.

"Yes, of course you did," Ivanov added. "Because you were there, working as a government contractor, weren't you?" Ivanov stopped circling Morgan and stood in between him and AJ, who was next to Lisa. "And now," he continued, pausing for effect, "you're going to help me—how do you say—undo it."

"I'll never help you," said Morgan as he curled his lips in disgust.

Ivanov cocked his head. "Well, then I guess I'll just have to convince you." He drew his gun and, in one quick motion, turned around and pulled the trigger. AJ jumped and then felt Lisa let go of his hand.

27

I handed the page from the binder with the officer's information on it over to Chris to look at. "We need access to Anderson's apartment along with the other man I mentioned earlier, Anthony Lennox."

The woman furrowed her brow and turned again, reopening the cabinet behind her and grabbing a bigger three-ring binder. "He preferred AJ," she said, turning back around and, setting the binder on the desk, flipped through it until she found what she was looking for. "Don't expect to find anything in eight fourteen. It should be empty. The guy moved out already, though I don't think he returned his keycard."

The manager pulled on the metal tabs and handed me the resident packet with a picture of AJ and his vehicle. Chris stepped closer, and we looked at it together. AJ appeared to be in his early twenties.

"We still want to see it," said Chris. "We believe the man we're looking for came here to see him."

The manager stared at Chris for a moment and then shrugged. "Fine." Her voice cracked.

"Let's see Anderson's first," I said and watched her unlock a drawer and grab a worn-out-looking keycard.

"This'll get us in both," she said and motioned for us to follow.

Chris held onto the resident packet for Anderson, and I held onto AJ's. I didn't know who the man was yet, but Morgan seemed to care about him very much. And that meant I needed to care about him, too.

We followed the manager to an elevator. "How long did AJ live here?" I asked as we stepped inside.

"A while," she said. "Anderson's been in eight sixteen for the last six months, moved in over the summer."

"Right next door?" asked Reed, and we exchanged a glance as the manager nodded.

A minute later we arrived at the eighth floor. The doors opened and the woman exited, rushing us down the hallway until we got to the adjacent apartments. AJ's was on the left, and eight sixteen, Anderson's, was just to the right of AJ's. The two doors were next to each other, and I guessed that the apartments were mirror images of each other. Chris and I both took a good look at the resident packets for both of the men before we turned to the manager and handed both sheets back over to her to hold for us.

"Ma'am, let me have the keycard. We'll take it from here. Can you wait for us down the hall?" I whispered.

She shook her head. "You boys don't have a warrant. I'm doing this as a favor because of the man you say was assaulted here, but I'm going to watch what you do inside these apartments. I'm not going anywhere."

"Fine," I replied. "Chris, you take Anderson's while I check out AJ's real quick and make sure it's clear." Chris nodded in reply and I turned to the manager. "Please open them," I said and reached for my Glock.

She inserted the keycard into both doors quickly. First AJ's, then Anderson's. The light on both changed from red to green and we heard two clicking sounds as the doors unlocked. I nodded to Chris. "Go," I said.

"Federal agent!" I said as I entered AJ's apartment. I heard Reed do the same on the other side of me.

I went from room to room. I cleared the bedroom and another room next to it. Then I moved to the bathroom and finally the kitchen, where I noticed a landline hanging on the wall.

It was the only item left in the entire apartment. I thought it was odd that AJ had a landline when most people his age only carried cell phones. I thought it was even stranger that it was still there. I was about to press play on the control panel to see if there were any messages on it when I heard Chris yell for me.

I ran out of AJ's apartment and stood at the doorway to Anderson's. I couldn't believe what I saw.

The manager was standing in the kitchen, holding two hands up to her mouth, eyes wide. Chris was standing over a bunched-up rug, looking at a trail of blood that extended from a back room to the foyer.

"Are we clear?" I asked, still holding my Glock and looking around the room.

"Yeah, apartment's empty," replied Chris as I holstered my weapon and took a few steps closer. "There's some kind of listening device in the bedroom back there. Looks like Anderson was surveilling AJ."

"And it looks like there was a struggle," I said, staring at the dried-up blood. "Wonder if it's Anderson's."

Chris carefully stepped around the stain. "So the guy's a victim?" he asked. "He didn't take Morgan?"

I thought about it. "Something happened, that's for sure.

Do you have any security cameras up here?" I asked the manager.

She shook her head.

"Okay, when was the last time you remember seeing Anderson?"

She looked up, trying to remember. "Two or three days ago, I guess."

I noticed she had set the two resident packets on the counter. I picked up Anderson's and studied the pictures. Then I reached for my phone and placed a call to Jami. She answered immediately.

"Jami, ninety-one fifty-two is the car number for Metropolitan PD Sergeant Doug Anderson. He lives in an apartment at The Bartlett right next door to Anthony Lennox," I said, putting the call on speakerphone.

"Next door?" she repeated.

"Yes. Listen, I need to track down that police car. Can you find a way to locate it?" I asked and heard Jami start typing. I motioned for Reed to follow me. I stepped out of Anderson's apartment, walked into AJ's, and entered the kitchen area. Chris and the manager followed me inside as I motioned for Chris to look at the wall. "This is the only thing he left in here," I said in a low voice.

The manager looked it over. "Why would he leave his landline here and nothing else?"

"Blake," said Jami as I listened to the sound of her typing in the background, "I need a few minutes."

"Fine," I said and stared at AJ's phone. A red zero was on the display. I hit play anyway, and a voice said there were no new messages and three saved messages. My eyes flicked from Reed to the manager and back to the phone. I pressed play again.

The first message was from a DC moving company

calling to confirm an appointment AJ had set up. The next message was from the same company an hour later. One of the movers was standing outside the apartment, sounding annoyed, and saying that nobody was answering the door, so AJ would have to reschedule. The third message was from Morgan Lennox.

He sounded worried and asked why AJ wasn't answering his cell phone. I listened as the machine said the date and time of the call and realized that Morgan had called AJ right around the time he had called me as Jami and I were having dinner at Giordano's back in Chicago, six hundred miles away from here.

"Blake," said Jami, her voice echoing throughout the empty apartment, "the MPD has a GPS system for tracking their fleet of vehicles. Ninety-one fifty-two is offline, but I have an idea for finding it."

28

Chris and I looked at each other. "What's your idea, Jami?" he asked.

"On every MPD vehicle there's a camera that I might be able to access to figure out where it's located."

"But you just told us it's offline," I said.

"Yes," Jami replied. "The GPS locator isn't responding for some reason, but that doesn't mean I can't access the footage from the camera on the patrol car. I'm a little rusty, but DDC should have access to it."

Chris was shaking his head. "That's not gonna work, Jami. The footage from that camera inside the vehicle doesn't go anywhere. It just records on an endless loop to save on storage costs. They use a Panasonic Arbitrator camera, and it's only activated when the officer turns it on. Only if there's a recording of something substantial does the video footage get uploaded and archived at the end of an officer's shift."

"Great," Jami said in a defeated tone of voice as we heard the typing on the other end of the line stop.

I set my cell on the counter, keeping Jami on speakerphone. Still holding onto the two resident packets, I moved the page for AJ behind Anderson's, and I stared at the picture of the police vehicle. That was when I noticed there was something behind the photo. "How many pictures are in here?" I asked the woman.

"Two, one of the back of the resident's car and one of the side," she replied as I reached inside the plastic sheet cover, removed the resident packet, and pulled away the photo on top secured with a paperclip.

It revealed a picture of the side of the police car. I pulled it out and held it up to my eyes and studied it. Chris got closer to look at it with me. "Do you know what *that* is?" I asked, pointing to the top of the car.

He nodded. "License plate reader. It checks the plates of every car it passes so the cop doesn't have to."

"The ALPR, I forgot about that," said Jami, overhearing our conversation.

"Automatic License Plate Recognition," Chris added. "They installed them on a few vehicles at the Bureau. But not for us to run plates, really. We started using them to build our database for vehicle locations."

"Chris, does it have to be turned on like the Arbitrator camera? Or does it run continuously?" I asked.

"It just runs; you don't even have to think about it. It can scan up to three thousand plates an hour. It's continuously processing every plate an officer drives past, whether they're in a parking lot or on a four-lane highway. See that?" Chris said, pointing at another spot on the picture. "That's another camera. It's hard to see, but it's pointed to the left so it can scan vehicles in every direction that an officer's car passes. There's a processor that uploads the images to a database in real time in the back of every vehicle."

"Jami," I said, handing the picture to Chris and picking

up my cell, "if there's a database that stores every image the ALPR scans, can you get access to the most recent images from Anderson's vehicle?"

"We should have access, I'm just not finding anything on my end. Chris, do I just search for ALPR?"

"VeriPlate," Chris replied. "ALPR's the processor, but VeriPlate is the front-end application and database."

"Alright, hang on, I'm going to set the phone down," Jami said.

As we waited, I saw that the manager was getting flustered. "You okay?" I asked, and she shook her head.

"This is concerning. *Very* concerning." Her voice cracked. "What do I do about Anderson? Call the police?"

"We *are* the police," I replied. "Please don't do anything right now, ma'am. Let us handle this. If someone using Anderson's vehicle really did take the man we're looking for, then they likely have Anderson, too."

She didn't look convinced. And that worried me. If she called the MPD, that would complicate things.

"And what if Anderson's involved?" the manager asked. "I mean, he was in the apartment right next door. You're telling me he had a listening device set up to spy on AJ Lennox. Both men are missing and your friend was assaulted. What am I missing here?" she asked, holding her hands up, wanting an explanation.

I looked at Reed to get his take. He slowly shook his head, trying to understand the situation just like me. She was right. We *were* missing something, and I wasn't sure if Anderson was a victim or a villain.

"Ma'am, please give us a few minutes," I said. "We're going to figure out what happened to Sergeant—"

"Okay, Blake, I found the operating procedure, and I have access to the VeriPlate database," Jami said, interrupting me. "I started a search on car ninety-one fifty-two. I see results starting to come through."

"When was the latest tag scanned?" asked Chris.

"I think we need to wait for it to finish the search," she replied. "The images are coming back in the order of when the plates were scanned today. Looks like there's a picture associated with every tag. It's making the data dump take a while, but it's almost done, I think. It's already up to plates scanned an hour ago."

I thought about that and had an idea. "Can we figure out the location of the car based on the processor? How does it communicate with the database?" I asked Chris. "Does it send any kind of geolocation data?"

He thought it over and shook his head. "No, I don't think so. From what I understand, the ALPR uses air cards to operate over the same cellular networks as a cell phone. You could probably find the location based on that, but it would take a while. There isn't a number to plug into an application like Stingray."

"Okay, Blake. The search just finished," said Jami. "Do you want me to get the home addresses for the last few plates scanned? Maybe we can get an idea of the general area where the police car was last driving in?"

I thought about it. "No. I want you to look at the last image that it took. See if you can figure out where the car's located right now. Look for a nearby building or landmark that might tell us where we can find it."

"Looking now," Jami replied. Thirty seconds later, we heard her gasp. "Oh my God," she said softly.

"What?" I asked.

"The last image was taken from inside some kind of garage. The side camera must have snapped the picture of the tag from a white van parked next to it. Blake, Morgan's in the picture next to another man."

I felt my heart start to race. "Okay, go back one image and tell me what you see."

Chris and I stood huddled around my phone, waiting for Jami's response as the manager watched us both.

"Got it. Looks like a car drove by as it backed in. I see a street sign. Crossroad is Forty-Sixth and Lafayette Place."

29

Chris Reed stared at me. "Where's Forty-Sixth and Lafayette? DC?" he asked, massaging his temples with his hands. I looked up at the manager and saw that she was nervously biting her lip. The three of us stood frozen, feeling anxious and impatiently waiting for Jami to respond as she searched for the location.

"Jami?" I said as I lifted my arm to check the time.

"I'm working on it, okay? I'm not Morgan," she snapped. I knew she was feeling as stressed as we were. We waited another thirty seconds in silence, listening to her type, and wondering where Morgan had been taken. "Alright, it looks like Forty-Sixth Avenue dead-ends into Lafayette Place. The crossroad is in Hyattsville."

"Maryland," I said, looking over to Chris. "Jami, how far away is that from where we are now?"

"Checking. Looks like twelve and a half miles whether you take fifty or two ninety-five. Twenty minutes."

"We need to take two ninety-five and stay south of the city," said Chris.

I nodded. "Jami, can you get an exact address based on that image and send it to my phone?"

"I'll get you close. I need to go," she whispered and hung up. I wondered if Landry had stopped by.

Knowing Bill Landry and how he loved to throw a wrench in my plans anytime he could, that concerned me. Chris and I shot each other a look as the manager walked out the door. "I have to call someone about this," she said, her voice cracking. "In the best interest of our residents, I have to make sure they're safe."

"Ma'am, we're twenty minutes away from the federal agent we're looking for," I said as Chris and I walked into the hallway and I closed the door to AJ's apartment. The woman followed me to Anderson's door, and I pulled it closed, too. "If you make that call now, you're going to put this entire operation in jeopardy."

"Fine," she replied. "Then you have twenty minutes before I make the call. I do not feel safe right now."

I looked at Reed, then back to the manager. I nodded. "Fine. Chris, we need to go."

We took the elevator to the first floor and ran outside. I pushed the door open, and the cold air hit my face, making me flinch as I ran to the SUV to climb inside. I looked at my phone and saw that Jami had sent me the second-to-last image that Anderson's car had taken as it backed into the building in Hyattsville. Based on the angle of the picture, I felt confident that we could figure out which building it had been taken from.

Jami had also sent me an address close to the intersection of Forty-Sixth and Lafayette Place. I drove the SUV hard and fast. Fifteen minutes later, we exited the highway and drove another few miles on surface streets. Chris and I didn't talk those last few minutes. The engine roared as we approached.

Two minutes before we were set to arrive, Chris reached over and showed me the aerial view on his phone. There was no good way to get to where we needed to be without being noticed, because Forty-Sixth dead-ended into Lafayette Place, which was a dead end itself. I realized that we'd have to park a block south and walk there.

I turned right on Ingraham Street and made a left up Lafayette and parked. "Looks like an old factory, two hundred feet northwest of us," I said, grabbing Chris's phone and zooming out on the map to explain the approach. "Damn it. Doesn't look like there's a back door, only two entrances on the front of the building."

"Okay," he replied, looking up to keep an eye on the street as we talked. "How do you want to play this?"

I tapped on an option to show us the street view and pointed at the front of the building. "There are two bays and two entrances, one outside each bay. How many explosives did I see in the back of the truck?"

"Enough," he replied.

"I need a timed charge on both doors. We'll enter left."

"Blake, what if Morgan's near one of the doors? A blast like that can be fatal if he's standing too close."

For a moment, I thought about Jami's sister and I knew why. I tried to push the words that Kate had spoken to me out of my mind to focus on the operation. "We're running out of time, and I don't see any other options, do you?"

Chris shook his head.

"Okay then, let's roll," I said as I climbed out of the SUV and walked to the back of the vehicle. Chris opened the hatch and unlocked the drawer. He pulled it open and I once again saw the explosives we'd need to blast the two doors open. He checked his gun and holstered it before grabbing a field bag to transfer the material from the drawer over to the building.

I called Jami's cell. She didn't answer. I checked my call history and saw that her last call was from a DC number. I figured it was the conference room she was working from, so I tapped the number to call her there. "Hey, it's me," I said as the call was answered. "You figure out who's in that picture with Morgan?"

"Jordan, this is Bill Landry." I tapped Chris on the shoulder and motioned for him to lean in to hear the conversation. "I'm assuming Chris Reed is with you. I've had my people tracking your location for the past fifteen minutes. Care to tell me what the two of you are doing in Hyattsville?"

"Bill," I whispered into the phone, not wanting to blow our cover, "we believe that Morgan Lennox was abducted two hours ago, and we tracked him down to this industrial park. We're going in to get him back."

"If that's true, then give me ten minutes. I have an agent en route. Let us handle this when we get there."

"And what's he going to do when he gets here? Are you going to green-light this operation or stop it?" I asked and waited for a response.

Landry didn't say a word.

"That's what I thought. He's not going to do anything when he gets here except try to stop us from doing this. That's what you do best, isn't it, Bill?"

"Jordan, we'll be there in ten minutes. I need you and Agent Reed to stand down. Do you hear me?"

"Let me talk to Jami," I said. There was another pause on the line. "What did you do with her, Bill?"

"Agent Davis is unavailable right now. But you can certainly talk with her when you get here, okay?"

"Bill, I'm working under the authority of the president. So is Chris Reed. You know that."

"And *you* know that counterterrorism efforts are under the jurisdiction of DDC and the FBI. Last time I checked, Jordan, you were *neither*," said Landry. "You haven't done anything wrong yet. Stand down. Wait where you are. Let the FBI handle the situation with Morgan Lennox. We'll be there shortly."

I stepped back and looked at Chris. "Last time I checked, Agent Reed is FBI, too," I said, disconnecting the call and slipping the phone back in my pocket. Chris put the last remaining items in the field bag and closed the drawer. We stepped back and I pulled the hatch closed. "You sure you want to do this?" I asked.

"Landry's not sending a tactical unit, just a Bureau guy to force us to stand down. If Morgan's in there, we have to get him back. But, Blake, you know if we do this, there's no going back. Everything changes."

"I know," I said, tugging at my sleeve again to check the time. "We have ten minutes. We need to go now."

30

WE APPROACHED FROM THE SOUTH. CHRIS HAD HIS FIELD BAG with the explosives strapped over his shoulder. I ran next to him with both hands wrapped around my Glock, heading north on Lafayette Place toward Forty-Sixth. When we got to the cross street, I saw the red-brick building appear around the corner.

I made a fist with my left hand and held it up, signaling to Reed that we needed to hold up for a second. We knelt behind a tree as I quickly checked the area up ahead. A single streetlight ten yards in front of us lit a portion of the street. Everything else was dark, including the factory we needed to gain access to.

"Clear," I whispered. We stood and ran west twenty more yards on Forty-Sixth and knelt behind another tree. "That's it," I said, confirming that the building number was the same as on the picture Jami had sent. "Fifty-three forty-two," I said, staring at our target and looking all around, searching for any movement.

"Blake, we have less than eight minutes now until they get here."

"How long will it take to set the charges?" I asked, looking left and right, still scanning the building.

"Sixty seconds each."

"Let's move," I said, and we jogged across the street. When we got to the other side, I held my left hand up. We needed to slow down if we wanted to do this right. Directly in front of us were the two large bay doors with an entrance beside each of them. Chris approached the door next to the left bay first and got started.

I stayed back and knelt in the snow that had accumulated along the driveway, providing cover for Reed, still watching for any kind of movement from around each side of the abandoned factory. I thought about Morgan and what Chris had said, about how anyone near the doors could be fatally wounded when the explosives were detonated. And that made me think about Kate again and the words she had said.

She had told me I was cursed, that anyone I cared about either ended up dead or in the hospital. As I watched Chris working on the first door, I thought about my reaction to what Kate had said. I hadn't had a chance to reject it. Jami had walked back into the room with Matthew after cleaning up the broken glass. Kate told Matthew to get his things because they were leaving. I never had a chance to respond to Kate.

Maybe that was why I couldn't stop thinking about it.

I watched Chris move to the door on my right and get to work, but my mind was six hundred miles away.

Chris had been shot and almost died in the hospital eleven months ago because of me. President Keller had been kidnapped under my watch. My father died because of my actions. And my wife, Maria, was killed on the streets of Chicago. I wasn't even there to stop it.

Now Morgan was in danger and somewhere inside the factory.

I thought about his phone call, asking me to help him look into the DC murder. But I had dismissed him. If I had just listened instead of rejecting his call for help, Morgan might be safe right now. Maybe Kate was right.

Maybe I *was* cursed.

"Blake," Chris whispered, motioning for me to join him.

I got up and walked quickly to the side of the building. I stood in between the two large bay doors and held onto the Glock tightly, aiming it at the ground as I kept my back up against the wall. Reed did the same. "Ready?" I asked, and Reed nodded. I looked to my left, then my right, checking both doors. "How long?"

"About thirty seconds," he replied. "The door on our right will go first, then the left one ten seconds later."

I nodded. "We'll enter right, following the blast. I'll lead us in. Cover me," I said and closed my eyes.

The door on my right exploded, causing me to flinch. We heard shouts from inside the old factory. To our left, we heard someone starting to open the second door. I looked to my left and saw the door swing open, and I knew it would expose us to the blast. "Move!" I yelled and ran to my right, entering the building.

Chris had just made it in when we saw a man inside the factory standing at the other door, carefully peering outside as the second explosive detonated. A bright flash of orange reflected off the snow outside the building, and I watched the blast force the door closed on the man as he tried to exit, killing him instantly.

We saw another man emerge, running out of a room to our left. I fired one shot and took him down.

I turned and looked around the inside of the factory.

With a hand, I motioned to the left at the room the man had just appeared from. Chris ran from behind me and headed in to check it out. My heart was racing. I watched, providing him cover as I slowly moved toward another room directly in front of me.

"Clear," he said, and as he ran to catch up to me, I swung my Glock to the door I was approaching.

Another man appeared to our right. Reed turned, firing two shots from behind me, and the man fell to the floor. I pointed to the room and we started moving again. When we got to the door, Chris ran up beside it and waited for me. I stepped forward and kicked it open. I couldn't believe what I saw inside.

A man and a woman appeared in front of me, each with an arm wrapped around their chest, and each with a gun aimed at their head. The young woman had come into view first, so I entered the room aiming my Glock at the man holding her. Chris followed. Out of the corner of my eye, I could see he had his weapon trained on the man behind the younger guy. The next few seconds felt like an eternity and unfolded in slow motion. I thought about what Jami had told us about AJ Lennox and Lisa Evans.

It was them. "Put the gun down!" I yelled at my guy and noticed Lisa struggling to stand. She looked hurt.

"You drop your weapon, or I'll put a bullet in her brain," the man holding the young woman replied.

I looked at Lisa. She was fighting back tears and shaking. My eyes flicked to my right. AJ looked terrified as the man standing behind him held a gun to his temple. I looked back at the man who was holding Lisa.

"Put the gun down," I said. "I don't want to kill you, but I will if I have to."

He didn't move.

"Put it down!"

The man smiled and shook his head slowly. "You won't take the shot. It's too—"

I closed an eye and squeezed the trigger. The man's head snapped back from the impact of the bullet and he fell to the floor. Lisa screamed and recoiled in fright. I turned to my right and aimed the Glock at the other man. Now there were two guns aimed at his head. "Drop it or you're next," I said in a low voice.

The man holding AJ stared at me. His eyes moved to the dead man on the floor to his right. He looked back at me, and I started to close an eye. "Okay," he said with a faint accent and aimed the gun in the air. Slowly, he let go of AJ and took a step backwards. He bent down and dropped the gun. I took five steps closer and, using the weight of my gun, hit the man's face. He was knocked out cold. I kicked his gun back to Chris and checked the man for weapons. I found a cell phone and knife and put them in my pockets.

"Are you okay?" I asked, turning to Lisa.

She nodded and limped over to AJ, wrapping her arms around him.

"My name is Blake Jordan. This is Agent Reed," I said, looking at Chris. "Where is Morgan Lennox?"

Before either of them could answer, I heard the sound of footsteps. Someone was heading straight for us.

31

As the footsteps grew louder, I holstered my weapon and raised my hands. They weren't after Chris. They were here for me. I stepped forward and squinted as I looked out into the large room, waiting to see the agent Landry had sent to intercept me. I lowered my hands as soon as I saw the man come into view.

"Blake? Are we clear?" asked Agent Mark Reynolds as he lowered his weapon and cautiously walked toward me.

I nodded and met him at the door and shook his hand.

"What the hell happened here, man?"

"Hostage situation," I replied. "You alone?"

"Just me. Landry's bringing some of us back in from Union Station. He asked me to come up here instead, said Reed was caught up in some trouble with you, Blake. Guess he doesn't know you and I are tight, too."

I turned around to look at Chris, but noticed that Lisa had taken a seat on the couch. Her face was white. I walked closer and knelt down and held her hand. It was cold and sweaty. "Are you in pain, Lisa?"

She shook her head and looked down to her thigh. Her

black jeans were damp with blood. I could see where a bullet had grazed her and broken the skin. I reached into my pocket and grabbed the knife I had taken from the man on the floor in the corner, still unconscious. I opened the blade and carefully cut open part of the jeans. "You're lucky," I said. "Another half inch to the right, we'd have a bigger problem."

"Guess I'm just shaken up," she replied and turned to her right. I could see why she was feeling ill.

"Let's move to the other room," I suggested as I noticed Lisa glancing at the body of the man who had held her at gunpoint. The scene out there wasn't much better, but the color quickly returned to her face.

I motioned for Lisa to take a seat against the wall just outside the room we had exited. She sat down on the floor and AJ joined her. I knelt again to get down to their level and help them feel more comfortable.

"So how do you know my name? Are you FBI?" asked Lisa.

"Something like that," I said. "Morgan disappeared a few hours ago. We tracked him down to this building. It looks like he was trying to find both of you. We think he got kidnapped. We followed the trail here."

Lisa nodded, satisfied with the answer. "Morgan's his uncle," she said, looking at AJ. "He came for us."

"Lisa Evans, DoD," I said and turned to my right. "You're Anthony Lennox, but you prefer AJ. Also DoD."

AJ shook his head. "I *was*. Last day there was Friday. I was supposed to start at the NSA on Monday."

Chris had stepped out and walked up behind me. I looked up to see if he had heard what AJ just said. "What do you mean you were *supposed* to?" I asked, turning back to AJ to understand what he meant.

"The cyberattack," he began and paused for a beat, "the train crashes, I'm responsible for both of them."

Reynolds emerged from the room and stopped at the doorway. "How?" asked Chris, as confused as I was.

AJ shook his head. "I don't know. I was at a bar with my friend. We left; I was going to walk him home."

"Shawn Beckman?" I asked.

AJ looked at me with surprise and nodded. "A man named Nikolai Ivanov shot him dead. I was in that police car over there and watched it happen. Another man was there with me. He hired me at the NSA."

"What's his name?" asked Reynolds, trying to get caught up with the conversation we were having.

"Mr. Wolf. That's what he asked me to call him. He's an American. I interviewed with him for the NSA job. He's involved in all of this somehow." AJ paused for a second. "They found Lisa and brought her here. They made me do terrible things, saying if I didn't do as they asked, they'd hurt her. Then they found Morgan somehow and brought him here. They said he needed to do something for them or they'd kill me."

It was hard to believe that AJ had executed the terrorist attacks. But he had, and now they were using him as leverage to force Morgan to do something else for them. "What did they tell Morgan to do?" I asked.

AJ looked unsure. "The man named Ivanov wasn't very clear. He said something about the United States spying on Russia for years. He asked Morgan if he remembered being a part of that project ten years ago."

"Did he?" I asked.

"He seemed to," replied AJ. "Ivanov said he needed Morgan to undo what he did. Whatever he was working on,

Ivanov wants it shut down. Before they left, I heard Ivanov say it had to happen by midnight."

I heard a groan from the man inside the room. He was coming to. Reynolds reached for his handcuffs and walked inside to put them on the man. I turned back to AJ. "What was Morgan doing ten years ago?"

AJ looked up at Chris, then turned back to me. "I don't know who he worked for, but I know where he was living. New York City, Midtown. I know because I lived with him when I came to America for university."

"That helps," I said. "Do you remember anything else? Were any other names or locations mentioned?"

Before AJ could answer, I heard what sounded like a cell phone ringing out by the two large bay doors. I stood and turned. I walked closer to the body of the man at the door to our left. But by the time I got there, the ringing stopped. Ten seconds later, I heard the sound again. This time, it was coming from my pocket.

I grabbed the cell phone that belonged to the man Reynolds had just restrained and ran into the small room. Reynolds had the guy cuffed and sitting on the couch. Mark looked to me as Chris followed me in.

"You're gonna answer this. Ask for his location or you'll end up like your friend over there," I said, looking over at the dead man on the other side of the room. I answered the call, placed it on speakerphone, and held the phone to his face. He stared at me and I nodded for him to speak. I narrowed my eyes and waited.

"Sergei?" a man with a Russian accent said, followed by a short pause. "Sergei, are you there?"

"I'm here," the man replied. But that was all he said. I reached for my Glock and held it against the man.

"Sergei, why is Alexei not answering his phone?"

I pushed the Glock harder against his throat. He opened his mouth to speak and I waited. "Because he's dead," he answered. "They're here, Nikolai! Three agents and they have the prisoners!"

I looked down and saw the line disconnect. The man smiled at me as Chris lunged from behind and held me back. I pulled away from him and walked away in frustration as I realized we'd lost the one and only lead we had.

"Wait," AJ said as I walked past him. I stopped, took a deep breath, and turned. "I remember something," he said. "A name. Claudia. I heard the man named Ivanov say that she had warned him about Morgan."

32

Jami Davis sat in the cold, steel chair and waited. There was no clock inside the room and she wasn't wearing a watch, so she estimated how long she had been in there alone. Thirty, maybe forty-five minutes.

She could see the white shirt of a guard standing on the other side of the door through a small vertical windowpane just above the doorknob. It came in and out of view as the man fidgeted on the other side. Jami had been surprised to find Bill Landry at the door to the conference room as she reviewed the last few images taken from Anderson's car. She was just about to run the last image, the one with Morgan and an unidentified man, through DDC's facial recognition program when she looked up and saw Landry.

He disconnected the line as a guard appeared in the doorway. Landry told her to get up and leave the room. She did as she was told and followed the guard down the corridor and was ushered into the room where she now sat alone, waiting for Landry to return and explain what was happening.

Jami watched the guard turn and enter a code into the

door. A second later, Landry entered the room. "Why are you detaining me?" she asked loudly. "A DDC employee was kidnapped, do you get that?"

Landry smiled and approached the table. He reached for an old gray Polycom unit used for conference calls and moved it so that it was in between them. Then he sat down. "First off, you're not being detained."

"It sure as hell feels like it, Bill."

"Second," he continued, "we know about Morgan Lennox. I've just spent the last thirty minutes reviewing the security tape. We got him leaving the building. We also checked the servers and saw that both of you accessed Stingray to locate two cell phones. Care to share with me what the two of you were doing?"

"I didn't know what he was doing," replied Jami. "I was on that conference call with you and Shapiro. When I came back, he was gone. He called, it sounded like there was a struggle, and I tracked him down."

Bill Landry rested his elbows on the table. "We need to call Roger Shapiro. But before we do, you need to understand that we *are* going to help look for Morgan. In fact, I have Mark Reynolds in the field right now up in Hyattsville. Shapiro wants him back, too, so we're going to do whatever is necessary. Okay?"

Jami didn't look convinced.

"Let me call Roger," Landry added and pressed a button to get a dial tone.

Landry entered the eleven digits, sat back in his chair, and stared at the Polycom as the line rang. "Shapiro," Jami's boss said, answering the call.

"Roger, it's Bill. I've got Davis with me."

"Agent Davis," Shapiro began, "I need you to leave Washington and head to New York City right away. If you leave now, you can get there by noon. As you know, we don't have a DDC field office there yet, so Bill's been kind enough to work with me and help get you set up at the FBI's field office just south of Midtown."

"I can't do that," answered Jami. "I need to run an image to identify and find the man who took Morgan."

"Bill, you want to give her the update on that?" asked Shapiro, his voice echoing inside the small room.

Landry cleared his throat. "We know who he is, Jami. My team down the hall has been monitoring your network activity for two hours. We ran the image. He's Nikolai Ivanov, been on our watch list for a few years. We're working on it. In the meantime, we think an attack is planned for tonight in New York based on chatter we intercepted. It's New Year's Eve. The entire world will be watching Times Square."

"What kind of chatter?" asked Jami. "What did the communications say? Are there any other details?"

"Might be a truck bomb," said Landry. "Or a repeat of the terror attacks in Europe where Islamic militants intentionally drove trucks into crowds. We're going to have two million people in a very small space."

Jami shook her head. "Why aren't we evacuating the area? Why wouldn't we just cancel the whole thing?" She glanced at Landry's watch. "It's not even eight o'clock in the morning yet, we still have plenty of time."

"We don't want people to panic. The NYPD has sixty-five sanitation trucks filled with sand and placed in strategic positions, along with over a hundred smaller 'blocker' vehicles to stop an attack," said Landry.

"That's not all," Shapiro's voice boomed from the Polycom. "They'll have heavily armed police teams, bomb-sniffing dogs, helicopters, and bag searches in subways in addition to coast guard and police vessels patrolling the waterways, along with several other layers of plainclothes officers, cameras, and rooftop observation points. It's all being set up this very moment all around the heart of Times Square."

Jami cocked her head to one side. "Sounds like you've thought of everything. Why do you need *me?*"

"Because," said Landry, "we have reason to believe that Lennox is on his way to New York right now. You were onto something with the license plate reader database we watched you log in to. But those readers aren't just on select police and government vehicles. They're everywhere, Davis, including major highways all across the nation, installed earlier this year, in fact. They feed location information on hundreds of thousands if not millions of vehicles each and every day. We've been looking for the plate from the van in that last image you pulled down from the database. We got a hit a few minutes ago."

Jami thought about his response and nodded in agreement with the approach. "Where's the vehicle now?"

"Last seen headed northeast on I-95," replied Shapiro. "We lost track of it just north of Baltimore."

"And we don't know *why*," said Landry, anticipating Jami's next question. "Maybe they switched vehicles, or decided to exit the highway and take surface streets, or stopped and took the damned plate off the van."

"Davis, I need you in New York," interjected Shapiro. "Based on what you were able to find over the last few hours, you were right. We're on the same side. Lennox is missing and we need to get him back. Bill and I have spoken, and I've made it perfectly clear that I need his full support if we want to get him back."

"And you have it," insisted Landry. "You have my full

support." Bill Landry sat up, folded his arms on the table, and leaned in. He raised his eyebrows and waited. Shapiro stopped talking and the line was silent.

Jami looked down. "Fine," she said. "I'll go."

"Okay," replied Shapiro. "Bill will coordinate everything and get you what you need. Call me when you get to New York," he said and disconnected the line as Landry pressed the button on the Polycom to hang up.

"I think you're going to be an asset for us up there," he said. "We'll get you a Bureau-issued vehicle and firearm. We have a field office at 26 Federal Plaza. Are you familiar with New York?"

Jami nodded.

"Good," Landry added and stood, motioning for Jami to follow him. "I'll coordinate with Curt Willis, the special agent in charge over there, and I'll get the name of who you'll be working with before you arrive."

Jami stopped at the door. "You know what I think, Bill?" she asked as Landry turned around. "I think you're trying to get me out of Washington. I don't believe you care about Morgan Lennox at all."

Landry stifled a smile and nodded toward the end of the dark corridor. "Come on, Davis. Let's go."

33

President James Keller opened the door to the executive residence on the second floor of the White House, located between the East Wing and the West Wing. He quietly shut the door behind him and walked slowly by his wife, Margaret, trying not to wake her up as he passed. Keller made it into the bathroom, gently closed the door behind him, and walked to the mirror. After looking at his reflection for a brief moment, he turned the knob on the faucet and bent over to splash some cold water on his face.

Thirty seconds later, he looked back up at his reflection and was surprised to see Margaret behind him.

"Good morning, my dear," said Keller as he turned the faucet off and turned around. "You sleep okay?"

The first lady looked up to her husband from the wheelchair she had been confined to for over a year now. Medication had helped with the symptoms of Parkinson's, yet she still felt better using the chair. Margaret had fallen twice since moving into the White House eleven months ago, so it had been almost a year since she had attempted to move around without the chair or help from Nurse Cheryl.

"You look worried," Margaret whispered and turned around, pushing herself back into their bedroom.

"Of course I'm worried," the president admitted, following her out. "Two major terrorist attacks happened yesterday. One to the infrastructure of our intelligence agencies and another claiming innocent lives." Keller went into the sitting room and took off his jacket, carefully resting it on the back of a chair that looked like it had been in the room since the seventies. Then he sat down, closed his eyes, and exhaled.

Margaret rolled herself in front of her husband and reached for his hands. "Look at me," she said, and Keller looked up and stared at his wife. He offered a smile, one that said, *Don't worry, everything's fine.*

He imagined his wife offering some sage advice about how he'd been through this kind of thing in the past. About how he should lean on the good people he had surrounding him. About how he'd know what to do.

So he was surprised when she abruptly let go of his hands and backed away.

"What's wrong, honey?" Keller asked.

But his wife just pressed her lips together and shook her head slowly. "I've known you long enough to know when you're lying to me. Something happened. Not the two attacks. Something else. What is it?"

Keller leaned back in his chair. He looked outside and saw the sun coming up over Washington. Its sunbeams entered one of the windows and streaked through the room. It reminded him that while the day was just beginning, in a matter of hours it would be nightfall. And with it would come yet another attack.

"Jim, I'm talking to you," Margaret said harshly. "I'm your wife. You can talk to me, you know."

Keller took a deep breath and let it out slowly, looking sideways and shaking his head as he did. "I just met with Mike Billings. Early this morning, we learned that we had been warned about the attack at Union Station. A prisoner tried to warn us that it would happen. Nobody took her seriously. And now she's come forth with new information." Keller paused and added, "Another attack will be taking place very soon."

"Well, at least you know about it. If the intelligence community takes it seriously, they can try to prevent it. Right? They can do what they do best and keep it from happening. What about Blake? Does he know?"

Keller nodded slowly, but something about the way he answered the question told Margaret there was more he still wasn't sharing with her.

"What is it? What are you not telling me?" she asked.

President Keller leaned in and extended his hands and waited for his wife to return the gesture.

"The prisoner is Claudia Nazir," he said, feeling his heart start to beat faster as the words came out.

Margaret Keller's eyes narrowed as she studied her husband. "Why did you meet with Mike?"

The president didn't respond, just shifted in his seat and let go of one of her hands to wipe his brow.

"Jim? Why did you meet with him?" she asked again in a voice both louder and higher in pitch.

"Because she says she knows where the attack is taking place. And she'll tell us if we grant her clemency."

Margaret squeezed her husband's hand and shook her head. "No, you can't do that. What about Blake? And what about Ben Jordan? You told me months ago that Bob Wagner would see to it that she makes it to her trial, that she'd be held accountable for her actions, her involvement in Ben's death."

"I know what I said," Keller snapped, dropping his wife's hand and standing. He walked to the window and held a hand up to shield the sun from his view and looked out onto the snow-covered lawn.

Margaret turned herself to the right to face the president. "Did you sign it yet?"

"No," Keller whispered.

"Have you told Blake that you're moving forward with this?"

"No, honey, but it's already in motion. You need to understand that—"

"Then take it back," Margaret said, interrupting her husband. "Tell them you changed your mind, say—"

"We don't have time," the president said, staring at his wife. "Blake just called me. We're out of options."

Margaret returned the stare, looking up to her husband as he reached for his handkerchief and mopped his brow once again. "You should go back in that room and take a longer look at yourself in the mirror."

"What's that supposed to mean?" asked the president.

"Exactly what it sounds like. You haven't even been in Washington for a year and you've already changed."

"I haven't changed."

"You used to tell me about the time you spent as a SEAL. The way they taught you to think. You told me more than once that there's always a third option, you just had to find it. Are you *really* out of options?"

"Honey," the president said, taking two steps closer to his wife, "it's New Year's Eve. I've just learned that the attack is taking place *tonight*. We don't know more than that, and the only way to get the information is from Claudia Nazir.

She knew about last night's attack. She knows about tonight's. Do you understand?"

Margaret nodded. "I understand plenty," she said and turned herself toward the door.

"Life is about choices. Sometimes you have to choose the best bad choice. That's my job, day in, day out."

The first lady stopped and turned herself around, fighting back tears. Keller walked across the room, knelt next to his wife, and held her tight. "I'm sorry," she whispered softly. "I just want justice for Ben. I know I'm not alone."

The president nodded at his wife.

"Please try to find it, Jim. Find the third option."

34

After calling the president, I spoke with AJ again. There wasn't much else said between Ivanov and his uncle. But what he'd told me about Claudia warning Ivanov about Morgan was more than enough for me. Claudia was more involved than I thought. And I needed to figure out why.

Reaching for my cell phone, I saw that I had a missed call from Jami between when I spoke with Keller and when I talked with AJ Lennox some more. I took my phone off silent mode and walked toward the bay doors and called her back. I told her about Ivanov and Wolf. She told me about Shapiro and Landry.

I looked up and saw that Reynolds was motioning for me, so I told Jami I'd call her back when I could and hung up. "What's going on, Mark?" I asked as I walked across the factory floor.

His brow was furrowed. Something was wrong. "I need to call Landry with a sitrep," he said, using military-speak for situation report. "What do you want me to say? That you were gone when I got here?"

I thought about it, but before I could answer, we heard

the low rumble of vehicles approaching outside the building. I reached for my Glock and stepped backwards, unsure who had arrived at the factory or why.

"Hold up, Blake," Mark said from behind me. "Just backup, man," he added when additional FBI agents walked inside. I recognized some of them. Reynolds walked past me to speak with the men ahead of us. "It's okay," Reynolds yelled, his voice echoing throughout the room. "We got four dead, one captured."

I turned to talk with Chris Reed. "It's over," I said. "We should have gotten out of here when we could."

Looking back, I saw a medic enter, and I directed him over to Lisa. He cut the rest of her pant leg off and wrapped the wound with some gauze. The agent asked her if she could walk, and Lisa said she could.

He helped Lisa get to her feet and walked her toward the exit. She turned around and said thank you to me. I smiled and watched AJ join her as they disappeared outside. More agents arrived and entered the building. Two of them were checking out the police car parked inside the bay. Three entered the smaller room behind me to talk with the terrorist Reynolds had handcuffed earlier. They brought the man out and walked him to one of the black SUVs parked just outside the front of the building and sped off with him.

Then shouts came from the men standing behind the police car. The agents had popped the trunk and were looking inside. I stepped closer to see what they found. It was the body of Sergeant Doug Anderson.

"So they're cop killers, too," I said, turning to Reed, who had joined me next to the car. "Chris," I continued, "Ivanov knows Claudia Nazir. We need to find the connection between the two of them."

Reed shook his head. "Can Jami help? Maybe she can run a cross-check on Nazir, Ivanov, and Wolf."

"Landry and Shapiro sent her to New York. She's been driving for an hour, said she'll be there by noon."

"New York?" he said. "Why would they send her there?"

"Because of a terrorist threat," I replied. "But it's more than that. They wanted to separate her from us."

"You mean from you?" Reed asked.

I looked over his shoulder and watched Mark Reynolds across the room, leaning against the wall, talking to someone on the phone and looking at me. I knew who he was talking to. I figured it didn't matter anymore. The FBI got here too fast. This was Bill Landry's show now.

Reynolds nodded, disconnected the call, and walked over to Chris and me, and we stood in a circle.

"Let me guess," I said to Reynolds sarcastically. "That was Bill Landry and he wants you to bring me in?"

Mark shook his head. "Yeah, that was him, but that's not what he wants me to do."

My eyes flicked over to Chris, then returned to Reynolds. "Okay, what does he want you to do?"

He hesitated for a few moments, like he'd been warned to proceed carefully with me.

"Mark, what is it?"

"He wants me to pick up a prisoner from the DC Central Detention Facility."

"Claudia Nazir," I said.

Reynolds nodded cautiously. "He told me that the president just sent him a signed document offering her conditional immunity. Landry wants me to go get her now and bring her back to FBI headquarters before her scheduled pickup and transfer to another federal prison. He said if I can beat the transfer, it will be less complicated. If she helps us stop the attack, she's free. Landry said that's the deal Keller's offering."

Mark turned to Reed. "Landry wants you and Jordan to head back to the Hoover Building." Reynolds then looked at me. "He's going to let you talk to her, Blake. Landry said one of Keller's conditions is that you, and only you, can broker the clemency deal with Claudia Nazir. I'll meet back up with you two there."

"I have a better idea," I said and turned to Reed. "Chris will head back without me. When he gets there, he'll check on AJ and Lisa and convince Landry to let him debrief them."

Chris looked confused, not sure where I was going with this.

"Tell Landry about Wolf, see if he can help get you access to NSA employee headshots. Show them to AJ and Lisa and see if they can help us identify who the man is."

"And what are *you* going to do?" asked Reynolds as I turned to face him before responding.

"I'm gonna ride with *you*."

"No, man," Mark said, shaking his head and holding both hands up. "That's not what Landry said to do."

"I *know* what Landry said. But do you really think he's gonna let me get anywhere near her?" I asked.

"Blake's right," added Chris. "I've known Bill Landry a long time. Things never go like he says they'll go, especially if Blake is involved. And he doesn't agree with the president on much of anything, either. Whenever Keller says he needs Bill's assistance, Landry gives him the runaround." Reed turned to look at me. "I'm with Blake on this one. If we want to get some answers from Claudia, he needs to ride with you."

"Please, Mark," I added. "Let me talk to her before it's too late. I'm just going to ask her a few questions."

Mark looked at Chris, then back to me as he decided what to do. He knew Landry wouldn't be happy if he agreed to this. But Mark had a knack for being able to handle his boss. Reynolds also knew that what Chris and I were telling him made sense. Landry couldn't be trusted, and if we wanted a chance to try to get some more answers, I needed to talk to Claudia Nazir one more time.

"Fine," he finally said. "Let's go."

35

Twenty minutes later, we arrived at the DC Central Detention Facility. Instead of parking across the street where we had left Reed's SUV earlier, Reynolds pulled right up to the front door. Mark got a call and found out we were thirty minutes ahead of the transport vehicle, which was a relief to both of us.

"Leave it running," I said. Mark had the heater cranked, and I wanted to stay warm and loose as I started to think through what I was going to do when he brought Claudia out.

He nodded and stepped outside.

I watched him walk up to the entrance and disappear inside. I imagined him talking with the woman Chris and I had met with. I wondered if she'd make him empty his pockets out into the gray basket. I figured that was probably something just for visitors, not for federal agents on official business like taking custody of a terrorist like Nazir. I thought about the visit earlier and walked through the path that Chris and I had taken to get to the holding area in my mind. It would take at least ten minutes in and out.

Unbuckling my seatbelt, I reached for my cell phone and called the White House. Emma Ross answered.

"I need to speak with the president," I said.

"Just saw him a second ago, Blake. Hang on for me while I track him down for you, okay?" she replied.

I waited, looking at the clock on the dashboard, and watched as two minutes passed. *Eight to go*, I thought.

Another few seconds passed and I heard Emma's voice. "Blake Jordan for you," she said in the distance.

"Blake?" Keller said.

"Why'd you do it, Mr. President?" I asked softly. "Why'd you decide to offer her immunity?"

"*Conditional* immunity," Keller said, correcting me. "If she doesn't deliver, if she doesn't give us the information we need in time to stop the attack she claims is taking place tonight, she gets *nothing*."

I was silent, unsure how to respond to that.

"I had to do it, Blake. And I realize this decision is unpopular with you after all you've been through, but if I have a chance to save American lives, I'm going to take it."

"I understand, but I *know* Claudia Nazir. She wants nothing more than to see our country brought to its knees. I saw it in her eyes when she told me there would be another attack. She *wants* it to happen, sir. But she wants safe passage out of the United States even more. If you want to believe that she's going to agree to a deal where she gets to walk *only* if she prevents the attack, fine. But that's not how she works."

"But it *is* how I work," Keller said. "It's the only way we can win here. She's going to have to play ball."

The clock on the dashboard caught my attention again. Five minutes had passed. Halfway there.

"What if there's another way, Mr. President?" I asked,

turning to my left and looking over my shoulder out the back window to make sure Mark Reynolds wasn't returning yet. I heard the president take a deep breath and let it out slowly. I did the same, trying to keep myself calm as I thought through my plan.

"You mean a third option?" Keller finally asked after several seconds of silence.

"There's a man named Nikolai Ivanov. I just found out that Claudia Nazir has been working with him."

"Who is he?" asked the president.

"The man responsible for the cyberattack and the train crashes at Union Station. He also murdered a cop, abducted a DDC analyst, and has ties to Claudia Nazir. There's a connection between them, and I have a chance right now to figure out what it is," I said and turned back around as I waited for Keller's response.

"We need to get Ivanov," he said, followed by a long pause before he continued. "Where are you, Blake?"

"I'm sitting outside the DC Central Detention Facility. The Bureau agent I rode with is inside taking Nazir into FBI custody right now. He's going to transport her to the Hoover Building for me to broker the deal."

"Which I want *you* to handle, and I made that perfectly clear to Bill Landry." Keller paused again. "Do you want to tell me what you're thinking? I get the feeling there's a reason you're telling me all of this."

"Because there might be another way to get her to talk and figure out what the link is between her and Ivanov, but once she's at the Hoover Building, I won't have full control of the situation. I have less than five minutes if I'm going to make this work, but I need to know that I'll have your support if I do this."

Keller paused as he thought it over. "That depends.

What are you going to do?"

"Mr. President, it's better if you don't know the details," I replied and saw that eight minutes had passed.

I waited, keeping my eyes on the clock, feeling my heart beating hard and keeping time in my chest as I waited for the answer.

Keller finally said, "Blake, if you have a third option I'm not seeing here, and if you believe it's going to get us what we need without having to fulfill our end of the bargain, then do it. But you need to be sure about it. Because the way I see it right now, that immunity deal is our best shot."

"Thank you, Mr. President," I said, knowing that I did have a third option available to me. "I need to go."

"Godspeed," he replied and disconnected the line.

I dug into my jacket pocket and found the cell phone that belonged to one of the terrorists Ivanov had tried to make contact with earlier. I reattached the battery I had removed at the factory when no one was looking to prevent Ivanov or any of his men from following me. I powered up the phone and waited.

Just as the clock on the dashboard hit the ten-minute mark, I navigated to the phone's call log. I stared at the number Ivanov had called from, realizing that he most likely would have ditched his phone by now with the FBI on his trail. I dialed, pressed the phone to my ear, and waited as the line started to ring.

The call was answered. I heard what sounded like road noise; then the line was disconnected. "Damn it," I whispered and turned around. Reynolds was walking out of the detention facility with Nazir in handcuffs.

He pointed in my direction and walked behind Claudia. I turned back around and dialed again. This time, the call went to voicemail. I heard a short tone and took a deep breath. This was it, my one and only shot.

"My name is Blake Jordan," I began. "I know who you are. And I know that you have a man named Morgan Lennox in your possession. For the next ten minutes, I'll have Claudia Nazir in mine. After that, she'll be in FBI custody. They're gonna cut a deal and offer her immunity in exchange for information. Information that you and I both know will lead the Bureau directly to you. And trust me when I say they're going to do whatever it takes to get her to talk and stop you from carrying out another attack.

"Now, Morgan Lennox happens to be a friend of mine. I don't know why you've taken him, or what you plan on using him for, but I'm willing to make a deal. You give me Lennox; I'll give you Nazir." I turned around again and saw that Reynolds and Nazir were just a few feet away. "You have ten minutes." I disconnected the line and shoved the phone into my jacket pocket just as Reynolds opened the back door.

36

Morgan Lennox knew something was wrong when Ivanov's phone rang and he didn't answer the call. It made him wonder who was calling the man sitting in the passenger seat and why he chose to ignore the phone call. For the past two and a half hours, Morgan had sat quietly next to one of Ivanov's flunkies while the man named Wolf drove the van five miles over the speed limit. Slow enough not to cause suspicion. Fast enough to get them to their destination as quickly as possible given the situation.

The steel handcuffs were beginning to dig into Morgan's skin as his body swayed from side to side every few minutes as the van barreled down the interstate. Thirty minutes earlier, Morgan had watched Wolf merge onto two ninety-five from the long stretch of highway they had been traveling on since leaving DC.

Morgan knew where they were headed. And he knew what he'd be asked to do once they got there.

He thought about his last government contract job before leaving the city. A lot had happened over the past ten years. Morgan had landed a job in Chicago and moved to the Midwest, leaving his nephew behind after he had graduated from college. It was a fresh start in a new city. Nine years after that, he joined the Department of Domestic Counterterrorism to work in data analytics and help stop domestic terrorism.

Can't believe it's been ten years, Morgan thought to himself and turned to look out the window as the vehicle steadily approached the city that he'd first called home after leaving his home country of Australia to settle in a faraway land with no family or friends. America, the land of opportunity, he had believed.

And he still believed it, even now. That was why he had encouraged his nephew to join him and come to America for university. Morgan had promised to look after him, to help him any way he could, and to be a father figure for someone he saw was just like himself, only eighteen years younger. It was why he invested so much of his time in helping AJ become as good as he was at the craft of system security and forensics.

And it was why Morgan knew the moment he stepped out of that police vehicle in the factory in Maryland that AJ was the person responsible for the cyberattack and the train crashes he was investigating.

Ivanov had made him do it. Just like Ivanov was now using AJ as a pawn to force Morgan into destroying the system he and his colleagues had worked so hard to build inside that skyscraper ten years ago.

Morgan kept his gaze focused out the window on his side of the van, watching the snow-covered rooftops of the small towns as they sped down the interstate, approaching the city. It wouldn't be long until he'd start to see the familiar buildings up ahead of them. An hour, maybe an hour and a half depending on how heavy the traffic would be as they got closer. Morgan knew that with it being New Year's Eve, the city would be packed with visitors from all over arriving to party in the streets and watch the famous ball drop.

When Morgan faced forward, he saw Ivanov with his cell to his ear. He wasn't speaking. Only listening.

Who called him earlier? Morgan thought, studying the man. He watched Ivanov lower the phone, turn to his left to give Wolf a concerned look, and then turn around.

"Who is Blake Jordan, Mr. Lennox?" asked Ivanov, turning to Morgan with an intense look in his eyes.

Adrenaline pumped through Morgan's body. He thought about the phone call Ivanov had ignored and seemed to have sent to voicemail and the message he appeared to have received and listened to. Morgan wondered if the FBI or DDC knew that he was captured and if they were trying to track him down.

"Mr. Lennox, I thought it went without saying, but maybe I need to be a little more explicit with you."

Morgan shuffled in his seat and turned to his right to look at the man seated next to him before shifting his gaze back to Ivanov, who curled up one lip, enjoying the game he was playing with his prisoner. He raised an arm to look at his watch, as if he was making a mental note about what the current time was.

"You are to cooperate with anything that I ask of you. That includes answering my questions, Mr. Lennox. You're smart enough to figure out why I left your nephew behind, aren't you? Do I really need to explain to you what will happen to him should you not cooperate with my requests?" Ivanov asked and paused for a beat to let his words hang in the air for a few moments before continuing. "I didn't think so."

"He works for the president," admitted Morgan.

Ivanov's eyebrows rose in surprise, and he turned to exchange a look with Wolf. "The *president?*" Ivanov asked in a tone mixed with curiosity and delight. "And what exactly does he do for the president?"

Morgan paused before responding, remembering the terror he'd seen in his nephew's eyes. Morgan didn't want to say more, and knew he shouldn't, but he had no choice. Ivanov and Wolf were in control, not him.

"Mr. Lennox?" Ivanov said, his voice ending on a higher pitch than where it had started.

"He works as an advisor on domestic counterterrorism. He's just a government bureaucrat."

Allowing a few moments to pass, Ivanov said, "Either there's more to it than that, or you're lying to me."

Then he turned back to look at Wolf and exchanged a few words with the driver in Russian. Morgan listened in frustration. He couldn't understand a word of what was being said, but he listened anyway.

Ivanov barked an order. He stared at Wolf, waiting for a response. Ivanov repeated it and Wolf nodded.

The men spoke for several more minutes before Ivanov pointed at the clock in the center console in between the two front seats and asked Wolf a question. Wolf answered, and Ivanov turned to his right to look out the passenger window. Although Morgan had no idea what the men were discussing, the rhythm of the conversation followed a familiar cadence common in any language. Two men, trying to weigh the pros and cons of a decision, with a deadline. Morgan turned to his left again to stare out the window at the passing scenery when a word was spoken that he *did* understand. But it wasn't just a word, it was a name.

Klavdiya.

Morgan's mind raced as he wondered why the men were discussing Claudia Nazir. Something had happened, or it was about to. He tried to imagine what had been communicated to the madman seated just four feet away from him. Whatever it was, it appeared to have left Ivanov unsettled and agitated. Morgan looked straight ahead and cocked his head to the right to try to gauge the reaction from Wolf after the heated conversation. Morgan could tell that the man driving the van had disagreed with Ivanov.

Who is this guy? Morgan thought to himself. Wolf looked American, yet spoke the Russian language perfectly. Morgan understood what Nikolai Ivanov wanted him to do, but why was the American with him? What was his personal agenda for what he was doing, and why was he helping the Russian terrorist?

One way or another, Morgan figured that once they arrived, all of his questions would be answered.

Ivanov held his cell phone up to his face and stared at the number that had called him twice just a few minutes earlier. Morgan couldn't help but wonder who had placed the call and if his nephew and Lisa were okay. He kept his eyes on Ivanov, watching the man continue to look at his phone, weighing a decision in his mind. Morgan sensed that he knew what that decision was.

Will Ivanov return the call?

37

Reynolds guided Nazir into the backseat, placing one of his large hands on top of her head to keep it from hitting the frame as she sat down, and he closed the door. A divider between the back and front seats ran along the width of the vehicle. The first two feet from the ceiling were made of glass. I stared over my shoulder as Claudia got settled, felt my presence, and looked up at me as her eyes locked onto mine.

She looked confused, then panicked. Claudia had been told she was being transported to another facility. But the FBI had arrived to take her into custody. She hadn't thought that she'd be face-to-face with me again.

Agent Reynolds climbed into the SUV. My already racing heart started beating faster. Would Ivanov get my message? My eyes moved back to the clock on the dashboard. The window of opportunity was closing.

"You okay, brother?" Reynolds asked, sensing that I was feeling stressed. "How do you want to do this?"

I turned back to face the front, and as I did, I heard my cell phone ring. "Go ahead and head back. We'll find a place along the way where we can stop, and I'll talk with her. I gotta take this call," I replied. "This is Jordan," I said as Mark nodded, put the SUV in gear, and pulled away from the facility, heading back to the office. There was only silence on the line. "This is Blake Jordan. Go ahead, please," I said and waited.

"I received your message," the caller said. I knew it was Ivanov. "Very interesting proposal, Mr. Jordan."

"And?" I said, trying to keep my end of the conversation as vague as I could with Mark there next to me.

"We have a deal. You give me Nazir; I give you Lennox. No police, no FBI. Just you and me. Is that clear?"

"Where?" I asked, looking out the passenger window, trying my best to remain calm and coolheaded.

There was another pause and I knew why. Giving me the location for the trade would show his hand and reveal his plans. To my surprise, he answered, "Brooklyn, the pier at Red Hook. Five o'clock."

"How will I find you?" I asked as I looked ahead to see how far out we were from the Hoover Building.

"I'll find *you*," replied Ivanov before disconnecting the call. I slipped the phone into my jacket pocket.

"Stop the car," I said as Reynolds turned to me, confused by the phone conversation that I just had.

He pulled into a shopping center on the right side of Pennsylvania just before we got to Independence. Reynolds parked and turned to me. "What is it, man?" he asked. "Who the hell were you talking to?"

I looked back over my shoulder at Nazir. "Can she hear us through the glass?"

He shook his head.

"Okay," I said, deciding where to begin. "I need to bring you in on something. I just spoke with Ivanov."

"How did you—"

"I kept the cell phone from the man you handcuffed earlier inside the factory. I used it to contact him when you went inside to take Claudia Nazir into FBI custody. He confirmed that he has Morgan Lennox in his possession, and he's willing to trade him for Nazir." I paused for a beat before adding, "I know they're working together, and I know he wants to get her back. I think he needs her for what he has planned."

"What do you mean?" asked Reynolds as I slowly moved my hand behind me to reach for my gun.

"I believe Ivanov's behind the attack that's happening sometime tonight."

Mark looked back to the front, thinking, and shook his head.

"Think about it," I continued. "She knew about yesterday's attacks. And based on where Ivanov wants to make the exchange, it lines up with the only lead we have right now. It's all connected, Mark."

"Where does he want to meet?" asked Reynolds as my hand found and slowly gripped my weapon.

"Brooklyn. And based on what AJ told us earlier about Ivanov mentioning Claudia's name, I'm willing to bet that whatever he's planning to use Morgan for has to be the same attack Claudia knows about."

I looked to my right out the passenger window as an older woman pushed a grocery cart past the vehicle. When I turned back, I looked down and was caught off guard to see Reynolds with a hand on his weapon.

"I know how you work, man," said Reynolds. "I've been Chris Reed's partner at the Bureau for over a year. He's told me stories."

My eyes flicked left. Nazir was watching us through the glass and looked concerned. I turned back to Reynolds.

"I know what you're thinking, Blake. Don't do this," he said and looked down. "I have orders to bring her in. We're going to let you broker the deal; then we're going to stop this attack."

"Mark, you don't understand. She's not going to accept a conditional immunity deal. If I let you take her in, I won't be able to get her to Brooklyn for the trade with Ivanov. Think about Union Station. Do you want a repeat of that?" I asked and paused for a moment. "I can't stop this unless I take her with me."

"You really think you're gonna take my vehicle from me and drive four hours with a terrorist in the backseat and the Bureau won't stop you? It's the FBI, Blake. You won't even make it out of Washington before they take your ass out. The only chance you have of getting Claudia Nazir to New York is to go back to the Hoover Building with me and make your case to Landry. Think about it, brother. It's the only way."

I sat in silence. Mark was right. There was no way I could make it all the way to New York without the Bureau finding me. It would be four long hours on the road, plenty of opportunity for the FBI to track me down and stop me somewhere along the way. I could call Emma Ross and try to charter a private flight. That could work, but it would also implicate the president, which was something I simply could not do.

"I'm on your side," Reynolds added, breaking the silence. "So is Chris Reed. But you're going to have to work with us to get what you want. You can't sidestep the Bureau like you always have in the past. We're not all bad guys,

Blake. Work with us for once. You don't really have any other option right now, do you?"

My heart sank in my chest. I thought about Morgan and what Ivanov might be planning on using him for.

I let go of the Glock and watched Reynolds slowly let go of his weapon as well. Then it hit me. He was right. I was so intent on looking for the third option that I failed to see that one was staring right at me.

In that moment, I realized there *was* another way for me to get Claudia to New York. And if it worked, it would not only lead me to Morgan, but I just might be able to figure out how to stop the attack.

"Well? You still want to talk to her and try to get the information you wanted, since we're here?"

"No. I have a better idea. Let's head back. I'm gonna have a little talk with Bill Landry," I replied.

"Just like that?" asked Reynolds as he put the SUV in gear and pulled back out onto Pennsylvania. "Thought for sure I was gonna have to take you down right here, man, all those stories Reed told me."

I turned my gaze back out onto the street outside the passenger window as Reynolds picked up speed and drove us to the Hoover Building.

The answer was so simple. And it was hidden in plain sight.

38

We arrived at FBI headquarters a few minutes later. Reynolds rolled down his window and talked with the same man, whom Chris and I had seen hours earlier, posted at the guardhouse. He let us inside. But instead of finding a spot, Mark stopped his SUV in front of the back entrance and turned the ignition off.

Reynolds stepped out of the vehicle and I did the same. "Be right there," he said, and I nodded.

As I walked around the back and headed toward the entrance, I looked back and saw Claudia being helped out of the backseat, still in handcuffs, still in a daze as she tried to make sense of what was happening.

Mark cleared me through security as I headed into the lobby and pressed the button for the elevator. Back behind me, I watched as Reynolds walked Claudia down a hallway, where I figured he'd bring her upstairs by a private elevator used in situations like this one. Soon, he'd have Nazir inside one of Landry's holding rooms, waiting for me to broker the deal that would give her the clemency she wanted.

Only she wouldn't take the deal. I knew that much. She'd want immunity with no strings attached.

After a short ride up to the third floor, I stepped into the dark hallway and approached the next security checkpoint. I pulled my cell out of my pocket and placed a quick call to Chris Reed to let me inside.

A minute later, Reed pushed open the door to let me in and gave a nod to the guard at the entrance.

"We looked into Ivanov," said Chris as I walked into the hallway and he handed me a folder. "Our profiler in New York wrote this up."

I slowed down and came to a stop as I thumbed through the documents.

"We have a problem, Blake."

"What is it?"

"You know the other guy AJ told us about? He doesn't exist. There's no one named Wolf at the NSA."

I closed the file and looked up at Chris. "That doesn't make any sense," I said. "Did you check the DoD?"

Reed nodded. "We checked both. During AJ's debrief, he told me Wolf interviewed him at the NSA building in Fort Meade. He said the man provisioned his systems access and gave him everything he'd need to carry out the cyberattack and the Union Station train crashes. So I'm thinking Wolf does work for the NSA. We just need to figure out exactly who this guy is and what he does for them."

"And how are you gonna do that?" I asked. "Could Anderson's vehicle have taken a picture of the guy?"

"I thought about that. I was hoping maybe his car might have taken a picture of Wolf from inside the factory up in Hyattsville. I couldn't catch Jami before she left, but I was able to get access to the data dump to review the last few images that she downloaded. All we have is the one image with Ivanov in it."

I handed the file back to Reed. "Alright, keep me posted," I said as I headed down the hallway toward Bill Landry's office.

"Blake," Reed called, and I turned back to face him. "You don't look so good. What's going on?"

I looked down the end of the hallway. A few Bureau employees buzzed from office to office. I turned back to Reed. "I talked to him, Chris," I said, crossing my arms. "Ivanov. I offered to trade Claudia for Morgan."

Reed slowly shook his head. "How are you going to do that?"

"I'm not exactly sure yet, but I have an idea," I replied and turned back toward Landry's office.

I knocked on his door and pushed it open. Landry looked up at me. "I need to speak with you," I said.

He lifted a hand to wave me away and raised the volume of the call he had on speakerphone.

I walked inside, closed the door behind me, and proceeded to lift and drop the receiver back in place and sat down.

"What the hell do you think you're doing, Jordan?" Landry demanded.

"I said I need to speak with you, and this can't wait," I replied.

"You have two minutes," he said and leaned back in his chair.

I nodded and paused for a moment. "Bill, have you been brought up to speed on Nikolai Ivanov?" I asked and set the folder on the desk in front of him, expecting him to pick it up. Instead, Landry just stared at it.

"We know more about Ivanov than you probably do.

We've been looking for him for quite a while. I called Reynolds earlier, and he brought me up to speed on your little factory fiasco up in Maryland." He looked down at the folder I had set in front of him. "And I already read that thing. There's no new information in there."

"What about Wolf?" I asked, and Landry slowly shook his head in response to my question.

"I know we can't find anything on the guy. Reed's going to pull NSA and DoD employee photos and run them by Anthony Lennox to see if he can ID him. We believe Ivanov and Wolf are headed to New York."

"You're right. They are headed to New York. In fact, they're going to be in Brooklyn at five o'clock."

Landry stared at me coldly. "And how the *hell* do you know that, Jordan?"

I shrugged. "Because I just called Ivanov."

Landry furrowed his brow and looked confused.

"Bill, I called him using the cell phone from one of the men taken into custody at the factory. I left a message and said I have something he wants and to return my call if he wants to make a trade."

"What do you have that he wants?"

"Claudia Nazir. I told him that I had a chance to grab her before she was taken into FBI custody."

"And what were you going to do when you got there, Jordan? Just hand her over to them?"

"No, I was going to trade her for Morgan Lennox. That was the deal Ivanov agreed to."

Landry tried to contain a laugh. "You know he sure as hell isn't going to just give you Lennox."

"I know he isn't, but that's what I asked for to get him to the table. He had to believe I wanted Morgan back and that I was willing to do anything I had to do to make that happen, including kidnapping Nazir from the FBI for a trade. He believes I'm headed to New York right now to make this deal with him." I paused before continuing. "Bill, we have leverage on both Ivanov and Nazir. We can stop this attack."

Landry leaned back in his chair again and studied me for a moment. "This is unlike you, Jordan."

"Let's work together on this, Bill. Give me your support and your resources. I'll get you Ivanov and Wolf."

39

AT ELEVEN THIRTY IN THE MORNING, JAMI DROVE THROUGH Jersey City, quickly approaching New York. She had spent much of the four-hour drive fuming over the assignment given to her by Landry and Roger Shapiro. Jami thought about the vague background that she'd been given about intercepted chatter leading the two agencies to believe that a terrorist attack might take place somewhere in the city.

The Department of Domestic Counterterrorism didn't have a presence yet in New York. And with the Washington field office under construction, the young agency only operated from Chicago, so Shapiro relied heavily on his friendship with Bill Landry to get things done in tandem with the FBI, using their vast resources and presence. If there was a credible threat, Shapiro was obligated to send an agent to the area.

Jami understood that. But she also knew Landry had a tendency to slow down DDC agents, either because he didn't like them or because he wanted his Bureau agents to appear superior to other agencies. And the long drive away from DC, where a terrorist attack had actually taken place, to a city with a possible terrorist attack looming made her wonder if she'd been sent on nothing more than a fool's errand.

Jami made three calls when she emerged from the Holland Tunnel and navigated the busy streets of Manhattan's lower east side. The first was to Shapiro, letting him know she had arrived. The second was to Landry to get the name and number of the contact that he wanted her to work with while in New York.

The third was to the woman Landry had instructed her to call before arriving at Federal Plaza. Jami told her that she was ten minutes out, and the Bureau contact gave Jami instructions on where she should park the vehicle that Bill Landry had loaned her. She said she'd be waiting for Jami in the main lobby.

When Jami got to the building, she parked underneath the NO STANDING/AWM sign across the street.

She stepped out of the vehicle and turned around. Behind her was a small park with young children wearing heavy jackets and playing as parents sat on nearby benches keeping watch. Jami turned back to face the street and stared at the tall government building that she was about to enter. She stepped to the curb, and when there was a break in traffic, she jogged across the one-way street and headed for the lobby.

A Filipino woman wearing black-rimmed glasses was waiting for her when she entered.

"Agent Davis?" she asked, extending her hand as she approached.

Jami nodded.

"I'm Veronica Hillstone."

Jami shook her hand and smiled. "Just call me Jami. I can't stand the formalities."

Veronica pursed her lips. "You can call me Veronica. Not Ronnie, Nicki, Verna, or Vera. Just Veronica."

The sharp tone to the woman's voice made Jami feel uneasy. She sensed Veronica was either stressed out or frustrated, maybe even both. "Follow me," Veronica continued and handed Jami a visitor badge and motioned for her to enter through a turnstile to her right, directly adjacent to a guard's desk.

The man sitting behind the desk looked up, watched Jami pass through, and nodded his approval. Then he lowered his head to turn his attention back to a row of monitors spaced out in front of him that streamed a live feed of the area outside the perimeter of the large government building. Veronica walked Jami to an elevator at the far end of the lobby and, once inside, pressed the button marked twenty-three.

"You park under the NO STANDING/AWM sign?"

"Yeah," Jami replied. "One space left. Never seen that sign before today. What does AWM mean?"

Veronica smirked. "It doesn't mean anything. Those signs are posted all over the city. Years ago, a couple of Bureau agents drove up to Canal Street to arrest a guy over in Little Italy. When they came out of the building, their vehicle had been towed." Hillstone grinned as the elevator rushed to the twenty-third floor. "So we had those signs put up to keep that from happening again. That's where we park while in the city."

Jami nodded and grabbed the long metal bar that stretched along the width of the elevator to keep herself steady as it rapidly came to a stop. When the doors opened, Jami followed Veronica down a maze of hallways and over to a group of small cubicles in a far corner of the floor.

"We're here," said Hillstone when she arrived at her

cubicle and stood over her desk, rummaging through an overhead compartment that contained extra computer equipment. Jami looked over Hillstone's workspace as she waited. Pictures lined her desk, including a family photo of Veronica with her husband and young daughter. Jami looked up and noticed a framed certificate hanging on the wall with the words SNARKIEST PERSONALITY on it.

Veronica found what she was looking for and, when she turned around, caught Jami looking at it. "Last year I won 'bubbliest personality.' *Whatever*, right?" she asked as Jami forced a smile. "Let me get you set up at the empty cubicle next to me," Veronica added, and Jami turned to follow her to the workstation.

Hillstone carried a docking station that she had found and set it on the empty desk. She turned and gestured for Jami to hand over her DDC laptop, and Jami complied. Veronica attached it to the docking station and confirmed the two external monitors were working before she took a few steps back.

"Go ahead and log in. I'll get you connected to the Bureau's network so you can get online," said Veronica.

Jami nodded, unlocked her computer, and stepped aside for Hillstone to log in to the Bureau's network. Veronica looked at her watch as Jami sat down and entered her log-in credentials. "There's lunch in the boardroom if you're hungry. Might be our last chance to get some food in us before this supposed attack."

"Thanks, but I'm not hungry. And I heard it would happen by midnight, so it could be a while."

Jami swiveled around in her chair and looked up at Veronica.

"Well," Hillstone replied, "based on the intelligence

we've pieced together so far, they're thinking if it happens, it'll definitely be sooner than that."

"Who is they?" asked Jami.

"The ops team. They've intercepted several nearby communications over the last few hours that suggest something might be going down somewhere in the city. The team just doesn't know where it's happening."

Jami leaned back in the chair and squinted her eyes. "You mean you're not part of the ops team?"

Veronica shook her head.

"*Great*," Jami added. "Landry sent me on a four-hour drive only to pair me up with someone who can't help me. I knew I couldn't trust him. I should have just stayed in Washington."

Hillstone crossed her arms and cocked her head to the right. "What makes you think I can't help you?"

After pausing a beat, Jami said, "I assume you guys are aware of Nikolai Ivanov and a man named Wolf?"

Veronica nodded. "Yes, and I know about Claudia Nazir and the immunity deal that's being brokered."

"So you know about the situation with DDC analyst Morgan Lennox?" asked Jami, and Veronica nodded again. "Okay. Well, on the way over, I learned that Ivanov mentioned something that Lennox was involved in ten years ago. I don't have a way of getting that information through DDC channels, but I need to get it somehow."

Veronica furrowed her brow and bit her lip.

"Morgan's a friend of mine. Can you help me?"

Veronica's smirk returned along with a mischievous expression. "Come over to my desk. Let's find out."

40

I FOLLOWED LANDRY OUT OF HIS OFFICE AND DOWN THE LONG corridor. After a few attempts at locating Reynolds and Reed, we finally found them in a huddle room. They stopped talking as Landry entered. I figured they must have been updating each other on the information I had shared with them earlier.

"Listen up," said Landry after I walked inside and he pushed the door closed behind him to keep the conversation we were about to have just between the four of us. "I'm assuming you're both aware of the situation between Ivanov and Jordan?" Landry looked down at his two agents, who were seated across from each other at a small table. Chris and Mark stared at each other for a beat before turning to me.

"Yes, they're both aware of the phone conversation I had with Ivanov," I answered on their behalf.

"Good. But I want to make sure we're all crystal clear on where we stand," Landry continued. "Nikolai Ivanov is under the impression that Jordan has taken Claudia Nazir from FBI custody and is traveling to New York to make a trade for DDC analyst Morgan Lennox. What's the time and location of the trade?"

I took a moment to think about my response, knowing full well how Landry operated. It wouldn't be unlike him to use the information I'd share to his advantage and still keep me out of the operation.

"Jordan?" he pressed. "You gonna tell us what you know so we can work together on this, like you said?"

"Red Hook, Brooklyn," I answered. "He wants to meet me at the pier at five o'clock." I felt my heart start to beat fast as I waited for Landry to respond. He studied me before turning to his two agents.

"Red Hook," Landry repeated, crossing his arms and leaning against the wall. "Fine. What do you need?"

Looking at my watch, I saw that it was just past one in the afternoon. "I need to get Claudia to New York as quickly as possible. And I need to bring Reed with me," I replied, turning to my left to look at Chris.

"No," said Landry. "I can send Reynolds, but Reed stays here. I need him to keep working with Anthony and Lisa. Mark, keep your eyes on Nazir and oversee this operation on our behalf. Understood?"

Reynolds shot me a glance before his eyes flicked back over to his boss. "Understood."

"Good. Where is Claudia Nazir now?" asked Landry.

Reynolds gestured to his left. "Holding room down the hall. She believes an immunity deal is being prepared as we speak."

Landry paused for a moment to think about that. "Tell her there's been a change of plans. The deal will be brokered in New York since that's where we believe the attack will take place. Maybe that'll motivate her to tell us what she knows while we figure out just how the hell we're going to play this meeting at five." Landry looked at his watch. "I can get you, Nazir, and Jordan on a plane within the hour and get you into New York by two forty-five, maybe three. And that'll give us about an hour to get information out of her."

"Bill, I'm telling you, she's not going to talk unless she gets *full* immunity," I said. "Even if we can't get her to give us any more information in New York, you still need to let me take her to the meeting at five."

"Keller's team drafted the immunity deal, so talk to them. I'll coordinate the transfer to the New York field office. I'll also demand we get some boots on the ground over at Red Hook as soon as possible."

"Damn it, Bill. Ivanov was clear about this. He told me I needed to come *alone*. Just Claudia and me. You start putting agents around that pier, Ivanov's going to know, and this will not end well for any of us."

Landry stood up straight and walked up to me. He jabbed his finger in my chest and said, "Jordan, you're asking me to let you leave this building with a known terrorist and take her two hundred plus miles to another state to trade her for an inept DDC analyst who has screwed me over *several* times over the years. And you expect me to just let you walk out of here?" He paused for effect, his deep voice hanging in the air as the three of us listened in silence. "I've read the file on Ivanov. I know based on the conversations Reed has had with Anthony Lennox and Lisa Evans that he's behind the Union Station attack and most likely planning something in Manhattan. Why would I ever let you meet with him alone?"

I took a half step forward and stared into Landry's eyes. "Because you have to, Bill."

"What the hell is that supposed to mean?"

"The president's immunity deal for Claudia. It's not just conditional on *her* behalf, requiring that she help us stop the attack for us to honor the agreement. It's conditional on *my* behalf, too. Did you read it?"

Landry's eyes flicked to the right and landed on Chris Reed, then returned to me.

"Well, you should have. No one can broker the deal with her except me. You want me to move forward, you're gonna have to let me take her to Brooklyn to meet with Ivanov regardless of whether or not she gives us the information."

"Can't do that, Jordan. Claudia Nazir must remain in FBI custody at all times. I can't just let you take her."

"Fine," I said. "Send Reynolds with me, but he has to stay out of sight, and no boots on the ground, Bill."

Landry shook his head. "What will you do if Lennox is there, if Ivanov actually brings him? Are you just going to hand Nazir over and let the two of them walk away and execute whatever it is they're planning?"

"Morgan isn't going to be there, Bill. Neither is Ivanov. I'm taking Claudia for a trade that you and I both know will never happen. I'm using her as a pawn to draw out his men. I'll force them to take me to wherever Ivanov and Wolf are keeping Lennox." *Then I'm going to stop this attack*, I thought to myself.

Landry shook his head again. "Fine," he said and looked at Mark. "Reynolds will accompany you to Red Hook. I'll call the special agent in charge in New York and get things ready for you. This is going to be on a need-to-know basis, so we'll need to keep Nazir's transfer between the four of us and New York."

Bill started for the door, grabbed the doorknob, and turned around. "Reynolds, prepare Nazir for transport. I'll make some calls and will coordinate a flight out of Dulles. Be ready to go in fifteen minutes."

Landry stepped out and slammed the door behind him as he left.

I remained standing, trying to process the conversation I'd just had with Landry. I couldn't believe my plan had actually worked. Reynolds pushed his chair out, stood, and headed for the door. "Meet me downstairs in fifteen minutes, Blake. I'll have her ready and we'll head out to the airport. Get ready, man."

Reynolds walked out, and I watched him head down the hallway in the direction of the holding room. I took his seat at the table, rested my elbows on its surface, pressed my hands together as if in prayer, and held them against my face as I began to think through everything I'd need to do when I got to New York.

"You really think he's going to let you run this operation your way?" asked Chris. "You trust him?"

"Right now, you and Jami are the only ones I can trust," I answered. "But we're gonna need a better plan." I reached for my phone and dialed Jami's number to let her know I was on my way to join her.

41

"Sorry about that," said Jami as she returned to Hillstone's desk and sat down in the chair she had pulled over from the adjacent cubicle. "That was the guy I was telling you about. He's on his way here." Jami lowered her voice before adding, "They're on a chartered flight. And he's bringing Nazir with him."

"What?" asked Veronica, turning from her screen to face Jami. "She's coming here? To New York?"

Davis nodded. "Guess they want to bring her into the city. Maybe that'll encourage her to talk to us."

Hillstone furrowed her brow and looked away, thinking about the news Jami had shared. "Maybe we'll have some information by the time they get here," she said and looked at her watch. "Sorry this is taking so long. I located the files I was looking for on Lennox, but I had to request a retrieval while you stepped away. The Bureau does this thing where they archive anything older than seven years. Why seven years is beyond me. I think it's a storage-expense reduction thing. They'll do anything to save a buck around here."

Jami pushed her chair closer. "You found his file?" she asked. "Well, that only took ninety minutes."

Hillstone stifled a laugh and turned to Jami. "You'd think they would make things easy for us, but *no*. There's absolutely no organization of the records we keep on people, even across federal agencies." She turned to face Jami and sighed. "And now we wait for the retrieval to be done. Should be soon."

Jami took a deep breath to calm her nerves. "So how long have you been a profiler?"

"A few years. I did a lot of government contract work overseas. When we found out we were expecting Elizabeth, I looked for something a little more family-friendly. So now I sit here writing reports on serial killers and terrorists all day. Trust me, it's a dream come true," she said sarcastically.

That made Jami smile as she looked over Hillstone's shoulder, watching the status bar on the retrieval process inch its way closer to completion with every passing second. "Thanks for your help, Veronica."

"Call me Vee," said Hillstone, returning the smile as the two women heard a chime coming from the profiler's computer. That prompted Veronica to turn her chair back around to face her two computer monitors. She began toggling numerous screens and stopped on one of them. "Bingo," she said and turned to give Jami a high five.

Jami moved her chair even closer as she watched Veronica's screen from behind her. "Okay, looks like he was working as a contractor here in the city somewhere. The contract ended nine years ago, so maybe it was a twelve-month stint. Now we just need to figure out who he was working for and what he was doing here."

Hillstone continued to sift through Morgan's files and stopped when she found something of interest.

"What's PROJECT X?" asked Davis, reading the screen over Veronica's shoulder.

"Not sure. It's only mentioned once, but there's a reference ID associated with it. Looks like CR2007." Hillstone cocked her head to the right slightly. "See what I'm talking about? Seriously, why can't they just tell us what Lennox was working on in this file. Now I have to go and cross-reference that CR number."

With that, Vee accessed a Bureau application and stared at the screen for a moment before entering her log-in credentials. A LOG IN SUCCESSFUL message flashed on her screen, followed by a prompt for her to enter a CR number into the cross-reference field. "You'd think they would make this process easier, but no, they don't care about people like me. Whatever. I'm over it," she said and entered CR2007.

The two women watched an hourglass icon appear on the screen. Thirty seconds later, the icon disappeared, and the document that Hillstone was looking for opened. "Finally," she said in frustration.

Veronica gave the document a quick glance, then shook her head slowly. "It's some kind of handbook," she said and scrolled through the file before stopping abruptly. "Look at this, every few words are redacted. How the hell am I supposed to do my job if I can't even get access to original documents?"

"Let's just read it," Jami suggested. "Maybe we can figure it out."

Hillstone sighed, scrolled back to the top of the document, and began reading from the beginning. "Temporary duty handbook. A guide for traveling to site. The purpose of this handbook is to provide proper procedures and guidelines when traveling on official business in support of the program.

"Traveler is not to identify him or herself as an employee of the National Security Agency or a member of the intelligence community. The program has vehicles available for visiting sites that require US government anonymity. Keys are available from REDACTED on the second floor of the REDACTED building in room REDACTED and in the file cabinet outside the program director's office."

"What is this, Vee?"

"I have no clue," replied Hillstone before continuing. "The cover vehicles are leased by the FBI through a commercial cover company. Personnel are aware of the FBI link, but have no knowledge of NSA's involvement. No one should ever have contact with the leasing company. These vehicles are for official use only to include the transport of NSA equipment and personnel who actively support NSA/FBI programs. These programs currently include BLARNEY, FAIRVIEW, STORMBREW, and OAKSTAR. In keeping with operational security purposes, the FBI recommends following an indirect route between NSA and covert sites. In the case of an accident, contact police and request an accident report.

"Identify yourself as a DoD employee unless reporting your identity can compromise an operation or site. In the event of an accident that could compromise an operation or site, use your personal identification. Arrangements will be made through the FBI to contact all parties to provide correct and accurate information. Check with the site point of contact for guidance on proper attire prior to traveling. Noncasual attire could cause an operational security red flag. No military uniforms or NSA badges should be worn. The employee should maintain a low profile, decline from venturing off on their own, and always follow the guidance of the program's security representative."

Veronica scrolled down through the rest of the document briefly to see how much more there was to the NSA handbook. There were only a few more short paragraphs left. She scrolled back to where she had left off and continued. "Visits to partner meeting facility TITANPOINTE and the FBI's New York field office," she said and stopped reading. "Wait. What? We work with an NSA office here in the city somewhere?"

"I didn't even know there was one," replied Davis. "I thought the closest NSA facility was in Fort Meade."

Hillstone nodded and continued, now with a whisper. "Coordinate with NSA point of contact REDACTED REDACTED prior to visit. The TITANPOINTE point of contact will be responsible for notifying the FBI site watch officer and coordinating security-related details with the partner. When approaching the facility, ring the buzzer and wait for admittance. When traveling to the partner's facilities or other program sites, such as TITANPOINTE, provide your family with a coworker's phone number in case of an emergency at home. Family members and coworkers who are not cleared can be given generic travel plans and general purpose for visit. That is, attend technical meetings, site visit, or install equipment. Always be aware of your audience. Remain cognizant of the clearance level of the persons you're speaking to or meeting with. Remain courteous to partners. Remember, this is a partnership out of contractual relationship."

A chill ran down Jami's spine as Hillstone turned to face her. "Vee, we have to locate TITANPOINTE."

42

At three thirty, Mark Reynolds and I finally arrived at the Bureau's New York City field office with Nazir. With the Ivanov meeting taking place in ninety minutes, I didn't have much time to try to broker the clemency deal with Claudia before we'd need to start heading over to the meeting spot in Brooklyn.

The field office was small. Curt Willis, the Bureau's special agent in charge, picked us up from the airport and explained to us on the drive over that the Bureau only occupied one floor of the government building at Federal Plaza. Willis said most of the office employees were behind-the-scenes types like profilers and analysts; the rest were agents. While the space was small, he assured me that his team was effective.

Willis looked to be around the same age as me, a man in his thirties with just enough experience to do his job effectively while at the same time not being in the system so long that he wouldn't question the status quo when he needed to. While he didn't ask many questions, I could tell the man had plenty of them.

Willis parked on a side street when we arrived at Federal Plaza, and we walked to an unmarked steel door in the back of the building. He swiped a keycard, we heard a clicking sound, and he tugged on the door. A second later, we were following Willis down a dark corridor, heading for security.

Five minutes after that, we arrived at the twenty-third floor.

Willis led the way, and Mark Reynolds followed close behind, keeping a hand on Claudia's back as the handcuffed woman stayed near the two Bureau men and glanced at me over her shoulder as we walked.

"Blake," I heard Jami say. She was with another woman in the back of a cluster of cubicles.

"I'll catch up to you," I said to Reynolds. He looked at Jami, then nodded at me and picked up the pace.

Jami turned to the woman next to her. "This is Veronica Hillstone. She's a profiler with the Bureau."

I extended my hand. "Blake Jordan."

Hillstone smirked and a corner of her mouth curled up. "Call me Vee," she said before turning to Jami. "Any friend of yours is a friend of mine," she added as she sat back down at her desk.

"What's going on?" I asked as Jami took a seat and pushed her chair closer to Hillstone.

"We've been looking into Morgan's background, trying to figure out what he was involved in ten years ago. There are a lot of documents out there, all of them archived. Vee requested a retrieval. They're becoming available now, but the one we looked at was heavily redacted. We're trying to piece things together."

"What do you have so far?" I asked, glancing at a clock on Vee's desk and starting to become anxious.

She shook her head slowly and answered on behalf of

Jami without breaking eye contact from her screen. "So far, just a handbook that gives guidance for traveling to sites under a program called BLARNEY."

"Not just BLARNEY," added Jami. "It covers visits to FAIRVIEW, STORMBREW, and OAKSTAR, too."

"BLARNEY?" I repeated. "Isn't that the NSA surveillance program that was made public by Snowden?"

Jami nodded. "This version of the handbook specifically references a site called TITANPOINTE."

I leaned against the cubicle. "You think TITANPOINTE is here? In New York?"

That caused Veronica to break her focus from the screen and turn to me. "It has to be. The handbook addresses all programs, like Jami mentioned, but it was customized for TITANPOINTE. It has to be here. It also mentions a partner. I'm not finding much information, so I'm going to have to try something else."

"What about under PROJECT X?" asked Jami. "Look in the Bureau's system. I'll do the same with DDC."

I turned to Jami, then Veronica. "What's PROJECT X?" I asked.

"If these damned things were more organized, we'd know already," answered Hillstone. "I swear, I don't know how they expect me to do my job with everything being so hard to find and impossible to read." Veronica took her black-framed glasses off and inspected them before continuing. "Sorry, that doesn't answer your question. I think PROJECT X is related to TITANPOINTE somehow. I just don't know how."

Jami pushed her chair back to the cubicle across from Veronica. I stayed standing in the short walkway that separated the two workstations as they both began typing. I looked up and saw Reynolds emerge from around a corner and motion for me to join him. "I have to go," I said. "Let me know what you find."

"She knows, Blake," Jami said from behind me when I got to the main hallway that would lead me to the holding room. I turned around and looked back at her. "Claudia. She knows where TITANPOINTE is."

I nodded. "I'll get her to talk," I said and followed the corridor to the holding room where Nazir waited.

When I arrived, Curt Willis was at the door. We stood together and looked inside the room through the two-way mirror. Claudia was seated at a table as Reynolds stood against the wall, looking at her.

Willis turned and handed me a black folder. "Did the president make the changes I requested?" I asked. The special agent in charge nodded as I opened the folder to confirm. "Then there's just one thing left to do," I said, closing the folder and gesturing to the door. "Let's get this over with."

With that, Willis punched in the access code. I watched Claudia Nazir turn to the door as she heard the code being entered. Willis pulled it open and shut it behind me once I had walked inside. I stood at the entrance to the holding room and stared at Nazir. Her eyes met mine. Reynolds walked to the opposite corner of the room, behind Nazir, to give me a little more room to work.

Feeling my heart begin to race again, I took a deep breath to try to calm down. A flood of memories rushed in. I couldn't help but think about Maria again. A scene from our wedding day flashed across my mind. I felt the hair on my neck stand on end. Claudia blinked, and I became fully present in the moment again. Maria was gone. Claudia was the last person on earth responsible for her death. With the stroke of a pen, I was about to authorize her clemency. She would never pay for her crimes. She would never feel the pain that haunted me every day of my life.

I took two steps forward, dropped the black folder on the desk, and opened it. I pulled the pen from its holder and signed the document. I set the pen down and turned the folder around for it to face Claudia. Then I pushed it to her. "Sign it," I said and watched Nazir lean in and read the details of the deal.

She shook her head and looked up at me. "This says I'm being given *immediate* clemency with guaranteed safe passage by midnight tonight to my home country in exchange for information that *might* lead to stopping a terrorist attack on the United States." She looked down at the document. "What's the catch?"

I smiled. It felt good to have the upper hand for once. "Sign the document and maybe we'll talk about it."

43

When the van approached the corner of Church and Thomas, Wolf carefully drove up onto the sidewalk next to the tall, Lower Manhattan building, and put the vehicle in reverse. Slowly, Wolf inched his way down the path designated for covert drop-offs of government surveillance equipment as the van finally disappeared behind a barrier wall designed to provide privacy and anonymity for NSA vendors.

Wolf killed the lights, engaged the parking brake, and turned off the ignition. He reached into the glove box, retrieved a Smith & Wesson M&P22 Compact, and attached a SilencerCo Sparrow suppressor to it.

"How long will this take?" asked Ivanov, who retrieved his own weapon and inserted a fresh magazine.

"As long as it needs to," replied Wolf as he finished twisting the suppressor onto his weapon. He reached for a UHF walkie-talkie and placed it inside his jacket and handed two more to Ivanov and the other man. "Take my seat," Wolf said to the man next to Morgan. "Any problems, drive to the rendezvous point."

The man got up and passed across Morgan as Wolf exited the van. Morgan watched as he climbed into the driver's seat, closed the door, and waited next to Ivanov as he had been instructed. Wolf stood for a brief moment just outside Morgan's window and checked his weapon before hiding it inside his jacket and disappearing behind the van.

Morgan knew where Wolf was headed, as he remembered there was an entrance into the building at the bottom of the loading area, having used it years ago to accept countless deliveries of surveillance equipment from the various NSA vendors that the agency had contracted with.

The clock on the center console caught Morgan's attention. He saw that it was already four o'clock. Although the sun would be setting in less than an hour, the city had already started rapidly growing dark since Ivanov and his small team had arrived as the tall buildings in Lower Manhattan shielded the sunlight.

"Why am I here?" asked Morgan, breaking the silence and prompting Ivanov to look over his shoulder.

"Mr. Lennox, you are a smart man. You know exactly why we're here," Ivanov answered and paused for a moment to collect his thoughts. "But I will entertain your question simply to make sure you are crystal clear on the purpose for our visit. For ten years now, your government has been collecting communications from the people of Russia, in addition to thirty-seven other countries around the world, in collaboration with numerous American telecommunications companies. A program you were responsible for implementing." Ivanov turned around again and stared at Morgan. "That ends today."

"You can't possibly believe I can stop something like this. I only dealt with a very small portion of—"

"Stop lying, Mr. Lennox," interrupted Ivanov. "I am a

smart man, too. I know exactly what you were responsible for, and we both know you're capable of much more than you care to admit."

Before Ivanov could continue, a voice came from the radio. It was Wolf relaying that he was ready.

Ivanov pushed open the passenger door and exited the vehicle. Morgan watched as the man walked around the front of the van, stopped to the left of where Morgan was sitting, and slid open the door. He gestured with his gun for Lennox to get out and move toward the back of the building.

Forcing Morgan to walk to the back door, Ivanov followed his captive while leaving the other man waiting inside the van. When he reached the door at the end of the inclined driveway, it opened on its own. Wolf stood in the doorway and let them inside.

The three men walked through the first floor with Wolf leading the way, followed by Morgan, then Ivanov. When they turned a corner, Morgan noticed a spray of red on the adjacent wall and, after a few more steps, realized it was blood. A security guard was dead on the floor with a weapon in his hand. Ivanov laughed as he stepped over the man. "How many more are there?" he asked as they continued to walk.

"Only one," said Wolf. "He's been taken care of as well."

Fifty feet farther, they entered an elevator and Wolf pressed the button marked twenty-nine. "Two men protecting one of the nation's most closely guarded secrets?" asked Ivanov in disbelief as the doors closed.

"That's the point," replied Wolf. "They don't know what this place is. For all they know, it's a telephone exchange building. No regular employees work here. Only occasional site visits," replied Wolf. "Isn't that right, Mr. Lennox?" he asked, and the two men turned to Morgan.

He didn't answer. Instead, Morgan kept his eyes fixed on the red digital display that showed the elevator's progress as it rocketed up to the top floor of the building. When the doors opened, Wolf stepped out, followed by Morgan, and finally Ivanov. They walked down a dark corridor and arrived at a steel door. Wolf swiped his keycard, the light above the card reader changed from red to green, and the men heard a clicking sound as the door unlocked. Wolf pulled it open. "Enter," commanded Ivanov.

As he entered the server room, a cold chill hit Morgan's face from the air conditioner that kept the massive amount of equipment cool. He stopped and looked around the familiar room as memories of countless hours spent at the location setting up, configuring, and testing communications equipment rushed in.

"Keep walking," demanded Wolf. Morgan instinctively felt that Ivanov was the man ultimately in charge, but based on Wolf's access and familiarity with the NSA building, he knew this was his part of the plan.

The machines stretched along both sides of the enormous room, which ran the full length of the building. The lights coming from the equipment created a blue hue that engulfed everything inside the room. Morgan turned around and saw that both Ivanov's and Wolf's faces were illuminated with the same color. Wolf lifted his hand and pointed to an alcove at the end of the room.

"I've prepared a workstation for you," said Wolf as he walked past Morgan and entered the dark space. The man unlocked a panel that released a tray, which slid out, revealing a closed laptop that was connected to the equipment. "This will give you access not only to this room, but to every machine from floors three through twenty-eight," said Wolf as he opened the lid and entered in the log-in credentials. He stepped away and held his hand out toward the laptop. "It's ready. Go ahead and step up to the terminal for me."

Ivanov shoved the barrel of his gun into Morgan's back, encouraging him to move toward the terminal. Morgan obeyed and stepped closer to the tray holding the laptop, which came to just above his waist. There was no chair for him to sit in, so Morgan would have to stand to do the work.

"You trained Anthony well," said Ivanov as he watched Lennox glare at the computer, still deciding if he was going to follow Wolf's demands. "But he's young and inexperienced. A cheap substitute for what you have to offer us, Mr. Lennox." Ivanov paused. "I suggest you follow my comrade's directives. Otherwise—"

Before Ivanov could finish his sentence, he was interrupted by a voice coming from the radios that he and Wolf were carrying. "Nikolai," the man sitting inside the van said, "we're ready for you. It's time."

Ivanov shot Wolf a knowing look and nodded. "I'm heading down now and will meet you at the door."

Wolf dug into a pocket and handed Ivanov a keycard. "Keep this," he said. Ivanov nodded again and headed toward the server room exit, which he had propped open with a chair, as Wolf turned back to Morgan. "Mr. Lennox, there are two actions we need you to take. Complete these assignments and your nephew lives."

44

Claudia Nazir stared at me. "What are you going to do to me?" she asked, looking at me coldly.

"Right now, I need you to focus on telling me how to stop this attack," I said, looking at my watch. "This offer is about to expire."

Claudia stared at the paper with the president's signature above mine. She took a deep breath, held it for a brief moment, and let it out slowly as a worried expression came across her face.

"I want a lawyer," she said. "And this says nothing about my children. I want them to leave with me."

"This is about *you*, Claudia. There aren't going to be any lawyers. Just you and me. Right here, right now."

Nazir glanced away from me, thinking, and finally said, "How can I trust that this deal you're offering will be held up at the end of the day without someone here representing *my* best interests?"

I forced a smile. "I guess you're just gonna have to trust me, aren't you? Now sign the damned thing."

Claudia looked back down at the document and shook her head.

"You were behind the funding of the man who kidnapped President Keller over a year ago. And you were also involved in the plot to assassinate him and the rest of his cabinet at the inauguration. Do you really think you have a better option right now?"

Nazir grabbed the pen and tapped it on the document, deciding what to do.

"We're running out of time. This is your one and only chance to get out of this. Help us stop this attack and you'll get your freedom."

Claudia stopped tapping the pen, clicked the end, and signed it. Once she was finished, she dropped the pen on the document, and I reached over and grabbed the black folder and closed it.

"Start talking," I said.

"Explosives," she began. "A shipment from Iran was redirected to the United States nine months ago."

"Where'd they come in?"

"New Jersey," she replied.

"How?"

"My government has been coordinating attacks in Bahrain and other countries for years. We smuggle thousands of pounds of explosives a year. It wasn't difficult to have part of that redirected to America."

"No, how'd you get it past the authorities?"

Nazir smiled. "Your country imports an incredible number of vehicles each year, Mr. Jordan. Well over a half million of them. When the cargo ships arrive, they are inspected quickly before authorities move onto the next arriving shipment. Contract workers drive the vehicles off the ships and park them in a nearby lot. We intercepted one of those ships before it arrived at port and moved the explosives. They were hidden in a select group of vehicles, and the materials were unloaded, one by one, at a garage in Newark."

"Where in Newark?"

"It's empty. You'll waste your time if you go there. By now, the explosives are inside a transport vehicle."

"Where's the vehicle now?" I asked. Nazir's eyes flicked over to Reynolds, who had moved behind me. "Damn it, Claudia. Where is the vehicle now!" I yelled, my voice reverberating inside the small room. I had a feeling I knew what the answer was going to be, and I paused as I waited for her to give it to me.

Claudia recoiled briefly, then slowly relaxed. "Here," she replied in a whisper. "It's in New York."

I set the folder down, rested my hands on the table, and leaned in close to her. "That's impossible," I said. "We have checkpoints looking for any suspicious vehicles entering the city. We would have found them."

"It's *not* impossible, Mr. Jordan, and it *wouldn't* be suspicious. We have an armored truck, stolen over a year ago. It was the idea of a man named Nikolai Ivanov. He had an associate kill the men driving the truck as it was en route for a cash pickup. He then took it to a rented garage and hid it there. The plan was to load the truck with the explosives and bring it into the city. I'm sure it's been here for some time."

"We know about Ivanov. But the associate—what's his name?"

Nazir slowly shook her head. "His name is Wolf."

"We can't find anything on Wolf. The man doesn't exist."

Nazir nodded knowingly.

"How's he involved?"

"All I know about the man is that he is with an intelligence agency and had access to what Ivanov needed."

"And what was that?"

"I don't know," Nazir replied.

I stared at the woman, reading her. For once, I couldn't tell if she was lying. "What do you know about PROJECT X?"

Claudia shook her head.

"What about TITANPOINTE?"

Claudia's eyes narrowed as she thought about it. "I may have overheard Wolf mention it once or twice."

"Morgan Lennox," I said. "You warned Ivanov about him. How do you know him?"

She remained silent and scowled at me.

"Ivanov has him. We think they're here in the city. What is he going to use him for?"

"I don't have answers to any of these questions," she replied, becoming flustered.

"Stop lying to me!" I yelled and shoved the document she had just signed off the table. "Enough games, Claudia. You're going to tell me what I need to know, or I promise, you're gonna wish I had let you spend the rest of your life in prison. Now tell me how you know Morgan Lennox and why Ivanov needs him!" Reynolds walked over to me and put a hand on my shoulder. I turned and pushed him away before turning back to Claudia. "I'm going to ask you one last time, *how is Morgan Lennox involved in this!*"

A moment passed before she finally spoke. "Nikolai was a good friend of my husband, Aasaal," she said. "After he was killed by *you*," she added with a glare, "I traveled to New York to find Nikolai, and I asked him to take me in. I had nowhere else to go. He offered his help, but needed *me* to do something for him in return. My job was to coordinate the explosives delivery. Wolf had a list of people who had worked on a secret government project. I just happened to recognize Lennox's name from another list I had seen, one kept by Aasaal and used by Marco Lopez. Everyone in your inner circle was on that list, Mr. Jordan."

That made me think of Maria and my father and how they had both been targeted by Marco before I killed the man. Then I thought about Jami and how she had captured Claudia Nazir. I prayed that Ivanov and Wolf didn't know about her. I picked up the black folder from the floor, turned, and nodded at Reynolds as I walked to the door. I pounded my fist on it twice. The faint sound of the entry code being punched in could be heard as Willis opened the door. "You get all that?"

Willis nodded.

"Good. Relay that to Bill Landry. He has people working on this. I'm sure you do, too. We need to find that truck. And I need a vehicle for the operation."

Curt Willis pointed behind his back with his thumb. "Take the loaner Agent Davis drove in."

I checked my watch again, then turned back to Claudia. "Get up," I said. "We're gonna take a little drive."

45

Before leaving the Bureau's field office, I stopped by Jami's desk and got the keys to her loaner vehicle. Jami followed me to the elevator and grabbed my hands. She said to be careful. I told her I would.

When I got to the ground floor, Reynolds was waiting for me with Nazir. She was in cuffs, and he had a tactical bag with him. We walked across the street, and I climbed into the driver's seat as Mark secured Claudia in the backseat before joining me in the front. I punched Red Hook into the GPS system and we headed out. Five minutes later, I saw the meeting spot in the distance as I drove over the Brooklyn Bridge.

Fifteen minutes after that, we arrived at the Red Hook neighborhood. Mark was looking at a map on his phone and suggested that I stop the SUV just south of Coffey Park. When I got there, I stopped the SUV and stepped out along with Mark, who stood outside his door, rummaging through the tactical bag as I opened the backseat door and looked at Claudia. "Get out," I said and reached into my jacket for my weapon.

"First, tell me why you've brought me here," she said as I checked the Glock's magazine and chamber.

"If you want your immunity," I replied, "you'll need to do something for me first. Now get out."

Claudia hesitated, keeping eye contact with me, and finally inched her way out of the vehicle. I closed her door as Reynolds walked around the back. I saw him insert an earpiece before walking over to join me.

"You're going to need all of this, man," he said, handing me an earpiece along with two extra magazines.

I stuffed the mags in my pockets and inserted the earpiece.

"Copy?" asked Mark as he stood next to me.

"Copy," I replied, confirming that I could hear him loud and clear. "Where are you gonna be?" I asked as I noticed Reynolds looking around the park and checking our surroundings before turning to look up and down the street. There was something about the way he was acting that bothered me. "You okay?"

"I'm fine," he said, but his body language was telling me something different. "I'll be circling the neighborhood." Mark turned to his right and nodded down the empty street. "Stay on Wolcott; follow it all the way to the wharf at the end." He removed the cuffs from Claudia and looked at me. "Be careful, man."

I nodded, deciding that Mark was acting strange because I was taking Nazir alone with me to the meeting. On the flight from DC, Mark shared that he had spoken with Landry, and his boss had changed his mind about me taking Nazir to the meeting spot by myself, even though she'd be out of FBI custody. I didn't think that was like Landry, but it didn't matter. My plan was to let myself be taken by Ivanov's men.

"Let's move," I finally said to Claudia, putting my left hand on her back while keeping my right gripped on my weapon. As we started to walk down Wolcott, I heard Mark climb inside the vehicle and drive away.

We walked quickly down the one-way street with old three- and four-story buildings on both sides of us. We crossed Van Brunt and continued to head toward the waterfront. I turned around and looked in every direction, remembering how Ivanov said he'd find me when I got here. When we got to Ferris Street, the Manhattan skyline came into view across the water, and I felt the hair on my neck stand on end. "Stop," I said. We were being watched. I pushed my gun into Claudia's back and looked around in every direction.

Claudia jerked away from me. "Mr. Jordan, tell me why you brought me here."

I ignored her and looked at an old red-brick building to our right. Iron bars covered the windows. I couldn't see anyone inside, but I still couldn't shake the feeling that we were being watched. The streets were completely empty. It felt like something was wrong.

"Tell me now!" she yelled as a strong gust of wind hit my face from the channel.

I grabbed Claudia, turned her around, and pushed her ahead of me. "Walk!" I yelled, and we pressed on.

I pushed the Glock into her back, and we continued to walk down Wolcott. She turned to glare at me before returning her gaze to the road in front of us, and I realized it was a dead end. We took a few more steps, then stopped. There was nowhere else to go. To our left was a massive abandoned building that must have been some kind of factory or warehouse with seven large garage doors. It took up the entire block.

A tall black fence with barbed wire stretched from the edge of the building and extended all the way down the street we had walked on. We were alone with no sign of Nikolai Ivanov. I reached inside my jacket and grabbed the phone that belonged to Ivanov's man and was about to call him. Then I had a better idea.

I let go of the phone, leaving it in my jacket pocket. I grabbed Claudia by the front of her shirt and walked her backwards, slamming her head into the fence. Her eyes grew wide and she screamed. I reached for my earpiece, removed it, and held it tight in my left hand to keep Reynolds from hearing the next few words I was about to speak. I pushed my weapon against her throat and leaned in close. "Is it true?"

"Is *what* true?"

"Your husband," I said and paused for a beat, choosing my words carefully. "The last thing he said to me was that you helped Marco." I started to breathe hard and fast as I stared into the woman's dark eyes. "He told me that *you* killed my wife, not Marco." I paused again, reading her. "I want to know if it's true."

I watched a smile slowly start to appear across her face. "I guess we're even, Mr. Jordan. A life for a life."

"Why?" I whispered as a flood of memories of Maria rushed over me. My hand was shaking and I blinked repeatedly, trying to keep myself calm. "Why?" I asked again. "She did nothing wrong. She was innocent."

Nazir's smile widened. "Maybe. And what about Agent Davis? Is she *also* innocent?" The words pierced me like a dagger. Jami had been responsible for Claudia's capture. *She knows Jami's name.* "I already told you," Claudia continued. "Aasaal had a list. We thought it would devastate you. We thought you would step down so Marco could take your job and help us." I pulled her forward and slammed her head against the fence again. She laughed. "We all have choices, Mr. Jordan. Some are just easier to make than others."

"You bitch," I said as I dropped the earpiece to the ground and grabbed her throat with my left hand and squeezed as I watched her struggle to breathe. I was so focused on Claudia that I didn't notice the vehicle approaching from the other end of Wolcott until it was too late. The truck's headlights turned on and illuminated Claudia's face. I turned to my right and became fully present again. I pulled Claudia away from the fence, moved the Glock from her neck to the side of her head, and forced her to stand next to me.

"Who *is* that?" she asked, gasping for air as the truck came to a stop with its bright headlights still on us.

"A trade," I replied. "You for Morgan Lennox."

"You fool," Claudia hissed as the noise from the idling engine echoed off the large building to our right. "You're smarter than this. Nikolai would never give up Lennox or meet you out in the open like this."

"I know," I said as the engine was cut and the driver's door slowly opened, followed by the passenger door. I lifted my left hand to block the light coming from the headlights and saw the rear doors open in the back.

The driver stepped forward. I could only make out his outline, as my eyes were still adjusting to the light. "Don't take another step," I said as I held Claudia at gunpoint. "You want her back, you give me Lennox."

The man laughed. "There's just one problem, Mr. Jordan. We don't want her. We want *you*." The man's arm disappeared in the light and I heard a gunshot. Claudia's body went limp and she fell to the ground.

46

I looked down at Claudia's body in shock and lifted my hands in the air, still holding onto my gun. The headlights from the truck continued to shine on me, though I could still make out the silhouette of the man's arm as he moved his gun from where Claudia had stood over to me. I looked away, blinded by light.

Suddenly, another shot rang out. The sound was loud and echoed all around me. I flinched in response, thinking for a moment that I had been shot. Then the man in front of me fell down next to Claudia's body.

Ivanov's men ran from me and took cover on the left side of the truck as four of the large garage doors to my right were quickly pulled open and Bureau agents rushed out. I looked to the top of the building, saw an agent on the roof, and realized he had taken the shot that had killed the man who had his weapon trained on me. The agent noticed me staring at him and looked away as he scanned the rest of the area.

I got into a crouched stance and quickly moved to my left, my Glock leading the way. "Put your hands in the air!" I yelled as I found the three men there taking cover. I forced them out into the open as Bureau agents caught up with them on the other side of the truck. The men were forced to the ground and cuffed.

Curt Willis appeared twenty yards west of me on Wolcott and approached, followed by Mark Reynolds.

Holstering my weapon, I ran back behind the truck and knelt next to Claudia. A pool of blood had formed around her body. I turned her over and looked in disbelief. She was blinking. *She's still alive.*

"Claudia," I said, grabbing her face and forcing her to look at me, "tell me where I can find Lennox." Her eyes were fixed on mine. "Claudia, I didn't know they would do this. Please, tell me where I can find him!"

She was struggling to breathe. I leaned in as Willis was getting closer. "Thomas," she whispered softly.

"Thomas?" I repeated just as she stopped blinking and stared at me. "Claudia! Who is Thomas?" I asked, but it was no use. She was gone. I stayed crouched on the ground for a moment before looking up and seeing Willis motion for a medic to check on Nazir. I stood and stepped out of the medic's way.

He checked her pulse and confirmed what I already knew. Then the man checked on the driver on the ground next to her. When he turned him over, I could see that he wasn't Ivanov. I turned toward Willis.

"Jordan, I need you to come with me," he said as he started walking away, and I caught up to him.

"Damn it, Curt. Why didn't you tell me about this operation? This wasn't the plan. I would have let them take me back to Ivanov. Reynolds could have tracked me using my phone," I said as we walked away from the scene and slowed as we passed the handcuffed men sitting on the ground. I looked, trying to ID them. They were all Russian, but none were Ivanov and definitely not Wolf, who AJ had said was American.

"Listen, Jordan," replied Willis. "Everything changed when we lost contact with you. Reynolds wasn't picking up audio from your earpiece. He tried communicating with you, but you wouldn't copy. We saw that man over there kill Nazir and then aim his weapon at you," he replied and paused to let that sink in. "We had eyes over the street but couldn't hear a damn thing. We weren't going to let the guy kill you, too."

"I get that," I said, "but you could have told me about the plan. I would have played this differently."

Willis stepped closer and stood right up in my face. "Jordan, Landry told me your history. You might work for the president, but you're not one of us. You're not in charge. Bill Landry and I call the shots around here." He turned back to look at Ivanov's men. "We'll take them in and see what we can get out of them."

"You won't get anything, Curt," I said as I noticed Reynolds standing next to the vehicle that the men had arrived in along with several other agents, who had surrounded the armored truck. Headlights from a number of Bureau SUVs were illuminating the truck as I pointed toward the vehicle. "That's the truck Claudia told us about," I said and started to move toward it, but Willis grabbed my arm to hold me back.

"It's empty, Jordan. We checked. Nothing's in there."

I shook my head in disbelief.

Willis paused for a moment before adding, "She was lying to you. They couldn't have fit all those men in that truck with the number of explosives she said they were transporting. I was standing outside the room when she said that. I believed her at first, thought maybe they'd try to drive the truck into the crowd up in Midtown, but—"

"She wasn't lying, Curt," I said, interrupting him. "I need to figure out where that truck has been today."

"No, *we* need to figure that out," he replied. "*You* need to head back with Reynolds. You're done here."

I almost told him about what Claudia had said, giving me the name Thomas, but I decided against it. As I watched Willis walk back toward the mass of New York Bureau agents, I stood alone at the edge of the street, taking in the entire scene. Red and blue lights reflected off the pavement and all along the side of the large building now to my left. Flashes of light came from an agent standing over the bodies of Claudia and the driver as she took photographs while Reynolds wrapped up a conversation with another agent.

Reaching for my cell phone, I tried calling Jami, but she didn't answer. Then I tried Chris Reed, but I couldn't get a hold of him, either. Looking across the channel, I saw the Manhattan skyline as lights inside the many skyscrapers began to light up the sky. I thought about the people in Midtown and wondered where those explosives were. I had read Claudia's body language when she told me about them. I didn't think she had been lying, as Willis claimed.

I thought about Morgan Lennox and wondered where in the city he might be. If I could just find him, I'd find Ivanov and Wolf. Checking my watch, I knew there wasn't much time left before it would be too late.

Then my thoughts drifted back to what Willis had said moments earlier. He was right. I wasn't one of them. But I wasn't a civilian, either. I was somewhere in between. A gust of wind from the channel hit my face, and I closed my eyes, trying to understand who I was and what I was supposed to be. I didn't know.

When the wind stopped, I opened my eyes and saw someone walking toward me. It was Mark Reynolds.

"Come on, man," he said as he approached. "I've been asked to take you back to Federal Plaza. Willis and Landry want you debriefed about what happened here. Willis says it can't wait. He wants it done now."

"*Then* what?" I asked.

"Then you're free to go."

I stared at the man. "You played me, Mark."

Reynolds shook his head. "I don't work for you, Blake. I work for Bill Landry. He gave me orders and I followed them. It's that simple, man. I know you get that." When I didn't respond, he looked down Wolcott to where he had parked his vehicle. "Let me see your weapon," he said as he held out his hand.

Reaching into my jacket, I grabbed my Glock and handed it over to him.

"You'll get it back when we're done," he said after accepting it. "Come on, man. We need to head back."

As we left, I turned back to look at the flashing lights one more time. Then we walked into the shadows.

47

We walked another few minutes down Wolcott as I searched for Jami's vehicle on the dark road. I asked about Anderson's involvement. Mark said the Bureau thought the officer was involved, but understanding how would take time. When we found the car parked at Conover, Mark got it started. As he navigated the dark streets of Brooklyn, I couldn't help but think about the last thing Claudia had said to me. I had gotten so close to finding Ivanov. Now, I didn't see how anyone would be able to stop him.

There was no sense of urgency to Reynolds. He drove at a slow and steady pace through the Red Hook neighborhood as I stared out the window, unable to accept that this was the end of the road for me.

Just then, I heard the sound of my cell phone ringing. I reached for it, looked at the screen, and turned to Reynolds. "It's the White House, Mark. I need to take this," I lied, and he gestured for me to take the call.

"This is Jordan."

"Blake, it's Jami. Veronica's here with me and we have you on speakerphone."

"Go ahead," I said and turned my head to look out the passenger window again, trying to remain calm.

"We figured it out," Jami continued. "It took a while, but Veronica was able to get access to Morgan's files. Ten years ago, he worked as a contractor for the NSA under two of their programs, one code-named BLARNEY and the other called SKIDROWE. BLARNEY's a surveillance program that collects metadata from international communications. SKIDROWE began operating along with BLARNEY about ten years ago and focuses on monitoring signals being sent to and from satellites around the world. It looks like Morgan helped start it up. Both programs operate out of a building owned by one of the NSA's partners."

"Who's that?" I asked as I looked straight ahead and noticed Reynolds turn to me, curious about the call.

I heard Veronica clear her throat in the background. "In all of the documents we've been reading, they're being referred to as LITHIUM," said Hillstone. "But based on a few things that have crossed my desk over the years, I'm pretty sure I know who LITHIUM is: it's the United States Telecommunications Company. They've been working alongside the government since the seventies. It has to be them. Anyway, that doesn't matter. New Yorkers refer to it as the Long Lines Building. I located the building's schematics. It was built in seventy-four. One document referred to the place as 'a skyscraper to be inhabited by machines.' The building's just creepy."

"The working title was PROJECT X," Jami added. "That's what the architect called the secret building."

"But the NSA refers to it as TITANPOINTE," said Hillstone. "From what we just read, it was built strong enough to withstand an atomic blast. It's got two hundred and fifty thousand gallons of gasoline and enough food and water stored to keep fifteen hundred people alive for two weeks. It looks like it could be used as a government shelter from nuclear fallout. Twenty-nine floors, absolutely no windows anywhere, just two sets of large air vents for God knows what. It blends in during the day, and there aren't any lights outside, so it disappears completely at night. The building's hidden in plain sight. Like I said: *creepy*."

Reynolds slowed the car as we came to a stoplight, and I tried to make sense of what I was hearing. "Where?" I asked as Reynolds turned right onto Atlantic Avenue and started to pick up speed.

"Here, in the city," replied Jami. "Two blocks away. It's outside our window. We're looking at it right now."

"No, *where?*" I asked again, trying to figure out where in Lower Manhattan the building was located.

Jami paused for a beat before saying, "Thirty-three Thomas Street."

"*Thomas?*" I asked in disbelief as Mark glanced at me briefly.

There was a pause on the other end of the line. "Blake?" said Jami. "Is everything okay?"

I thought about it. "I'm not sure yet."

Disconnecting the call, I dropped my cell phone back inside my jacket. Another traffic light at Henry Street changed to red as Reynolds slowed the vehicle down and brought it to a stop. "Keller?" he asked.

"No," I replied and noticed an orange clock to our left for pedestrians to cross counting down from thirty. "His chief of staff," I lied. "She just wanted to relay a message to me from the president. Not important."

Past the clock, I saw the headlights of a car approaching us. "We should have worked together," I said.

The car was slowing down. I watched the clock tick

down to ten, then five, then zero. "I'm sorry, man," Mark said as he looked up at the red light above us, expecting it to turn green before turning his head back to the left to look at the car stopped at the intersection. I coughed as I depressed the lock on my seatbelt.

"I'm sorry, too."

"For what?" asked Reynolds, still looking at the vehicle to our left, waiting for our light to turn green.

I threw the seatbelt off and reached my arm around the man's neck. "Don't fight it, Mark," I said as I squeezed hard while Reynolds struggled. He was such a large man, I wasn't sure if I had the leverage to be able to subdue him. If it worked, I knew he'd lose consciousness within ten seconds. I started counting. Mark continued to struggle. "Don't fight it," I repeated as I closed my eyes, squeezing as hard as I could.

Reynolds grabbed my arm, trying to pull it away from his throat and struggling to breathe. With my left hand, I grabbed my right wrist to counter his strength and pulled it tighter as I started counting again. When I got to five, the light turned green. At five seconds, Reynolds moved his leg and floored it, causing the SUV to spin out as the tires struggled to gain traction. The tires finally caught the road and started moving. At ten, Mark went limp as he lost consciousness, and I pushed him aside and grabbed the wheel.

I straightened us out and lifted Mark's leg and pushed it down on the brake. That didn't work and only slowed us down some, but I kept pushing until we got to a slow enough speed for me to move Reynolds out of the way and reposition myself so I could reach my leg over the center console and stop the SUV.

Putting it in park, I dropped back into the passenger seat, out of breath, my heart beating out of control. Mark's cell phone rang. I ignored it, trying to focus on what I was going to do next. I thought about trying to pull the man out of the vehicle, but realized he was going to be too heavy for me to do that.

I had less than a minute before he'd start to regain consciousness. I pushed his body aside to reach behind his back and grabbed my weapon. I found handcuffs in his belt and grabbed them. I set the Glock on my lap and reached to grab his arm and cuffed him to his steering wheel, and I opened the passenger door.

As I tried to figure out where I was, another thought occurred to me. Leaning back inside the vehicle, I turned off the ignition and took the keys, climbed back out, and closed the door as Reynolds started to stir. A single streetlight illuminated the otherwise dark street. I reached for my cell phone and called Jami. "I'm standing at Atlantic and Court," I said. "I don't have a vehicle. How do I get to Thomas?"

"Hang on," she said as I heard her typing. "Okay, head north on Court. There's a subway station close by."

48

"How far down?" I asked as I jogged north on the wide sidewalk on Court Street, weaving around a number of Brooklyn residents walking the street as I headed north. "Jami? You still there?"

"Four blocks," she replied. "I'm looking at Maps, and from what I can tell, once you pass Livingston, you'll see Borough Hall Station on your right. I think that'll get you into the city here by us at Federal Plaza."

"No, keep going north," I heard Veronica say in the background, her voice more distant than Jami's. "That's just for the 4 and 5 trains." Her voice became louder as Jami put me on speakerphone and Veronica moved closer to Jami's phone. "Blake, you'll need to keep heading north on Court another two blocks and take the 2 train." She paused for a beat. "That'll get you here quicker than the 4."

"I'm crossing Livingston now," I said as I jogged past a row of older buildings and pushed my way through a gathering of people standing outside the entrance to a restaurant. "Jami, have you heard from Chris?"

"I called him with an update earlier. He's with AJ and

said he'd try to figure out what Ivanov has Morgan doing," she replied and paused for a moment before asking, "Blake, why aren't you with Mark Reynolds?"

I thought about how to answer that, knowing Veronica was with the Bureau. "Long story," I replied. "Let's just say Claudia's dead, the Bureau has Ivanov's men, and Willis removed me from the operation. I'm on my own now."

"They're my people and I trust them about as much as you do, Blake," replied Veronica. "We're still here."

I was glad to hear she was on our side. "I need to call Chris," I said. "Tell me where to go from here."

There was a brief pause before Veronica said, "You're about two and a half blocks away. If you hit Montague, you've gone too far. To your right, you'll see the entrance with a sign that has a red 2 and 3 on it. Take the stairs underground and follow the signs for the 2 train. Take it all the way to Chambers."

"How long will it take for me to get there?"

"Depends," replied Hillstone. "I take that way into work. Usually twenty minutes, but it could be longer."

I stopped running. I was breathing hard and took a second to catch my breath. "That's not gonna work."

"It'll have to," replied Veronica. "The NYPD just finished setting up a security checkpoint at the Manhattan and Brooklyn Bridges. Traffic might not be backed up to where you are now, but trust me, it's going to be a mess trying to get into the city by car for the rest of the night. You *have* to take the subway."

"Damn it," I said and started jogging again. "I need to go. Jami, I'll call you back when I get to Chambers."

I disconnected the call and dialed Chris Reed. He didn't answer, so I left a message as I passed a large building and the entrance to the subway appeared in front of me. A short green railing in the middle of the sidewalk descended underground, with the red 2 and 3 posted on the stairs just as Veronica had described. As I approached, a couple of kids ran past me as I entered the stairwell and went below. I felt the presence of someone approaching from behind. I quickly looked over my shoulder and saw a teenager.

I kept going, descending another set of stairs, passing dirty white tile along the walls and ceilings as the sound of horns from cars above ground was replaced by loud screeching sounds from the trains below.

When I reached the bottom, I saw a huge subway map on my left. I walked over to it and studied it, running my finger along the red line from the YOU ARE HERE mark as it went under the East River between Brooklyn and Manhattan, emerging in Battery Park. I kept following where the train would take me, making note of all the stops along the way. It had been a long time since I had visited New York with my parents as a kid to see the Thanksgiving Day Parade. Even then, we hadn't ridden the subway.

To my right, I saw a set of metal turnstiles. Beyond them was a deck of kiosks for purchasing a MetroCard.

I grabbed my wallet and pulled out a few dollars. I looked up and saw a CCTV camera and realized I had made a big mistake. I thought about Mark Reynolds a few blocks away. I hadn't taken his cell phone. I'd heard it ring and meant to grab it, but in the midst of the chaos, I had taken the car keys instead. He'd be conscious by now and would have placed a call with his free hand. The Bureau had to be looking for me.

"Buy a ticket or move out of the way," said a younger voice from behind me. I turned and saw it was the teenager standing behind me as my phone rang. I reached for it and saw that it was Chris calling me back.

"Go ahead," I said to the kid behind me and stepped aside, answering the call and balancing the phone on my shoulder as I looked up at the MetroCard machine to see how much cash I needed. "This is Jordan."

"Blake, it's me," replied Reed. "I don't have much time. You need to know that we have your location."

"What do you mean?" I asked.

Before Chris could answer, a recording of a man's voice boomed from overhead. It said, "Next Manhattan-bound 2 train will arrive in two minutes." The teenager who had purchased a MetroCard walked past me and entered through the turnstile. I could hear the train approaching and knew I needed to hurry. Except for another CCTV camera pointed in my direction, I was alone. I shoved my wallet back inside my pocket, pushed myself over the turnstile, and quickly jogged in the direction of where the train was going to stop.

"Chris? You still there?"

"I'm here," he replied. "Listen, Reynolds called for help ten minutes ago. They're just now getting to him. The guys upstairs pulled your last phone call. They know you're taking the 2 or 3 train over to Chambers."

The recording boomed overhead again, saying, "Manhattan-bound 2 train approaching the station. Please stand away from the platform edge." Immediately, I realized why Chris was calling and what he was trying to do. I felt my heart starting to beat hard in my chest. I was going to have to make a very quick decision.

"I'm twenty minutes away from Chambers. Can I make it there before your people get there?" I asked.

"I think so," said Reed. "Curt Willis called for one of his agents up in Midtown working the crowd to intercept you when you arrive." He paused and added, "But he's delayed. You might be able to beat him."

The way he replied didn't sound like him at all. In that moment, I could tell Chris was lying to me, knowing that his colleagues upstairs were likely listening to him as he spoke. He was trying to warn me.

"I have to go, Chris. Thanks for the tip," I said and walked up behind the teenager as the train arrived.

I watched the train approaching quickly. A streak of metal rushed past me as the train hit the brakes, and I heard the screeching sound engulf the platform area. It reminded me of the footage Jami had played for us of DC's Union Station at the DDC field office back in Chicago, and I felt sick to my stomach. I tried to regain my focus and thought back to the map I had studied as I entered the subway station. I closed my eyes, trying to remember what I had seen. Then I opened them, nodded to myself, and made my decision. The doors opened and a few passengers exited as I approached the train.

49

CURT WILLIS DROVE HIS BLACK BUREAU-ISSUED SUV through the Brooklyn Heights neighborhood at a steady pace and slowed as he approached the Brooklyn Bridge. The trip into the city would normally take less than fifteen minutes. But with the additional security checkpoints added by the NYPD, traffic slowed to a crawl as he inched his way toward the bridge. Willis stopped the SUV behind a long line of vehicles and put his phone to his ear to listen to a voicemail he had received while he was picking up Reynolds.

"Who called?" asked Mark from the passenger seat, rubbing his neck and trying to look past the traffic.

"Bill Landry," answered Willis. "Trying to make sure we've got a man to make the intercept at Chambers."

"How does Landry know where he's going?"

"He put a priority on his phone and pulled the last call the guy received fifteen or twenty minutes ago. He's taking the 2 train to Chambers. Based on the time stamp of the phone call and when we think he got on the train, he should arrive in a few minutes. Landry also requested geolocation tracking, so with every subway stop, they're able to confirm his location as his phone connects to the nearest cell tower. He got on right back there at Borough Hall," said Willis, pointing behind the vehicle with his thumb. "You okay?"

Reynolds nodded. "Neck's a little sore, but I'll be fine." He paused before asking, "Where's he going?"

"We'll know soon enough. Landry's pulling the rest of the calls. He'll let me know as soon as he finds out."

Mark Reynolds paused again before asking, "So what's the plan? We pick up Jordan, *then* what?"

"Then we question him. We find out why he assaulted you when all you were going to do was debrief him."

Once Willis got onto the bridge and it opened up to two lanes, he turned his overhead lights on, trying to pick up speed, but it didn't help. Five minutes later, he got through the checkpoint with an NYPD officer waving him through, but remained stuck behind a mass of cars on the bridge, trying to get into Manhattan.

"All my men are either back in Red Hook or working the New Year's Eve crowd in Midtown. I pulled one guy back who said he thought he could make the intercept in time," said Willis as he looked back down at his cell phone and placed another call. Bringing the phone to his ear, he added, "This is our one shot to pick this guy up. If we miss him, there's no telling where he's going. Unless you know something I don't?"

Reynolds shook his head and looked out the window.

Another second passed before Reynolds heard the faint sound of Willis's cell ringing an agent in Midtown. "Allen, it's Curt Willis. Are you in position?" he asked as he turned the overhead lights off since there was nowhere for his vehicle to go on the three-lane road, anyway. He was stuck on the bridge, at the mercy of the rush-hour and holiday traffic just like everyone else. "Allen, do you copy? Are you in position yet?"

"Yes, sir, I just arrived at the Chambers stop," replied the voice, loud and sounding tinny to Mark Reynolds as he sat in the passenger seat, overhearing the conversation between the two men. "I was on with Bill Landry's people. They've sent the tracking information to my phone and said they were able to pick up his signal at Wall Street, Fulton, and Park Place. I watched as he got to Park and disappeared a few seconds ago. Chambers is the next stop; he'll be here any minute now. I'll know if he stays on or gets off."

"Good," replied Willis as he heard over the phone a recorded voice announcing that the train was approaching the platform. When it stopped, Willis added, "You don't let him get away, understand me? If he doesn't exit the train, I need you to get on and detain him. And if he does exit, you pick him up before he makes it onto the street. The guy's a former federal agent. He'll lose you if he knows you're tailing him."

"Copy that," said Allen as Willis's vehicle started moving again at a slow two miles per hour. Ten seconds after that, traffic stopped, and Willis hit his steering wheel out of frustration. "Here he comes," the agent said as the sound of the train's brakes caused Willis to move the phone away from his ear briefly until it passed. "Doors are opening. I need to put the phone down so I can monitor the tracking and see where he goes."

Willis kept the phone to his ear while he waited.

Reynolds ignored the traffic ahead of him and turned slightly to his left as he leaned in, waiting to hear what was going to happen at the Chambers stop. "Put it on speakerphone."

Willis nodded and changed the audio setting on his phone so Mark could hear.

"He's on the move," Allen said as he started to walk faster. "He's definitely getting off. Looks like he's at the back of the train. I have a visual, he's climbing the stairs. Moving in to intercept now." The sound of the agent running could be heard as Allen closed in. He was breathing hard as he said, "Jordan, stand down!"

Reynolds and Willis made eye contact, and both dropped their gaze back to the phone as they waited for an update. "Federal agent, I told you to stand down!" the agent said, his voice shaky as he was running hard. The audio immediately became muffled as Allen stopped running and began speaking in a low voice as he approached. Willis wiped his brow with his left sleeve as he continued to hold the phone in his right hand.

After another thirty seconds of inaudible dialogue, the agent finally came back on the line. "It's not him, sir. Looks like Jordan slipped his cell into a teenager's pocket." He paused and said, "He's not here."

"Damn it!" yelled Willis. "Ask if he saw anyone matching Jordan's description, and if so, *where*."

The agent asked the question and came back on the line a few seconds later. "He says he saw the guy back in Brooklyn. He says Jordan bumped into him right after the train arrived, but he stayed on the platform."

"I'll have to call you back," said Willis, who disconnected the line and turned to his right to glance at Reynolds as he started to dial another number. "Bill," he said when his call was answered, "he got away."

Up ahead, traffic started moving again, and Reynolds watched as the red brake lights started to disappear. Willis picked up speed, and the road noise kept Mark from hearing what his boss, Bill Landry, had to say.

"I know exactly where that is. Why would he be going there?" asked Willis as he made it to the end of the bridge and tapped the brakes as the three-lane road began to merge into two lanes, creating a traffic bottleneck. "I still have a man at Chambers, and Reynolds is here with me. We'll head over there now. We're only a mile out, but dealing with heavy traffic." Landry said something else and Willis nodded. "Then I assume you know how serious this is. Alert the NSA. I'll call in more of my men from Midtown."

Willis disconnected the call as Reynolds nervously shifted in his seat and asked, "What did Landry say?"

Navigating the stop-and-go traffic while scrolling through his cell phone, Willis replied, "They pulled another phone call. They believe he's heading to 33 Thomas Street. We're not too far from there." Willis took a deep breath and let it out slowly while moving his head to his left, trying to look around the traffic up ahead to see how much longer they might be stuck on the bridge. He wiped more sweat from his brow, cracked his window, and lit a cigarette. Turning to his right, Willis looked at Reynolds and said, "We might have to head over on foot if this damn traffic doesn't let up soon. It's only seven blocks north of us."

"What's at 33 Thomas?"

Willis took a drag of his cigarette and answered, "One of the nation's most closely guarded secrets."

50

As I climbed the stairs at the Brooklyn Bridge-City Hall subway station, I looked at the map on the wall. Veronica was right. The 4 train was slower, but it had brought me farther east than the 2 train would have taken me. I ran my finger along the map and saw that Chambers was three blocks west. I thought about Reed's call. He had warned me that the Bureau was set to pick me up at Chambers. After referencing my current position with where Thomas was located, I climbed more stairs and emerged onto Centre Street.

I ran north on Centre, past the courthouse, and crossed Chambers. Three blocks west were the bright lights of Broadway and also the subway stop where I was sure someone was looking for me. I thought about the teenager from Brooklyn and wondered if he had found my phone before the Bureau found him.

Continuing north, I passed a small park on my right, which I recognized from earlier in the afternoon. Looking to my left, I saw the tall government building at Federal Plaza. A few offices inside the building were lit up, but the lights were on all throughout the twenty-third floor, where I knew Jami was working.

I grabbed the cell phone belonging to Ivanov's man back in Maryland that I had kept, and held it in my hand as I continued to jog north. I wanted to call Jami. She was expecting my call when I arrived. I knew I could use her help, and given her experience, I knew that she could handle any situation she'd be given.

But I stopped running when I got to the edge of the building, remembering once again what Kate had said.

I let go of the phone and reached down to the outside of my pocket and rested my hand on the ring box. I looked up one more time to the twenty-third floor and started moving again, turning the corner at Worth and again at Broadway before arriving at Thomas Street. Up ahead I saw what Veronica was talking about.

The building was tall, dark, and ominous. There were absolutely no lights on its exterior. I only saw it because of the streetlights and surrounding buildings. I stopped walking and just stood there, staring at it. I was looking at TITANPOINTE, a government secret hidden in plain sight in the heart of New York City.

And somewhere deep inside the massive windowless building was Morgan Lennox.

As I started walking again, trying to understand how I could get inside, I heard footsteps behind me. I turned around and saw the outline of a woman approaching from Broadway. "What are you doing here?"

"You were supposed to call me," replied Jami and stopped to catch her breath. "Landry has Willis looking for you. Veronica said they pulled your phone calls. I thought for sure they'd get you at Chambers."

"I took the 4. Chris called and warned me," I replied and paused. "You should have stayed with Veronica."

"Why, Blake? So they could keep me back to question me? Vee said I had to go before they came back to the office. I thought I was going to have to do this myself," she said and looked up at the dark building. "I'm glad you're okay, Blake," she added and put an arm around me and gave me a quick embrace.

"Did Veronica tell you anything else about this place? It's a big building. Morgan could be anywhere."

Jami nodded. "You know how we told you earlier that it's owned and operated by a partner called LITHIUM, a telecom company? Vee got access to the building's schematics. People don't really work here. The entire building is made up of massive amounts of communications equipment with a bunch of satellite dishes on top. The NSA taps, records, and archives domestic and international communications here."

"But where do we go? The building's twenty-nine stories high. That's a lot of ground to cover, Jami."

"Top floor," she replied. "That's where we need to go. Veronica was sure of it."

I turned and started walking toward the building, looking for a way to get inside, and Jami followed. As we approached, we saw a few cars parked out front. Jami pointed out the NO STANDING/AWM signs and explained their meaning. Besides a lobby entrance on Thomas, the building was surrounded by a black metal fence with no other way inside. We walked up to the lobby doors and saw they had bars over them.

"Let's try the other side of the building," I suggested, and Jami agreed.

We continued walking west on Thomas until we got to

Church and turned the corner when to our right, I noticed a barrier wall. I held my left hand up for Jami to stop when we got to the edge. I reached for my weapon and aimed it at the ground as Jami did the same. "I hear a car running," I said in a low voice.

I waited for a car to pass us on Church and moved the gun to my left hand, aiming it in front of me, as I slowly started to turn the right corner to take a look at the vehicle. "The driveway slopes down into the building," I said. "I see a white van parked backwards, with the cabin light on. Someone's in the vehicle."

"What are we going to do?"

Turning back around, I kept my back against the wall and said, "Find out who this guy is. Ready?"

Jami gripped her weapon and nodded. Using a combination of the crisscross and buttonhook entry techniques, I crouched down and stayed low as I turned the right corner and Jami covered me. Once we turned the corner, I stood, aiming my weapon at the driver, and descended the driveway toward him.

With the cabin light on, I could see the man's face as he looked up and noticed us approaching. He panicked, reached for something, and revealed a gun. I closed an eye and fired, shattering the windshield.

"Get down," I said to Jami as I continued to move toward the vehicle. Coming around the side, I could see the man's body was limp. I opened the door, grabbed the weapon out of his hand, and checked his pulse.

I pressed a button to unlock the rest of the doors, walked to the back of the van, and opened the doors. It was empty. "Clear," I yelled as I moved back around to the front of the vehicle where Jami was waiting.

"Who *was* that guy?" she asked as we heard the crackle

of a radio. Jami looked inside and found a walkie-talkie clipped to the man's belt. "Why would they need radios?" she asked as she pulled it off to inspect it.

"You said the building is fortified to withstand an atomic blast. Cell phones probably don't work inside."

I turned to look back down the sloped driveway and noticed something before looking back at Jami.

"What?" she asked.

"I think I know how we're going to get inside. Stand back and cover me, okay?"

I walked back to the driver's side door and looked at the driver's body, trying to figure out if I could pull him out of the vehicle. He was thin, a sharp contrast to Mark Reynolds's build. Using the height of the van as leverage, I grabbed the driver's body, slowly pulled him out of the cab, and set him on the icy ground.

I climbed inside, put the vehicle in drive, and pulled it up to the top of the driveway. I rolled the window down, adjusted the driver's side mirror to help me see where I was going, and put my seatbelt on. "Don't try this at home," I said to myself as I put the van in reverse and floored it. The wheels spun for a few seconds before the rubber finally caught the concrete and I raced down the driveway, leaving Jami behind.

51

THE IMPACT THRUST MY BODY FORWARD. I LOOKED UP AND SAW Jami at the top of the inclined driveway. I felt pain in my head and closed my eyes for a moment. When I opened them again, Jami was next to me, opening the door and unbuckling my seatbelt. I blinked a few times, trying to stay focused.

"Are you *crazy*?" she asked and gently put her hand on my forehead, and I flinched in pain as she did. "Blake, you're hurt. There's a bruise on your forehead. I think you hit your head on the steering wheel."

"We're inside, aren't we?"

Jami grabbed my arm and started to help me out when something caught her eye. She let go of me, grabbed her weapon, and started firing. I jumped out of the vehicle with my gun in hand and aimed it down the hallway where she had fired. Jami had taken the man out, but another appeared to our right.

I fired two shots and the man dropped to the floor. I walked over to check for a pulse as Jami checked the man she had shot. We searched them for anything we could use.

My guy had a pack of cigarettes on him. I tossed them, but found a lighter and kept it. I took his gun and stuffed it inside my jacket, next to my knife, and found another radio. I kept it in my hand as I walked over to where Jami was standing. "Now we have two," I said, holding up the second radio for her to see.

Jami nodded, placing her hand on the radio now clipped to her belt.

"We don't have long. I'm sure the Bureau's gonna be here any minute."

"Why don't we wait, then? If they pulled your phone calls, then they'll know what we're trying to do here."

"I tried working with them," I replied as I looked down and clipped the radio to my belt and aimed my weapon at the ground in front of me as I cautiously started to walk down the hallway. "They used me, Jami. I thought Mark was different, but he's just like Landry." My words hung in the air as I kept moving. "They don't trust me, and I don't trust them."

We stopped talking as we walked down a corridor and approached a corner. I briefly held my left hand up in a fist and we stopped. I held my gun with both hands, slowly turned the corner, and saw a man on the floor. Checking the rest of the area, I saw that it was clear, but then my entire field of vision became blurry. I blinked a few times, trying to shake it, but couldn't. "Check him," I said to Jami as she passed to my left, and she crouched down and looked the man over. I shook my head and closed my eyes for a moment. When I opened them, my vision returned. In that moment, I knew something was wrong and I was hurt.

"I think he's security. Vee told me their station's on the second floor," said Jami, checking the man's pulse.

Ahead of us were two elevators. "Top floor, right?" I

asked, and Jami nodded. I walked over and pushed the button while aiming my gun at the elevator doors. Once they opened, I stepped inside and pushed the button for one of the top floors. It lit up briefly, for less than a second, then turned off. Nothing happened. I noticed a card reader underneath the row of buttons. “Looks like we need a keycard to get upstairs.”

Jami, still standing in the corridor, turned to her right to look at the body of the security guard.

We walked to him and I looked him over. Attached to a belt loop was a retractable reel with a keycard on it. Pulling it off, I stood and returned to the elevator, hit the button again, and swiped the keycard. This time, the button illuminated and remained lit. The elevator doors started to close as Jami tried to enter.

“No,” I said. Jami had proven many times that she could take care of herself. But I wasn’t sure what I’d find upstairs and, remembering the words Kate had spoken to me, I had to keep her away from me. “You were right,” I continued. “Willis will be here soon. We should tell them what we’re doing. Stay here.”

“Blake, don’t be ridiculous. You can’t do this by yourself.”

“It’s *my* fault Morgan’s in this mess. I should have listened to him,” I said. “Please, just stay here. There aren’t any other exits. If I flush them out, they have to pass you. If we both go, we could miss them.”

Jami took a deep breath and let it out while nodding slowly. “You’re right.”

Holding onto my gun with my right hand, I reached for the radio and held it out in front of me and looked at the other radio still clipped to Jami’s belt. “Only use it if you have to, okay? They might not know—”

"Viktor, *u nas yest' problemy,*" a man said on the radio, a voice I recognized immediately. "Viktor?"

It was Ivanov. We heard a response in Russian as I stared at Jami. "I have to go," I said.

Jami slowly backed away from me and nodded. "Be careful, Blake."

I kept my eyes on her as the elevator doors closed. As soon as they did, I shook my head and tried to focus. The elevator started racing up to floor twenty-four. I knew that if I took it to twenty-nine, I'd be a sitting duck if Ivanov was waiting for me. I felt the elevator start to slow as I approached. I moved to the left side, crouched, and aimed my weapon as the doors opened. No one was there. I stood and slowly moved to the right and saw nobody in my direct line of sight. I quickly moved out into the hallway and looked around.

Turning back to the elevator, I looked up and noticed a marker above both elevator doors noting the floor the elevators were on. I thought about Ivanov and wondered if he might be monitoring their locations. Before the door could close, I stepped back inside and pressed the button for the second floor. I swiped the keycard, confirmed that the button remained lit, and exited.

Down the hall was a door with the word STAIRS outside it. I carefully entered. Aiming my Glock in front of me, I cleared the area just inside the stairwell, turned to face the next flight of stairs, and paused. It was completely silent. Carpeting covered the steps, allowing me to move quickly, but quietly.

A minute later, I reached the twenty-ninth floor. My heart was beating hard as I stood outside the door leading from the stairs. I looked down and saw my shirt moving underneath my unzipped jacket. Just as I started to reach for the handle, my vision became blurry again. "No," I whispered to myself, closing my eyes and shaking my head, trying to make it stop. When I opened my eyes, my vision was back to normal.

There was another card reader outside the door. I took a deep breath, swiped the keycard, and opened the door with my left hand while gripping my gun with my right. I entered the floor and saw that nobody was there. Quietly, I closed the door and walked farther down the hallway. I looked both ways. On my left was a set of double doors with vertical windows on both, leading to what looked like a conference room.

To my right was a steel door marked AUTHORIZED PERSONNEL ONLY. I had found the server room.

I immediately felt the presence of someone watching me. I turned around, swinging my gun around the room. Nobody was there. Then I looked up and saw a security camera in the corner directly behind me.

I had to move quickly. Turning back around, I approached the server room, swiped the keycard again, and entered. "Put your hands in the air!" I yelled to a man on the other side of the room. "Get them up!"

"Wait! Don't let the door close behind you!" the man yelled back to me. Keeping my Glock fixed on the man on the other side of the room, I stopped moving toward him and turned to see the door start to close. "Hold the door!" he yelled, but it was too late. It closed before I could see that there wasn't a card reader on this side of the steel door, only a keypad. I turned back to the man and realized what had happened.

52

I TOOK TWO STEPS CLOSER TO THE MAN. "STEP BACK FOR ME," I ordered and watched the man back away from an alcove on the other side of the enormous dark room.

"Don't shoot," said the man, crouching on the floor and cowering as I started moving closer to him.

When I was ten feet away, I stopped and asked, "Who are you?"

He didn't answer.

"Who are you!?"

"Clayton," he finally replied and looked up at me, both hands high above his head. "Jeff Clayton."

He was badly hurt with a busted lip, broken nose, and hair matted down with blood. "Why are you here?"

The man paused, nervously looked toward his right, then back to me. "I handle operations for this building. We have an inspection tomorrow morning. I came in tonight to make sure we were ready for it."

"Who is *we?*" I asked and paused for a beat before clarifying my question. "Who do you work for?"

"That doesn't matter," he replied and turned his attention to his right again. The man looked terrified.

"I'm not going to ask you again. Who do you work for?"

"FBI," he finally replied. "Listen, you need to help me. There's—"

"Your identification," I said, interrupting the man and taking two more steps closer. "Show it to me."

Clayton stopped talking, nodded slowly, and lowered one of his hands to reach inside his jacket. He pulled out his credentials and tossed them. They slid along the floor and stopped in front of me. I bent down, keeping my weapon aimed at the man, and picked them up.

"My name is Blake Jordan," I said as I looked over his ID, lowered my weapon, and approached the beaten Bureau man. "What happened to you?"

"I can explain all of that later. Right now, we have bigger problems," he said as he lowered his hands.

As I handed his credentials back to him, I looked to my left. Against the wall, in another alcove mirroring the one on the right where the man had been standing when I entered, was an incredible number of explosives. A clock counting down with a red digital display ticked brightly in front of us. We had twenty-nine minutes until it detonated. "My God," I whispered as I looked at the ticking bomb in front of me.

"We're trapped. That's why I didn't want you closing that door. Now we have no way to get out of here."

I knelt down to study the bomb and carefully tugged at some of the blasting caps that had been inserted into the malleable bricks of C-4.

"Careful," said Clayton as I tried to understand the triggering mechanism.

"I need to know who did this to you," I said, turning from the explosives to look at the man on my right.

He nervously stared at the explosives and said, “Fine. I heard gunshots and tried to escape. I made it to the ground floor, but two guys found me and handed me over to two more men, one was Russian, the other American. They had a man working at this computer terminal over here, Australian accent.”

“What happened to that man?”

Clayton didn’t answer.

I leaned in and asked again, “What happened to him?”

“He did what they needed him to do. They had no further use for him and took him away to kill him.”

53

I STARED AT CLAYTON, UNABLE TO MOVE. "HOW LONG AGO DID they take him away from here?"

He shook his head and looked over to the countdown timer. "I guess about half an hour ago, maybe." He looked back at me, visibly panicked. "Please. We're running out of time. We have to get out of this room."

"No, we have to get off this floor," I said, correcting the man. "There's enough C-4 in here to take out the entire corner of this building and destroy everything two or three floors down, plus the roof above us." Pulling the sleeve of my jacket back, I set a countdown timer on my watch to match the bomb's clock.

"Can you think of anything?" asked Clayton as I turned my attention back to inspecting the bomb.

"I'm trying," I replied and noticed my hands were sweaty as I continued to gently tug at some of the blasting caps inserted into the many bricks of C-4, trying to find some that were loose. As a former SEAL, my experience with bombs was with detonations, not defusing them. But having watched Chris Reed work with C-4 earlier, I had an idea.

"Why didn't they kill you?" I asked as I gently pulled two loose blasting caps from a brick of C-4 and inspected the wires attached to them. "Why leave you here instead?"

Clayton paused a beat before replying, "The Russian man was concerned that I had alerted the authorities. He asked me who I was and I told him. He argued with the American about what they should do with me. They spoke in Russian. It sounded like they were arguing. I guess he wasn't sure if he'd need me."

"He's a dangerous man," I said as I carefully moved the brick of C-4 that had the two loose blasting caps. "The Russian is a known terrorist named Nikolai Ivanov. We think the American works for the NSA."

"Who is he?" asked Clayton as I turned back and saw him wiping blood from his face onto his pants.

"That's a good question," I replied and set the brick of C-4 on the floor next to me. "He's also very dangerous. He goes by Wolf and is responsible for the train crash that happened down in Washington."

I turned back to the two dangling blasting caps and pulled the wires out of them. Reaching into my jacket, I grabbed my knife and marked two spots at both ends of the C-4 that I'd need to remove to make the explosive material smaller while leaving the middle section where the blasting caps had been intact.

"What are you doing?" the man asked nervously as I prepared to cut into the material.

"Trying to get us out of here," I said as I cut off one side of the brick, followed by the other side. I pushed the two ends that I cut off to the side and carefully reinserted the caps back into their original position.

Looking back at the rest of the bomb, I considered for a moment trying to remove the remaining blasting caps. Then

I noticed another device I didn't recognize attached to the timer. I wondered if it was there to trigger the explosion if any tampering was detected. I knew I had taken a big enough risk already by removing one of the bricks and decided against touching the rest of the explosives if I didn't have to.

The timer on the bomb showed that I had just over twenty-four minutes left until it would detonate.

I grabbed the small chunk of C-4 with two hands and stood. "Stay here," I said and headed back to the door on the other side of the room. When I reached the entrance, I looked for something I could set the brick on. I needed it to be close to the middle of the door to minimize the chance of blasting through the floor or the roof. I found something I could use and carefully set the C-4 on the floor while I pulled a metal filing cabinet out from the wall and pushed it in front of the door. Then I reached into my jacket.

Finding the lighter I had taken from the dead man on the ground floor, I bent down, grabbed the chunk of C-4, and with my thumb, flicked the lighter. I looked at the yellow glow from the flame and closed my eyes for a moment, praying that this was going to work like I needed it to.

Opening my eyes, I moved the flame underneath the edge of the chunk of C-4.

"What are you doing?" Clayton yelled nervously as he watched me from the other side of the room. "You're going to kill yourself!" The flame wouldn't catch, so I broke the lighter and poured the lighter fluid on it.

"I know what I'm doing," I yelled back and paused a beat before whispering to myself, "I think."

The flame caught hold, then danced at the bottom of the material as I felt perspiration start to form on my forehead.

Airflow from the air conditioner keeping the room cold made it hard to keep the flame steady and concentrated in one spot, so I turned my body slightly and brought the explosive closer to shield it from the air. The side finally burned steadily, turning from a grayish color to black as it started to smoke.

I stopped depressing the broken lighter with my thumb and dropped it onto the ground as I stood and turned the small chunk of material that I was still holding to allow more of it to catch on fire. The flame started to get bigger and brighter as the brick became hotter and more difficult to hold. When I couldn't stand the heat anymore, I set it on top of the filing cabinet next to the door and walked back to Clayton.

He had both hands to his head, visibly distraught at what he saw me doing on the other side of the room.

"Easy, Clayton," I said. "C-4 is highly stable. You can cut it, burn it, and throw it. My partner likes to keep some in the back of his SUV in case he ever needs it," I said and looked at the bomb: twenty-one minutes left. "This setup uses blasting caps and an electrical current attached to that timer to set it off. I'm not sure what the other device is attached to the bomb, but we got lucky that we could remove a brick from it."

Clayton was staring over my shoulder at the material burning near the entrance. "So if this needs a charge and blasting caps to detonate, what do you need to set off the piece burning against that door over there?"

I reached inside my jacket and turned around to face the entrance door.

"A bullet," I replied.

"But that's at least forty, maybe even fifty meters away."

I nodded. "I'm a pretty good shot. Now stand inside the

other alcove opposite the bomb," I said as I took my position at the opposite wall, ten feet in front of the bomb that was ticking behind me.

"Can you get hurt out in the open like that?" asked Clayton as I checked my Glock, confirming how much ammunition I had left, and remembering that I still had the other gun from the man on the ground floor.

"There could be a concussion wave," I replied, turning back to make sure I had enough clearance between myself and the bomb in case a wave did knock me over. "If there is, I'll try to take the hit to keep the tampering device on the bomb from triggering." I watched the timer tick past the twenty-minute mark.

I turned back around and knelt, resting my left elbow on my left knee, and aimed my gun just above the flame against the wall. I took a deep breath and let the air out slowly as I closed an eye and felt my heart beating hard, knowing I'd need to pull the trigger in between beats to have a chance at hitting the mark.

Suddenly, the fire alarm went off. Water sprayed down from overhead, throwing me off. "Hurry before it puts out the flame," yelled Clayton from behind me. I closed my eye once again and focused on my heartbeat.

54

I SQUEEZED THE TRIGGER AND BRACED MYSELF, BUT NOTHING happened as I realized I had aimed too high.

"Hurry," repeated Clayton, over the loud fire alarm. "I thought you said you were a good—"

I pulled the trigger again before he could finish, and I was knocked backwards from the force of the concussion wave, hitting the back of my head on the server room floor. I looked up and saw Clayton recoiled inside the alcove, startled by the loud sound of the C-4 exploding across the room. He looked blurry to me as I realized I had hit my head twice in the last few minutes, first in the van, and now.

"You okay?" I asked, sitting up and reaching for my weapon that I had dropped on the floor next to me.

"Yeah," he said as I watched him look around the corner before looking back at the bomb still behind me.

"Did it work?" I asked, sitting up and straining to see across the room as the fire sprinkler turned off.

"I can't tell with all of the smoke and the water dripping down," replied Clayton. "You took the hit, though. The bomb's okay."

I turned back, still on the floor, and narrowed my eyes: just over eighteen minutes left.

"We need to move," I said, getting to my feet and handing Clayton the gun from the man I had killed downstairs. I raised my Glock to lead the way as we headed to the entrance to the server room. We walked through white smoke from the detonation. Moving forward, water dripped on both of us as we passed through the remaining smoke and saw the end of the room. The door had been destroyed, and all that remained was a large hole and a smoldering hunk of metal on the floor that used to be a filing cabinet.

"Where do we go?" I asked as we exited the room, and I noticed that the overhead sprinklers outside the server room weren't on. Then the fire alarm turned off, making it easier to hear Clayton's response.

"Let me think about it," he said as I lowered my gun, walked to the elevators, and looked up.

I studied the display over both elevator doors, blinking repeatedly, trying to fix my vision and get the numbers to come into focus so I could figure out where Ivanov and Wolf might have taken Morgan.

I heard the radio crackle, followed by Ivanov's voice. "Viktor, *u menya yest' zhenshchina*." I froze in terror as I realized what was happening. "Viktor," Ivanov screamed again into the radio. "Do you copy, Viktor?"

It wasn't *what* Ivanov said, but *how* I heard him say it that caught me off guard. His voice was coming from the radio clipped to my belt.

And it was also transmitting from another radio right behind me that I realized was being carried by Jeff Clayton.

I stood frozen and heard the sound of the slide on a gun being racked to chamber a round. My heart sank.

"Drop the gun and turn around for me, Mr. Jordan. Nice

and slow," said the man standing behind me. "Do it now!" he yelled as I continued to face the elevators with my weapon in my right hand, realizing there was nothing I could do but obey his command. I slowly bent down, set my gun on the floor, and turned around to face the man I had just helped escape. "Kick it to me and put your hands in the air."

I turned the face of my watch inside my palm as I kicked my gun to Clayton. As he bent down to pick it up, I checked my watch. I was running out of time.

"We haven't been properly introduced," the man said as he slipped my gun in his jacket and aimed his weapon at me. "I prefer to go by Wolf," he added with a smile.

55

"WHO ARE YOU?" I ASKED, DEFENSELESS, AND STARING AT THE man standing ten feet away from me.

"Site officer and liaison between the FBI, NSA, and the United States Telecommunications Company."

"LITHIUM," I said.

"That's right," answered Wolf, raising an eyebrow as his smile widened. "You've done your homework, Mr. Jordan." He paused for a moment, collecting his thoughts before continuing. "I'm in the very unique position of having privileged access to FBI and NSA offices across the East Coast that work with partners such as the USTC for conducting foreign and domestic surveillance on innocent citizens. It stops *today*."

I looked past him into the server room, watching the smoldering remains and hearing the dripping from the sprinklers and wondering where Wolf was going with this. "Why do you care so much about Russia?"

"I *don't* care about Russia," answered Wolf. "It's *Ivanov* who cares about Russia, Mr. Jordan. Which I can understand. He's a very patriotic man and is passionate about protecting his country. But so am I."

Shaking my head slowly, I turned my gaze back to Wolf and said, "I don't understand. What did you and Ivanov have Lennox do? And why are you hurt? Who left you in that server room to die like this?"

Wolf checked his watch as I kept my hands behind my head, estimating how much time had passed and how long we had until the explosives in the other room would detonate. Wolf's smile disappeared. "Nikolai approached me with a proposal. If I got him access to this building and into this room," he said as he nodded over his shoulder, "then he'd get me access to someone who could shut the whole thing down."

"Morgan Lennox," I said, and Wolf nodded.

"Nikolai told me that all I had to do was convince Lennox to come to New York. Easier said than done. I used my own contacts within the FBI and NSA to lure the man to the East Coast. But he doesn't care about money or working for a big government agency. He wanted to stay in Chicago with DDC, the field office that you helped launch." Wolf studied my reaction and nodded to himself. "I've done *my* homework, too. Lennox is a very loyal man, so I knew it would take some convincing by way of his nephew, Anthony."

"What about the trains?" I asked. "We know you and Ivanov forced Anthony to cause the crash. *Why?*"

"It's called a diversion, Mr. Jordan," replied the man, cocking his head to one side. "If our goal was to maximize casualties in Washington, we wouldn't have crashed the trains at midnight, would we? Besides, we needed to test the kid for what we needed done here if we were unable to lure his uncle from Chicago."

"So you and Ivanov had Morgan shut down the systems collecting data on Russia. Now you're destroying the evidence and the hardware along with it." I paused and added, "How'd you get trapped in that room?"

Wolf used his hand to wipe away some blood that had started to run from his broken nose while keeping his gun fixed on me. He looked at the blood and sniffed as he brought the hand back to his weapon. "Lennox started destroying the foreign surveillance protocols that are controlled from this building, for Nikolai. I ordered him to initiate the same procedure on domestic data collection. Ivanov took me by surprise. There was a struggle. Nikolai said the surveillance on American citizens would not be disrupted."

As Wolf paced, I lowered my hand to glance at my wrist to check on the timer. He stopped walking and took two steps closer to me. "That bomb's gonna detonate in sixteen minutes," I said.

"Then you'll need to decide quickly, won't you?" replied Wolf.

I narrowed my eyes and shook my head, not understanding what the man was saying.

"There was one thing that Nikolai and I both agreed on, Mr. Jordan. When we found out who you were and who you worked for, we did a little digging in your past. You work for the president. He's been a personal friend and mentor of yours since you were a teenager. He trained you and helped you become a SEAL. Over the last ten plus years, you've garnered an incredible amount of knowledge and experience in counterterrorism. That's extremely useful to someone like me. What's even *more* useful is your *relationship* with the president. I might not have Lennox in my control anymore," he said and paused for effect. "But I have *you.* I need you to leave with me right now."

"I'm not going anywhere with you."

Wolf looked down to his weapon, admiring it while collecting his thoughts again. "Before Nikolai and I arrived in New York, we made a few phone calls. We know about your past, Mr. Jordan. It's a shame what happened to your wife. You wouldn't want anything like that to happen to anyone else you care about, would you? The people closest to you—we know who they are. Work for me and I will make sure that nobody gets hurt. Don't work for me, and their blood is on your hands. Those are your only two options."

He aimed his gun at me. There was no way out of the situation. As I took a deep breath, the lights flicked off for a moment and then came back on. Still keeping my hands behind my head, I turned to my left and noticed a security camera on the ceiling, pointed straight at us. I turned to face Wolf again and watched him turn to look at the camera. When the lights went out again, I lowered my body and lunged forward.

We hit the floor and Wolf fired the weapon twice. I felt around for his arm, and when I found it, I held it back behind him as the lights came back on. With his free hand, Wolf punched me twice in the face. I punched back, hitting the man in his already broken nose. He screamed in pain as I grabbed his free hand and held it back behind him while using my other hand to slam his arm holding the gun onto the floor.

He let go of the weapon and, using the strength from his legs, pushed himself off the floor, turning over to try to get on top of me. I pushed him away, rolled over, and tried to get to my feet, but he kicked me in the stomach before I could. I felt extreme pain in my ribs. He kicked again, knocking the wind out of me.

"Two options, Mr. Jordan," he yelled as I struggled to breathe and glanced down at the inside of my wrist. "We're running out of time," he added, walking over to me. "I need your decision and I need it *now*."

I was sprawled on the floor, the gun out of reach, watching him approach. I pulled my legs closer to my chest as the man walked next to me and bent over to pick up the gun. As he did, I kicked the back of his legs, causing him to fall on top of me. His head hit my chest, and as it did, I reached my arm around his neck.

Wolf struggled to break free, but I kept squeezing until his body went limp and he was unconscious. I pushed the man off me and sat up, out of breath and breathing hard. I felt inside my jacket and found the knife that I had kept. When I saw Wolf starting to move, I let go of the knife and quickly stood and reached to grab his gun from the floor. I walked to the other side of his body and stood over him as he started to blink and he began to regain consciousness. I aimed the gun at the man as he looked up at me.

"There's something they teach you as a SEAL, Clayton," I said as I took a few steps closer and looked him in the eye. Staring back at me, his chest heaved up and down, taking in deep breaths as I continued. "Something I'll never forget." I gripped the weapon with two hands. "There's always a third option," I said and pulled the trigger, sending several rounds into the man until it was empty. I kept squeezing the trigger, thinking about what he had said, until I finally stopped, lowered my arm, and dropped the gun.

I felt the distinct taste of blood in my mouth and wiped my face with the back of my hand, looked at it, then held my wrist up to my face to check the timer. I dropped my arm and stared at Wolf's lifeless body. Feeling the hair on the back of my neck stand on end, I slowly looked up and noticed the security camera. As I stared at it, the lights flicked off and on again.

Someone was there, watching, and trying to help.

56

I WALKED AROUND WOLF, GRABBED MY GLOCK, AND STOOD still as I tried to figure out where my helper might be. I thought about radioing Jami, but knew Ivanov and a man named Viktor would hear me.

Then I had another thought.

Security cameras were monitored by security officers. After seeing the dead officer on the ground floor, Jami had mentioned that based on the schematics Veronica had accessed, the security office was on the second floor. I turned my attention from the camera back to the two elevator doors on my left and looked at their locations based on the digital display above both doors. The elevator on the left was on the ground floor. The other was on the second floor. Right where I left it and the floor where I needed to be.

I pushed the button to call the elevator and watched as the one on my right started ascending. I checked my Glock and crouched in front of the door as it opened, aiming my weapon inside.

It was clear. Punching the button for the seventh floor, I

found the keycard, swiped it, and stared at Wolf's lifeless body as the doors closed. The elevator raced down to its destination, and I got into a crouch as the elevator slowed and the doors opened.

The area it opened up into was completely dark. I stepped out, using the light coming from inside the elevator to locate the stairwell. I walked toward it, and when I got halfway there, the elevator doors started to close. I picked up speed, as I was about to lose the little light I had. The doors closed before I reached the stairwell door. I had to walk in complete darkness, with my left hand extended and trying to feel for the door as my right hand gripped my Glock tightly.

Ten more steps, and I finally got to the edge of the room and felt around for the stairwell door. I reached for the keycard and moved it around the door until it located the reader and I heard the lock click. I found the handle and pulled it open. Once inside, I was relieved to see light again. Holding the keycard in my left hand, I looked up above me then back down toward the next floor below and aimed my weapon in front of me. I descended five more floors until I was standing outside the door marked for the second floor.

I took another deep breath, swiped the keycard, and carefully pulled the door open. It was clear.

Another few steps, and I saw a door with the words SECURITY PERSONNEL ONLY outside it. I again approached the door and entered just as I had at the stairwell. As soon as I pulled it open and entered with my hands gripped tightly around my Glock, I almost tripped over the body of a man on the floor.

I looked up and aimed my weapon in front of me for a moment before lowering it in relief as I exhaled. I quickly turned around and stopped the door from closing behind me, a mistake I had made upstairs. "Good call, mate," said Morgan as he brought a chair over to prop the door open and keep it from locking us in.

"You okay, man?" I asked as we embraced, and I noticed a row of monitors against the wall, each one toggling through countless cameras positioned all over the building every few seconds to monitor the area.

"Better than *this* bloke," he said, looking at the man at our feet with a LAN cable wrapped around his neck.

"Who is he?"

"A man named Viktor," replied Morgan. "Ivanov left me alone with him while he went looking for you."

I nodded and looked at my wrist to check on the timer. "Morgan, we have exactly ten minutes until the bomb in the server room detonates. Let's go find Jami and get out of here while we still can, okay?"

Before Morgan could reply, I heard the familiar crackle of a radio transmission beginning. "Mr. Jordan!" Ivanov yelled. My blood ran cold as his voice filled the room. "You have two minutes to show yourself."

57

I STARED AT MORGAN BEFORE MY EYES SHIFTED BACK TO THE monitors against the wall next to a computer-based control system that I guessed controlled the building's electrical system, including the fire systems, ventilation, and lighting that Morgan had used back when I was on the twenty-ninth floor fighting Wolf. The images from the many cameras toggled through the various vantage points from around the building and along each floor. I walked closer and said, "I need to see what's happening on the first floor, Morgan."

He followed me to the control panel and started typing, trying to isolate the cameras for me.

"Mr. Jordan," Ivanov's voice boomed following another crackle from the radio on my belt. I grabbed it and held it up to my face as Morgan finally got the monitors set to the first floor. "You now have ninety seconds. I need an acknowledgement that you are on your way. What is it you Navy SEALs say? *Hooyah?*" he asked with a laugh as a camera near the first-floor elevator found Ivanov holding Jami at gunpoint.

"Where are you?" I asked, trying to buy some time as I watched the madman and waited for his response.

"First floor. I have something I think you want," he responded.

"Don't listen to him, Blake!" Jami yelled as the transmission was cut off, and I watched Ivanov hit her.

"Damn it," I whispered, looking back at the propped-open door and then to the body of the man Morgan had killed. I reattached the radio onto my belt. I walked to the body and searched for another keycard, but he didn't have one. "Morgan, do you remember from when you worked here if there's a card reader in the stairwell to get access to the first floor?" I asked, turning back to look at my friend.

"No, mate. The readers only start at the second floor in the stairwell and are needed for any elevator."

"Good," I said, standing and handing my keycard to him. "I have an idea, and you're gonna need this." I handed him something else from my jacket that he'd need as I shared my plan for saving Jami with him.

Morgan followed me out of the security office as I stopped in the area between the elevator and the stairs. He pressed the button to call the closest elevator as I looked down to my watch again. "Wait five minutes," I said. "That should give me enough time, but you can't be late, okay?" I extended my hand and we shook.

"I'll use that time to try to kill the surveillance protocol deletion script they had me initiate."

"We don't have that much time, Morgan," I said as I took a few steps backwards toward the stairwell as the elevator doors opened and Morgan stepped inside. "I need you back in time for the plan to work."

"I'll be there. But I have to try to undo this. I worked too hard on this program to see it destroyed."

I nodded. "See you in five," I said as the elevator doors closed, and I turned around, reached for my gun, and slowly opened the stairwell door. Once inside, I descended one flight and kept my back against the wall. After counting to thirty, I gripped my weapon in my right hand, unclipped the radio from my belt, and depressed the button. "Ivanov, I'm coming down," I said, imagining him walking over to the elevator doors and looking up at the digital display to see where I was coming from. I turned the radio off, clipped it back onto my belt, and waited a few more seconds. I slowly turned the door handle and looked out onto the floor.

I was right. Ivanov was standing at the elevator door with his back to me. He had a gun to Jami's head and was looking up at the display, watching the number drop and believing that I was approaching from the twenty-ninth floor. I exited the stairwell, careful to close the door without it making noise, and approached from behind. Aiming my weapon out in front of me, I walked quickly to beat the elevator.

The elevator doors opened. Ivanov forced Jami to take a step closer as he saw that the elevator was empty.

"Drop the gun, Ivanov," I said, standing behind the man. I closed an eye, planning on squeezing the trigger to take him out, when my vision blurred again, coming in and out of focus. I couldn't get a shot.

Ivanov laughed. "Very clever, Mr. Jordan," he said, quickly turning his body so that his head and Jami's were inches apart as I kept my gun fixed on him. "Very, very clever. I'm glad you could join the party."

"Wolf is dead and you're next," I replied and paused for a beat. "But if you let her go, I'll let you live."

"That's a very generous proposal, Mr. Jordan," he replied. "You know what the problem was with Wolf? The man was narrow-minded. He didn't care about your government spying on Russia. He didn't care about Russia at all. He only cared about America. Said he was a patriot. Are *you* a patriot, Mr. Jordan?"

"Take the shot, Blake," Jami yelled as she struggled to break free from Ivanov's powerful grasp. My vision came back into focus, but it was too late. I couldn't take the shot now without the chance of hitting Jami.

Just then, I heard someone approach behind me. Keeping my Glock aimed at Ivanov, I looked over my shoulder and saw Mark Reynolds enter from the space I had crashed through, with his weapon drawn.

I turned back to Ivanov and yelled, "Stand down, Mark! I have this under control," as he reached me.

Reynolds stopped next to me and aimed his gun at Ivanov along with me. "I'm not here to stop you, Blake. I'm here to *help* you." He paused before adding, "Sorry, man. I should have listened to you."

"If you want to help me, go pull that fire alarm," I said, nodding to the small red pull station with the word FIRE on it across the room, as I remembered how loud the alarm was when I was in the server room. I needed a way to keep Ivanov from hearing the sound created by Morgan executing his part of the plan.

"Fire-rescue are outside the building already, Blake," replied Reynolds. "Willis is keeping them back."

"Just do it, Mark," I said and watched him slowly make his way toward the pull station. Keeping my eyes on Ivanov, I said, "You already got what you wanted. You had Lennox initiate the foreign surveillance protocol deletion on your country. You and your men set a bomb to destroy the surveillance equipment. You could have killed her and left without a trace," I said and looked at Jami. "Why are you still here?"

Ivanov smiled as I remembered what Wolf had told me upstairs, and I realized in that moment that I already knew the answer to my question. It was the one thing that Wolf said both men had agreed on. "You greedy son of a bitch," I whispered as Mark pulled down on the handle of the pull station, causing the fire alarm to trigger. "There's no way out of here, Ivanov!" I yelled over the pulsating alarm.

"Take them out!" replied Ivanov, loud enough only for me to hear as he looked at Mark on the other side of the room slowly making his way back over to us. "Him," he said, nodding at Reynolds, "and anyone else out there waiting for me. Do it and I'll let the woman go, unharmed, and we all get what we want, Jordan."

My eyes drifted to the left where, through my blurry field of vision, I saw what looked like Jami's gun at the other end of the room. With my vision blurred, I knew there was only one thing I could do. Reynolds returned and trained his gun on Ivanov. "What does he want?" he yelled over the loud alarm.

Lowering my gun, I looked at Mark and said, "He wants *me*." I gripped my Glock tight and slowly raised it, this time placing it underneath my chin. "Let her go, Ivanov, or I swear to you I'll pull the trigger."

58

Unable to see clearly for more than a few seconds at a time, I kept the gun underneath my chin and stared at Ivanov as we both realized we were in the middle of a Mexican standoff. He couldn't let Jami go, or Mark Reynolds would take him out. And leaving the building with Ivanov by taking out Reynolds, Willis, and any other Bureau guy out on the street wasn't an option, either. Not now, not ever.

"Blake! What are you doing?" screamed Jami, but I ignored her and tried to stay focused on Ivanov.

I raised my left hand and glanced down at my wrist, trying to see how much time was left. It took a few seconds for my eyes to adjust, but for a moment, I could make out the time. "We have five minutes until your bomb detonates," I said, knowing it also meant Morgan had run out of time. He wasn't coming.

Reynolds turned to me, shocked to hear that the explosives were there, inside the building somewhere.

"Mr. Jordan, you are forcing my hand," said Ivanov as I noticed blurred movement in the top of my field of vision as

I kept my eyes on the man. The plan was back in play. I just needed a little more time.

"Blake," said Reynolds with a concerned tone of voice, and I knew he was seeing the same thing that I was.

I held my left hand up. "It's okay, Mark," I said and removed my Glock from under my chin and raised both hands into the air while Reynolds continued to keep his weapon trained on the man holding Jami.

"Okay!" I yelled over the alarm that was doing its job of muting the sound that Ivanov would never hear. But now I had to keep him from seeing the light as well. I kept my finger on the trigger as I waited for the right moment, praying for my vision to become sharp again so I wouldn't miss my chance. "You win."

I could see Ivanov cock his head to the side. "Then you know what you need to do," he said, and I nodded.

Turning to my right, my eyes locked with Mark's as my vision became sharp again. "What are you doing?" he asked, looking concerned as I turned back to face forward, my gun still in the air, as the digital display counted down from three to one. I took a deep breath and let it out before responding to Reynolds.

"Stalling," I said just as the elevator doors opened, and I fired shots into the air, causing Ivanov to flinch.

I lowered my weapon and aimed it at Ivanov along with Reynolds, as I watched Ivanov open his eyes and look confused, trying to understand what I was doing. Suddenly, he realized someone was behind him. At that moment, Morgan Lennox stepped forward and plunged my knife deep into Ivanov's back.

Ivanov screamed in pain and loosened his grip on Jami. She twisted around and broke free, taking two steps toward me as she tried to understand what was happening. Morgan stepped out from the elevator car and Ivanov raised his arm. Morgan grabbed it and pushed it up into the air as Ivanov fired his gun.

I raised my Glock and closed an eye. With a squeeze of the trigger, I drilled a bullet through Ivanov's right wrist, causing him to drop his weapon. A moment later, Jami stepped forward and kicked Ivanov's chest.

The terrorist took a step backward, trying to regain his balance, but instead tripped over the gap between the inside of the elevator car and the threshold. Falling on his back, he drove the knife even deeper into his body. The door started to close, but hit Ivanov's leg and reopened as I checked the timer on my watch.

"The bomb's going to detonate in two minutes! You need to get out of this building *now!*" I yelled.

"We're not leaving without you," said Jami, turning to Morgan, who nodded his agreement.

"I'm gonna be right behind you," I explained. "Please, you have to go now. Get everyone out there away from the building." Jami said she would and ran outside as I turned to Morgan. "I need the keycard," I said as Lennox reached into a pocket and handed it back to me before following Jami out of the building.

Reynolds looked to Ivanov and said, "We need to get *him* out of here, too. The man's responsible for a lot of deaths over the last twenty-four hours. He needs to pay for his crimes."

Something about those words made me think about Claudia Nazir. I had used the very same words when talking about the woman just hours earlier. I shook my head. "No, Mark. Look at what Claudia did. She found a way out of the system, a system meant to protect innocent Americans. The system failed us."

"I can't let him die here," said Reynolds. "The man needs to be brought to justice."

I thought about it for a second before responding. "You're right," I replied. "Do you still have your cuffs?"

Before Mark could reply, Ivanov said something. I walked closer to the man and saw that he was laughing.

"Say it again," I yelled over the sound of the alarm.

Ivanov laughed again and took a deep breath before repeating himself. "Do you really think that you, or Agent Davis, or Chris Reed will be safe with me *dead?*" He turned his gaze from me to Mark. "And you, Agent Reynolds. Same goes for you and anyone else close to Jordan." He tried to laugh again, but coughed up blood as his life was draining from his body. Everything inside me wanted to help speed that up.

"What are you talking about?" I asked, looking down at my watch again.

"I've already communicated to my many affiliates exactly who you are and who you work for. This isn't going to end with me. Russia has a very long memory, Mr. Jordan. We're going to keep coming after you."

Reynolds said, "And we're going to be ready for them." Mark stretched out his hand. Inside it was a set of metal handcuffs. I looked up and saw Mark nod an approval to me.

I nodded back, took the handcuffs, and walked inside the elevator car. Grabbing Ivanov's left hand, I cuffed him to a long metal bar that stretched along the back of the elevator, to keep him from reaching the panel.

"What are you doing?" asked Ivanov.

I smiled, reached into my pocket to find the keycard that Morgan had returned to me, and swiped it.

Punching the button marked twenty-nine and seeing it

stay illuminated, I turned back to Ivanov and slowly backed out of the elevator.

"Hooyah," I said, watching the doors close and looking up to the digital display above, confirming that he was headed to his final destination.

"We need to get out of here!" yelled Reynolds as he ran toward the wrecked van that I had crashed into the building earlier, and looked back at me, motioning with his hand for me to join him before it was too late.

I ran hard and fast, trying to catch up to Mark as I heard a loud explosion from high above us, followed by the distinct sound of metal on metal as the entire inside of the building on the twenty-ninth floor was decimated. Just before I ran outside, I looked back and saw a flash of fire emerge from the two elevator shafts. I turned back around and ran up the slippery, inclined driveway, holding onto the guardrail as I did to keep myself upright.

At the top, I saw Curt Willis across the street, directing police and emergency crews while holding back his Bureau men along with Morgan and Jami.

They were safe.

59

THE EXPLOSION ON THE TWENTY-NINTH FLOOR ENDED UP BEING a nonevent for anyone standing outside TITANPOINTE. Jami reminded me that the architect had built the Lower Manhattan skyscraper strong enough to withstand an atomic blast. That same design had kept the NYPD officers, Bureau agents, and bystanders safe from what would have otherwise been a dangerous situation outside the building.

As I stared up at the dark, ominous building, Jami put her arms around me. “Blake, you saved my life in there,” she said as I wrapped my arms around her body and we held each other close. “Thank you.”

I smiled and said, “I guess we’re even,” thinking about how she had saved my life in a similar way once.

I turned to look behind me and saw Morgan Lennox standing next to Reynolds. Morgan stared solemnly at the building he had spent so many years of his life working from as smoke billowed from the large air vents on the sides of the skyscraper as fire-rescue crews along with NYPD and Bureau agents entered.

“Morgan,” I said, turning around as Jami let go and

joined me, "I'm sorry, I should have told you this earlier. AJ is okay." Morgan's expression changed from distant to fully present again. "So is Lisa."

"They're okay?" he asked in disbelief. "Where are they?"

"They're with Chris Reed back at the Hoover Building in DC," I said as I put my hand on his shoulder.

Before Morgan could ask any more questions about his nephew and Lisa, I noticed Mark look past Jami and me. I turned around and saw Curt Willis approaching with another Bureau guy with him. "Can someone explain to me what the hell's going on here?" he asked and turned his gaze from me to Reynolds.

"Yeah," replied Mark, turning to Morgan, Jami, and me. "They just took down Nikolai Ivanov and Wolf."

"All four of us did," I said, correcting Reynolds. "I'm not sure the plan would have worked without you."

Mark smiled and nodded as Willis asked, "Where are they?" referring to the terrorists.

"Dead," I replied, looking up to the tall building. "You'll find their bodies up on the twenty-ninth floor."

Willis narrowed his eyes and shook his head. "And what exactly were they doing up there?"

Jami, Morgan, and I spent the next several minutes filling in the gaps for Curt Willis and Mark Reynolds. Morgan explained his history with the secretive NSA building and what the terrorists wanted him to do. Being the guy in charge of the New York field office at Federal Plaza, Willis knew about the joint FBI-NSA relationship and the data center in the building known as TITANPOINTE. He knew Jeff Clayton, too.

Willis was surprised to learn that Clayton was the man referred to as Wolf, but said it made perfect sense to him. Being the liaison between the FBI, NSA, and the United

States Telecommunications Company who owned and operated the building, Clayton had unique and privileged access with all three organizations, making it easy for him to impersonate an NSA manager and "recruit" AJ Lennox for a job that never existed. Willis was glad to hear that the terrorists were stopped, but had another question, one we all needed an answer to.

"Lennox, were you able to stop the deletion of the surveillance protocol they had you initiate?" asked Willis.

For the first time in twenty-four hours, I saw a smile spread across Morgan's face as he winked.

Willis ordered the Bureau man listening in on the conversation to take Jami, Morgan, Mark, and me back to Federal Plaza for a full debrief and a formal after-action report meeting to be conducted with some of his agents.

Morgan explained on the drive over how he had watched Ivanov beat Wolf bloody while compelling him to continue working. Morgan had used that to his advantage, knowing that while Wolf had a background in computer forensics and understood what Lennox was working on, Ivanov did not.

In the five minutes that Ivanov and Wolf struggled, Morgan managed to stop the deletion and initiate a failover to the NSA's massive data center in Utah. When Morgan had gone back up to the twenty-ninth floor while I went downstairs to handle Ivanov, he had spent the additional few minutes confirming the data move was completed and began transferring temporary folders to the Utah servers, saying he could help recover the data within a day if the NSA would be willing to give him the opportunity.

Back inside Federal Plaza, the Bureau agents separated us for questioning. The agent debriefing me showed me a picture of Jeff Clayton, and I positively identified the man as

Wolf. He called Washington and spoke to agents at the Hoover Building, who had AJ Lennox ID the man as well.

During the debrief, a Bureau medic checked me over. She asked about my vision, and I told her I was having trouble focusing. She shined a bright light in my eyes and asked if I was experiencing any dizziness, nausea, or headaches. I told her only the blurry vision that seemed to have subsided. She placed a small bandage on my forehead over the abrasion from the steering wheel and went over the warning signs for concussions. She said if any developed, to let her know immediately. Once she left, the debrief continued.

After two hours of explaining everything that had happened since arriving in New York, I turned my wrist up and checked the time and saw that it was twenty minutes past eleven o'clock. I reminded the agent sitting with me that I worked for the president, which he said he already knew after making a call to Bill Landry earlier. I told him Agent Davis and Morgan Lennox worked for the Department of Domestic Counterterrorism and, unless the three of us were being charged with a crime, he needed to let us go.

The agent said he had to make a phone call and would be back. He returned fifteen minutes later with Jami, Morgan, and an evidence bag that he dropped on the table in front of me, containing my weapon. "Willis says you're free to go. They'll finish up in Chicago," the agent said, looking at Jami and Morgan. "You need to be back in Washington tomorrow to complete your debrief with Bill Landry."

I nodded and stood, reaching into the bag for my things, and left with Jami and Morgan. Veronica was outside the door, and Jami introduced her to Morgan. The agent who debriefed me said that the Bureau could order some food and had a spot for us to rest. "Thanks," I said. "But we need to step out for a while."

Morgan decided not to go, opting to stay back instead. He said he wanted to talk to AJ and make sure he was okay, so Jami and I headed downstairs by ourselves, and I called the White House on our way out. Emma Ross, President Keller's chief of staff, answered. I told her we needed her to coordinate a return flight back to Chicago. She said she'd get on it and handed the phone to the president. I brought Keller up to speed, letting him know that we had been successful in stopping the terrorist threat in New York. The president asked to see me tomorrow after I was done with Landry. I told him I'd stop by.

Ending the call, I slid the phone into my back pocket as we stepped outside. "What do you feel like?"

Jami and I checked our watches at the same time and saw that it was getting close to midnight. Looking up at me, she grabbed my hands and interlaced her fingers with mine. "Pizza?" she asked.

I nodded, feeling hungry and drained.

"We're running out of time on last-minute deliciousness points, you know."

I laughed and stepped toward a gentleman walking by us and asked where the closest pizza joint was. He said to go west two blocks, south on Church, and it'd be on our right. Ten minutes later, we were outside Dona Bella, sitting on the curb with two slices of steaming hot pizza, watching the fireworks illuminate the dark night sky as the clock hit midnight and millions of Americans rang in the New Year from Midtown.

60

We sat together for a long time, listening to the sound of music and celebration from the massive Midtown crowd while watching the endless fireworks overhead as they popped far away in the distance. Jami rested her head on my shoulder. We were both exhausted. I lowered my hand and felt the ring box.

As I did, an older model car drove north on the one-way street, slowly heading our way. Its headlights were blinding and made me think about standing at the end of Wolcott Street with Claudia Nazir. I had felt completely helpless in that moment back on Wolcott, as if I were floating on a sea without a shore, unable to ever make it back to the safety and security of land.

"You okay?" asked Jami as the driver approached. I let go of the ring box and slowly moved my hand behind me and gripped my weapon. The driver's window was lowered, and the man stared at Jami, then me before he nodded and said, "Happy New Year" with a smile, and Jami repeated the words back to him.

The driver continued north on Church Street before

disappearing. My thoughts drifted back to Nikolai Ivanov and what he had said about having communicated who I was and who I worked for to his affiliates. He had said that Russia had a very long memory and would never stop coming after me.

I believed him.

I realized then and there that I never could have kept my wife safe, just like I could never keep Jami safe. In the end, the people closest to me would pay the ultimate price. Just like Maria. And just like my father.

"Are you okay?" Jami asked again as I loosened my grip on the gun and turned to her, forcing a smile.

"I'm fine," I replied as I stood, helped her up, and started the ten-minute walk back to Federal Plaza.

Jami wrapped an arm around me and leaned her head on my side as we walked together and crossed Broadway. "I put in for a transfer to the new DDC field office in Washington," she said and looked up at me, waiting to see how I was going to respond. "We can finally live in the same city again," she added.

"You shouldn't have done that, Jami," I said, remembering that her sister, Kate, had told me this already.

"Why not?" she asked and stopped walking as I continued heading east, ignoring her. "Blake, *stop*."

I turned around and waited for her to catch up to me, unable to get the words that Ivanov had spoken out of my mind. We walked together, neither of us saying anything else, to Lafayette Street, where Jami and I turned the corner and headed north to Federal Plaza.

When we got to the front of the building, Jami started to climb the steps, but I stayed on the sidewalk. She turned around and walked back to me and held her hands out. I grabbed them and she smiled. "Blake, when Ivanov came up behind me and took me by surprise, he called me by name. He knew who I was." She paused for a beat before continuing, "And he said he wasn't going to hurt me, but needed me to lure you out. I didn't believe him." She paused again. "But I knew you'd come. I knew you would save me."

She pulled me in and said, "I love you, Blake. I love you so much."

We kissed. I closed my eyes and heard the faint pops of more fireworks exploding on the other side of the city. I opened my eyes and smiled as I finally had the one thing I wanted. It just wasn't what I needed.

I felt my smile slowly start to fade as I stared into her eyes, desperately searching for another way out. I had been trained to understand that there was always a third option. But for the first time in my life, I didn't see one. In that moment, all I wanted was to tell her that I loved her, to bend down on one knee and prove it to her.

But I couldn't. I had found my answer, one that, like TITANPOINTE, had been hiding in plain sight all along. I shook my head slowly and looked down, trying to find the right words to say. "I don't—" I finally got out and struggled to finish.

"You don't *what*, Blake?" she asked, furrowing her brow and holding onto my hands even tighter.

I took a deep breath and exhaled. "I don't know where to begin."

"I know," she replied with a smile and breathed a sigh of relief as I looked back up before continuing.

"Jami, I will always try to protect you and keep you safe the best I can. But I'll have to do it as a friend."

She shook her head and squinted her eyes. "I don't understand. You don't love me, Blake?"

"I'm empty, Jami," I replied, letting go of her hands and taking a step back. "There's nothing left to give."

Jami shook her head. "Blake, you're just tired. Let's get some rest. You'll feel better in the morning."

I took another step back and nodded. "You're right. I am tired." I forced a half smile. "Goodbye, Jami."

I turned and headed south on Lafayette, alone, leaving her standing on the steps of Federal Plaza. "Blake," she said, calling out to me. "Blake, please don't walk away from us." Her voice cut through the cold night air. I heard her walk down the steps, but she didn't come after me. And I didn't turn back.

Instead, I walked and kept on walking until Jami and Federal Plaza had disappeared far behind.

I thought about the conversation Jami and I had had in Giordano's, a life we had seven hundred miles away from here. "If curses *are* real," she had said to me as I stared into her eyes, "then they're meant to be broken."

I drew my jacket tighter around my body, trying to stay warm as I walked past dimly lit buildings emitting tall, white billows of hot steam coming from somewhere underneath the cold city streets.

One of the hardest decisions you'll ever face in life is choosing whether to walk away or try harder. I thought about the lyrics to a song I had heard once, how like a match being lit, or the sinking of a ship—sometimes, letting go gives a better grip. I had to find the courage to let go of what I could not change.

As I continued to walk, I thought about that third option I had so desperately searched for and finally realized why I couldn't find it. Sometimes your heart just needs more time to accept what your mind already knows. And sometimes, when you can't find a solution to a problem, it's because there was never a problem to be solved at all, but rather a truth to be accepted.

Kate was right. I couldn't have the girl and the job.

It wasn't the goodbye that hurt. It was the memories that I knew would follow and continue to haunt me.

But unlike a past that I could not change, I *could* change the direction of my future. For once, I had the chance to keep someone I loved safe.

I knew that walking away from Jami would leave me broken, but maybe that was what I needed to be.

Because only when you're broken can you start to heal.

Only when you're broken can you make peace with your broken pieces.

And only when you're broken can you see what you're really made of.

I hope you enjoyed book 3 in the Blake Jordan series. Go to kenfite.com/rules-of-engagement to start book 4.

Russian terrorists have brought America to its knees. Can Blake Jordan stop the next attack?

After he's given a warning by a dying man that Russian terrorists are coming after him, black ops agent Blake Jordan pushes everyone he cares about away to keep them safe. But Russia has a long memory.

When a cyberattack is unleashed against hospitals and government agencies, Blake teams up with his lost love to investigate. But he never expects her to be used as leverage for the release of the terrorist who Blake thinks is dead.

If he wants to protect the woman he loves, Blake must assemble a team to break out the prisoner. But the Russians don't follow the rules of engagement... and he'll have to make an impossible choice. RULES OF ENGAGEMENT is a fast-paced thriller you'll be reading late into the night.

Here's what readers are saying...

★★★★★ "...heart-pounding excitement."
★★★★★ "Suspenseful from beginning to end."
★★★★★ "...twists leading to a bittersweet climax."
★★★★★ "I was hooked from page one."
★★★★★ "Right up there with Baldacci and Thor."
★★★★★ "Another great Blake Jordan adventure."
★★★★★ "A totally unexpected ending!"
★★★★★ "The ending was great."
★★★★★ "...the action is nonstop."
★★★★★ "An excellent addition to the series."

Ready for a great story? Start reading now:
kenfite.com/rules-of-engagement

WANT THE NEXT BLAKE JORDAN STORY FOR $1 ON RELEASE DAY?*

*KINDLE EDITION ONLY

I'm currently writing the next book in the Blake Jordan series with a release planned soon. New subscribers get the Kindle version for $1 on release day.

Join my newsletter to reserve your copy and I'll let you know when it's ready to download to your Kindle.

kenfite.com/books

THE BLAKE JORDAN SERIES

IN ORDER

The Senator
Credible Threat
In Plain Sight
Rules of Engagement
The Homeland
The Shield
Thin Blue Line
Person of Interest
Abuse of Power

Made in the USA
Coppell, TX
05 April 2023

15280709R00184